A novel

EO-N

Dave Mason

Cover and book design by Pamela Kim Lee / Multiple Inc.
Printed and bound in the United States of America.
www.davemasonwrites.com
www.hellboxeditions.com

Library of Congress Control Number: 2020917758

ISBN: 978-1-7357064-0-5 hardcover
ISBN: 978-1-7357064-1-2 paperback
ISBN: 978-1-7357064-2-9 ebook

For all the good people.
You know who you are.

○

The late afternoon sun warmed her face,
the blanket was soft and comforting,
and she thought nothing but good thoughts.

1

The yelp startled him—a short, sharp cry that indicated something was most definitely wrong.

Panicked, the boy ran to catch up, cresting the ridge of snow over which his companion had disappeared just a few seconds before. She was crouched about fifty metres ahead on a wide flat plain, licking her front paw, the snow around it tinged ever so slightly pink.

"Laika! You okay? You hurt?" he asked breathlessly, speaking, as every dog owner does, as if his canine were completely fluent in human language.

The big black dog rolled onto her back as he approached, holding up her left foreleg for inspection. Maybe she did understand? As the boy dropped to a knee to look for signs of damage, something jabbed into him and he too yelped and jumped back, shocked more than hurt and wondering what could possibly be that sharp on the top of a slushy, snow-covered glacier.

Laika snapped to her feet, startled at her small human's vocal and physical recoil, but with her tail wagging furiously, having clearly reached the conclusion that both she and he were now in the same predicament. The boy pulled off a glove and poked a tentative finger through the small tear in his trouser knee, feeling around somewhat anxiously for any signs of damage. Relieved to discover that there was nothing of serious concern happening in there, he turned his attention to the mystery cause.

He'd fallen on the snow and ice out here thousands of times, so he knew that whatever had cut Laika's paw and torn a hole through his snow pants had to be something other than crystals of frozen water. A sharp rock, maybe? He began to dig, carefully scooping handful after handful of slushy snow away from the pain-inducing *thing*.

He uncovered the edge of a piece of metal, and as he dug a little deeper, it revealed its full self.

He guessed it to be about twice the size of his iPhone, but it was thinner, more like a piece of lightweight cardboard. Angular, gently curved, dull dark grey on one side and a kind of faded pea green on the other, the object had a line of raised dots and some small holes along one edge where it looked as if another piece of metal had maybe once been attached. He held it up in the weakening afternoon sunlight, trying to make sense of it, but of course he couldn't because it simply didn't belong there.

And, at that time of day especially, neither did he.

2

Alison loathed every second of this.

The funeral had been incredibly difficult but also, she hated to admit, a kind of guilty relief. Her mother had been pretty much out of it for about the last eight months, existing in a kind of suspended animation—not quite coherent, but not exactly incoherent. Not dead, but not really alive either.

Alison had tried her best to keep both of their spirits up, to be positive and to engage in meaningful conversation, but the woman who'd taught her to dance and sing and think—the woman who'd taught her how to live fiercely enough to win three state high school tennis championships and to hold her own in male-dominated corporate boardrooms—was simply no longer there. She'd been replaced by a gaunt lookalike who spouted mostly nonsensical fiction, a frail doppelgänger who'd apparently known different people and lived a much different life than her real mother.

But going through the odds and ends of her mother's life was necessary.

After Alison's brother, James, had been taken, after the pain and grief of that almost unbearable, staggering loss, her mother's illness had brought on the cold realization that it was just a matter of time until she'd be it. Until she'd be the only one left. And here she was, finally. Alone.

The shelves full of books and boxes full of papers and drawers full of stuff seemed endless, but Alison did what she knew she would do, even after having had years to try not to think ahead to this, the loneliest of lonely moments.

Despite the dull, relentless pain—despite the sad weight of it all—she felt obligated to work her way through her mother's belongings. To dig. To read. To acknowledge. To process. To file. To purge. To be sure she'd done her duty, fulfilled her obligation.

Obligation? But to who? To myself? she asked. *What's the point of that?* she replied, as she so often did, answering even her own questions with more questions.

3

Laika led the way, but she'd become a much wiser dog than she'd been the day before. She circled warily as Nils and his father walked across the whiteness. They stopped on the ridge above the flat plain and the black glove the boy had left on the still-visible pink spot. His father grabbed a tarp and a long, rectangular, black plastic case from the snowmobile's trailer as they dismounted.

"You really shouldn't have been out this far, Nils," said his father in his familiar instructional parental tone. "You know how dangerous it can be with the glacier changing like it is. What if you fell into a crevasse, huh? Who'd save you? Laika? Or maybe—what, you'd just text me from twenty-five metres down inside the ice?"

Nils knew his father was right. After all, the glacier did make him nervous sometimes, with its periodic booming and cracking, but it also drew him like a magnet. It was the very top of his world, and he loved the sense of freedom that came with venturing out with Laika and exploring its brilliant blue-and-white expanse.

He pulled the piece of twisted grey-green metal from his backpack and handed it to his father. "It was right there, over by my glove. That's where Laika got cut. It was kind of going straight down into the snow. You can still see the hole where I dug it out."

His father turned the mystery object over a few times before handing it back to Nils, then spread out the tarp, set the plastic case down, and kneeled to open it. "Okay. Let's see what we can find with this thing."

He placed the wide black strap around his neck, plugged in the headphones and slipped them over his ears, then flicked the power switch to On, triggering, Nils knew, the familiar, low electric hum. Mathias Eriksen had been "mudlarking"—as the British call it— since he was a kid. He'd told Nils endless stories as they'd prowled the pebbled beaches in front of his grandfather's cabin all summer long, desperately hoping to find that elusive Viking sword or helmet, but instead just turning up odd chunks of unrecognizable corroded metal and lost fishing paraphernalia. And now, like his father, Nils had come to associate that hum with the tantalizing chance of a magical discovery.

Mathias walked to the pink spot and lowered the detector's head until it hovered a few centimetres above the snow, then swung the device in a sweeping arc in front of himself and began to walk slowly to the west. When he'd travelled about thirty metres, he turned, re- traced his steps back to the pink snow, and began to walk slowly to the east. Another thirty metres out, he stopped and turned to Nils, who'd been pretty much holding his breath for the last ten minutes. Laika was, as usual, observing her humans with curious bewilderment.

"I'm not getting anything in either direction, Nils. I'm going to circle. Go and grab the rope."

The boy ran to the snowmobile and returned with a coil of thin yellow nylon rope and a wooden stake. His father drove the stake down into the pink snow, tied one end of the cord to it, and then walked, trailing the loose end of the rope through his fingers, to the first spot where he'd stopped. "Hold the pin steady, Nils. I'm going to walk around you." He tied the rope around his waist and began to walk, keeping the line taut and the lowered detector head close to the snow.

"Nothing yet," his father called out, head down. A few minutes later, "Still nothing." He completed a clockwise sixty-metre-diameter orbit, shortened his tether by about a metre, and began again.

"Nope. Nothing."

Nils tried to suppress a twinge of disappointment. He'd been with his dad many times when they'd found mysterious pieces of rusted junk buried in the sand: tin cans, car parts, door knobs, oar locks, even a couple of actual old coins once. The thrill of those discoveries—signaled by the change in detector tone his father had taught him to recognize—had always fired his imagination, and his excitement had only been slightly dimmed by the eventual reality of holding what amounted to an ancient lump of metal detritus. The real fun, he'd eventually come to realize, was mostly in the search. In the promise.

His father had pulled in another metre of rope and had just begun his third circumnavigation of the pink spot when he suddenly stopped. He backed up a few steps and swept the detector head over the same area three more times.

"Okay, Nils! Bring me a marker."

4

Alison shuffled the stack of papers. Digging into yet another over-stuffed file folder, she peeled back layer after layer of old phone bills, bank statements, and receipts one by one, not really sure what she was looking for exactly, but looking just the same.

She'd stopped to microwave her coffee for the third time, having worked her way through four more banker's boxes and three more shoeboxes. She leaned against the kitchen counter, stared out into the late Sunday afternoon steel-greyness—the Space Needle barely visible through the seemingly relentless drizzle and fog—and tried unsuccessfully to rub the burning fatigue from her eyes.

As she turned to face the next box of her mother's history, she caught a fleeting glimpse of a woman who almost looked like her in the plate glass. *Jesus*, she thought, involuntarily double-taking. She knew she'd been looking a little worse for wear lately—she'd sure as hell been feeling it—and dark rings under hazel eyes were certainly not her best look. She could have sworn she'd seen a grey hair or three hiding in the unruly mass that passed for her latest hairstyle, and she'd been lamenting her sedentary existence more and more.

Her mother's passing five weeks prior had basically been the capper on two and a half years of shit. Although it had only killed one of them, the sickness had effectively consumed two lives during its tenure. Beyond the pain she'd endured as her mother had faded to nothingness, Alison had also had too much time to analyze her own existence. She'd begun to chafe even more at the negative aspects of her status as a biotech CEO.

She'd absolutely insisted on the role from day one, believing— naively, she now fully admitted to herself—that the title would give her the control she thought she needed to best move the company forward. But after what had seemed like an incredibly brief honeymoon period and as the dollars had begun to disappear, the investors had begun to tighten the screws and ratchet up the expectations. She now clearly understood the double-edged sword of private equity in the biotech world, that failure would result in one kind of pain, success in another. She knew that when the day she'd been driving toward actually came—the day her team's hard work finally delivered an approved, effective drug that could actually save lives—the investment group's strategy would also become a reality. At that point, the profit motive would rule supreme over all further decisions, and the surgical extraction of maximum dollars from the bank accounts of the suffering and the desperate would become paramount.

The hard realities of the pharmaceutical business had seemed so abstract—so distant—when she'd started out. The excitement and energy and cockiness that had driven and empowered her as the company's founder—her team's early minor successes in oncology driven as much by her will as her intellect—had been slowly but inexorably supplanted by a constant, low-level state of worry and a nagging sense of guilt that had recently bloomed into sporadic episodes of almost crippling anxiety.

Deep down in her gut she still felt it, that innate, almost primal desire to help people, but it had become depressingly clear to her that being the CEO of a pharmaceutical innovator meant endless management meetings and stress more than it meant actually working with her lab team to try to develop breakthrough drugs. The constant battle in biotech, she now understood, was to fill the product development pipeline with enough viable drug candidates that the law of averages would result in one that might actually succeed. When a couple of early clinical trials had stalled and faltered, nagging doubts about her own abilities had begun to multiply, intellectual and emotional cancer cells fueled by the burning of other people's money.

As for life beyond the relentless demands of cancer? The last of her single friends had eventually paired up with significant others, leaving her to serve as a periodic third wheel, or to hang out from time to time with people who might once have passed for friends, if friends were the kind of people who cared only about themselves. And when it came to meaningful relationships, well, she'd kind of noticed—or rather it had been pointed out to her more than once—that she was usually the one to leave first. Her most recent potential, a tax lawyer named Daniel, had lasted all of five and a half weeks, as once again she'd cut things off before they'd really had a chance to go anywhere. Another instant distant memory.

Is leaving someone really better than losing someone? Shit, I don't know. The result is the same.

She turned to resurvey the task at hand, eyes eventually settling on the beige filing cabinet in the corner of her mother's office. She didn't see the cabinet so much as two or three more hours of god only knew what her mother might have stuffed in there, but she willed her thumb to push the button beside the handle and opened the top drawer, promising herself that when she'd gotten through this one she'd switch to wine.

Twenty-one minutes later, three drawers down, in a small manila envelope addressed to her grandmother Marie at her Halifax home, she found it.

The brittle paper, aged to a yellowish, greyish hue, was ragged at the edges, stained and wrinkled, and torn in the places where it had been folded and unfolded and refolded so many times that it was held together by only the most fragile of fibres.

Engraved in crisp black ink at the top of the document was the corporate boilerplate stuff.

CANADIAN NATIONAL TELEGRAM

D.E. GALLOWAY, ASSISTANT VICE PRESIDENT,

TORONTO ONT.

And debossed into its once-soft surface by the hammer strikes of an actual typewriter were the words that had dramatically changed the trajectory of her grandmother's young life, and which would, in turn, alter the lives of so many people who came after.

RAG11 32 GB 2 EXTRA=RCAF OTTAWA ONT 22 114A {PRIORITY - CC} MRS BARTON 7 PRINCE ARTHUR ST HALIFAX NS DEEPLY REGRET TO ADVISE THAT YOUR HUSBAND SQ LEADER JACK J BARTON M TWO EIGHT ONE EIGHT MISSING IN ACTION / OPERATIONS 22 APRIL 1945 STOP LETTER FOLLOWS PENDING RECEIPT WRITTEN NOTIFICATION FROM AIR MINISTRY STOP NO INFORMATION SHOULD BE GIVEN TO THE PRESS ***** . 404 SQUADRON RCAF L/I 7 6/7 1945 106++

She read the telegram three times, trying in vain to decipher the handwritten scribbles and numbers near its bottom right-hand corner, and noting the faded blue-violet rubber stamp on its top right:

Gently, she ran the tips of her fingers over her grandfather's name, imprinted into the paper's surface by someone who, Alison imagined, had once produced scores of equally gut-wrenching notifications every day. For years.

Without really knowing why, she brought the impersonal document close to her face. She closed her eyes, thinking for just a second that she might somehow detect some remnants of humanity there, some sense of sadness or loss. But as she knew it would, the paper just smelled old.

Alison had known about her grandfather at some point, had been provided with a vague memory that something terrible had happened to him when he was a very young man. She'd been a child when those hushed stories had been told, and as with most people who've acquired so little of their own, history did not really exist to her at that point in her life. But here, today, in the hands of a thirty-four-year-old woman who'd lately begun to feel the weight of her own life starting to pile up, was the decidedly dispassionate, matter-of-fact document that had left her grandmother Marie heartbroken and, not long afterward, alone with a baby girl.

That baby girl—Alison's mother—was Susan Elizabeth Barton Todd. Named in honour of her biological paternal grandmother, Susan had grown up never knowing her real father, raised instead by Marie and the wonderful man who'd been her "Dad" from the very beginning. A naval officer who'd survived his own war chasing German U-boats across the frozen North Atlantic, Commander John Bernard Todd had married the widowed Mrs. Marie Barton in the autumn of 1948, after the briefest of courtships, back when courtships were a thing. Shortly after the wedding, with his instant young family in tow, he'd made the move to Washington, DC, to take a new posting as RCN Naval Attaché.

Commander and Mrs. Todd had remained mostly happily in love for more than forty-five years, blessing Alison's mother, Susan, with the powerful sense of family and belonging that had always meant so much to her.

Susan had married Paul Wiley, her Boston University sweetheart, shortly after they'd graduated. An aeronautical engineer, Paul had been recruited by and accepted a job with United Aircraft, moving to a suburb of Montreal, where, to the best of Alison's recollection, he'd helped design helicopter engines or something like that. Susan had worked as an architect until James had been born, and Alison had come along just about four years after him, enough of a gap to be kiddingly referred to as "oopsie," although her parents had always been sure to let her know how much they'd hoped and hoped for her.

The family had relocated to Avon, Connecticut when Alison had turned eight, a difficult transition made a little easier by the presence of the big brother she knew had loved her as fiercely as any big brother possibly could.

She sat back, drained by her thoughts.

Life is easiest without them.

Get up, go to work, go home, binge-watch Netflix, sleep. Repeat.

Years, it seemed, had flown by that way, with what passed for happiness, hope, satisfaction, rage, frustration, and every other emotion all wrapped up in the work she put between herself and an actual life. She couldn't help but wonder sometimes—usually when she'd had a few too many and she allowed herself to think in such a way—if she was simply substituting the relentless and so often empty pursuit of career success for the sporadic and potentially empty pursuit of personal happiness.

She picked up the manila envelope and shook it one last time. A glossy, white-bordered black-and-white photograph, small enough to fit into the palm of her hand, fluttered like a leaf onto the jumble of papers scattered on her mother's hardwood floor.

She scooped it up.

Arms clasped behind him, a handsome young man stared into the camera's lens. His dark grey uniform jacket was crisp, belted at the waist, buttons shiny, with what looked to be a short row of ribbons and an embroidered wing emblem of some kind above his left breast pocket. His peaked cap was tilted slightly back on his head, revealing a short shock of dark hair, and his grin—he wasn't smiling exactly, but he wasn't frowning either—gave Alison the distinct impression that he kind of didn't give a shit. But absolutely everything else about his demeanour and his surroundings said that he did. A wide, flat field stretched out behind him, and off to one side, Alison could make out what looked like a couple of black trucks parked near the elliptical tail of some kind of black-grey, camouflaged, twin-engine airplane.

She turned the photograph over. There, in faded blue ink:

Bart

Scotland

March 1945

No empty pursuit there.

5

Twenty-seven fluorescent orange plastic markers dotted the snow, covering a huge area that appeared to fan out basically eastward from the pink spot and the wooden stake. The sun had dipped toward the horizon, and the night freeze had begun to claim the air.

Time to head back.

Nils and his father loaded their gear into the snowmobile trailer in silence as Laika waited and watched and wagged.

His father drained the last drops from his water bottle. "Well, I think this is really something, Nils. Something strange happened up here that needs to be understood. These sure as heck aren't rusty nails or pop bottle caps, son."

Deep in the pit of his stomach, Nils could feel an enormity starting to build.

Mind racing, he didn't really know what to think or what to allow himself to think. He knew only that he was incredibly happy to be up on the glacier with his father, sharing the beginning of what he imagined might be a true life adventure.

Doing his best to try to sound a little less over-the-moon excited than he actually was, Nils turned to his father. "So, uh, what do you think we should do, Dad? What's next?"

His father popped the front of his baseball cap up, scratched his forehead. "Well, I'll call a few people when we get back, tell them what we—I mean, what you and Laika found up here. And don't you worry, I'll smooth over your unauthorized glacier exploration with your mom."

Tucked in tightly behind his father as the snowmobile bumped and lurched over the crusted snow, Nils smiled the whole way home.

6

The man was up to his waist in ice and snow, sweating buckets in the warm sun.

Following a brief police investigation, Professor Jonas Lundeen and his young student assistant had made the trek from Bergen to the glacial plateau and its array of fluorescent orange markers at the request of the Norwegian Ministry of Defence and the Norwegian War Graves Service.

"Ah, for sure you got a signal in this vicinity, yeah?" said Jonas, squinting into the sun as he looked up at Nils and his father.

"Yes. Yes. Very clear. There would have to be something there to make that sound. It's unmistakable."

The professor scooped another shovel load of snow into the sieve held by his partner, watching as the second man shook and swirled its contents. As the last of the slushy whiteness dropped through the fine metal mesh, a small yellow-grey object materialized.

It was a crumpled, rectangular piece of brassy metal, about half the size of a playing card. Its curved, compound shape and four small holes along one of its edges implied that it might once have been attached to something else.

The man held it up in the bright sunlight, turning it over and over as he carefully wiped the moisture from it. Barely legible block letters stretched across its surface in faded red:

T UNI A P LE

"Well, well, well! What do you think of that?" Jonas asked, just a hint of excitement in his voice.

Three and a half days later, after the crew had been bolstered by the arrival of two additional student researchers equipped with some kind of expensive electromagnetic device, Professor Lundeen stood in front of two blue tarpaulins with his team, two police officers, the Eriksens, and a black dog.

Twenty-nine individual objects of varying shapes, sizes, contours, thicknesses, and colours lay in the sun. Each item, ranging from about five millimetres to more than sixty centimetres in length, had been photographed from every conceivable angle, assigned a code number, been tagged and bagged, and the GPS location in which it had been found had been logged into a database.

They each had their theories. Although they all agreed the bits and pieces were most likely from an aircraft of some kind, possibly even a satellite, no one had any real idea what it was they might actually be looking at. But, Nils noticed, it was one particular object that got the adults the most agitated.

That object, the adults said, coded 100916-65, appeared to be an eleven-millimetre-long piece of bone.

7

Robertson had really been on a roll.

"If we don't see the results we need in the next few months, the shit is really going to hit the fan, financially speaking. You know that, right? You really think I can go back to my people for more? Given the goddamn track record here? Jesus Christ, Alison. It's time to make it happen."

She'd heard it all before of course, about once a month for a year or so. And each time, she'd wondered at the craziness of it all. Jonathan Robertson, the company's belligerent lead investor and chairman, had apparently made a fortune in a prior venture involved in windshield wiper blades or hose clamps or something like that, and so he'd just naturally thought it would be a good idea for him and a few of his rich friends to back a fledgling biotech venture. *Motor oil meets Type 1 ultrapure water. Widgets meet molecules.* As she'd done about once a month for a year or so, she'd spent an hour calming him down. "Look, we're pushing as hard as we can, Jonathan, but it's a process. An extremely complicated process. You know that. And you also know we're very, very close."

By the time the video call had finally ended, with the usual phony smiles and "you know we all believe in you," and "keep the pedal to the metal" and "let me know if there's anything you need" bullshit, the ever-present but usually small knot between Alison's shoulder blades had once again become a large knot, and she'd slumped in her chair, drained.

Ninety minutes later, the voices droned on and her energy level had almost bottomed out.

As the finance committee meeting came dangerously close to entering its second hour and the productive portion of the conversation transitioned into the standard "rehashing what we've already covered twice" wrap-up phase, Alison mentally checked out of the proceedings. Her presence, however, was still unquestioned. Years and years of practice enabled her to simultaneously communicate intense focus—emphasized by periodic head nods, hmms, ah-has, and the odd scribbled note—while taking a mind walk elsewhere.

So, what's left to do?

In the nine weeks since the funeral, she'd pretty much wrapped up the legal issues, dealt with the life insurance stuff, and checked off almost all of the boxes on her executor to-do list, so as far as she knew, the paperwork was pretty much taken care of. The task of combing through and culling and sorting seven decades worth of her mother's accumulated physical life-stuff was substantially complete, and the real estate agent had called to let her know he was pretty sure he'd have an offer in the next day or so. She glanced down. *Where do we go from here?*

As she'd found herself doing at inexplicably random times over the past few months, she clicked the jpeg on her computer's desktop. And as he'd done for the past few months, from her open laptop screen, out of sight of the other basically checked-out meeting attendees, the young man with the I-don't-give-a-shit grin stared at her.

Six hours later, another day of spreadsheets and lack-of-progress reports and anxiety-inducing burn-rate presentations behind her, Alison poured herself a second glass of red wine, flopped down on the couch, and grabbed the remote. When an unrecognizable number popped up on her cell, her first instinct was to ignore it. By the third ring, it had dawned on her that she'd been communicating with an assortment of lawyers and accountants and adjusters and agents as she'd dealt with her mother's estate, so she took a chance and thumb-tapped the insistent green button.

"Hello. I'm trying to reach Ms. Alison Todd Wiley."

"Yes, hello. This is she."

"Good evening, ma'am. My name is Scott Wilcox. I'm a casualty identification investigator with the DHH, Department of National Defence, Ottawa. Do you have a few minutes to talk?"

The six days it took for her to get herself from Seattle to Oslo would not be nearly enough time for Alison to mentally process what Scott Wilcox would share with her over the next seventeen minutes.

o o o

They met in the restaurant of the Hotel Intercontinental.

"Miss Wiley? Nice to finally meet you in person, ma'am."

"Please, Mr. Wilcox, call me Alison. I must say, your call came right out of the blue, and I really haven't stopped thinking about our conversation ever since. I know it's, ah, maybe a bit premature for me to be here given your agency's protocols, but based on the evidence that you mentioned and, well, a few personal and professional circum-stances, I just felt I should make the trip."

Scott Wilcox smiled the briefest of smiles.

He was somewhat different than she'd imagined. From their initial phone call, she knew he was quiet and soft-spoken and most definitely to the point. But he was much younger than his job title and telephone demeanour had somehow intimated he would be. Calling her ma'am on the phone had made him sound midsixties. Working at the Department of National Defence had somehow made him sound midfifties at least. In person, Alison guessed him to be in his early forties at most.

His black hair, greying slightly at the temples, was cropped short. He wore black jeans and boots, and a black turtleneck under a black fleece jacket. And somewhat oddly, she noticed, he wore his watch with the face to the inside of his wrist.

She immediately regretted her business casual decision.

As he'd been on the phone, Scott Wilcox was certainly matter-of-fact. He covered off the general plan and the anticipated travel times—they agreed to meet outside the hotel lobby at 5:30 the next morning—and said good night.

As she left the elevator and walked down the hallway toward her room, Alison sensed something coming to life underneath her numbing fatigue, a slightly discomforting but also exciting sensation she couldn't quite get her head around.

As her head touched the pillow, she recognized it. The buzz. She'd always relished the unknown and been challenged and energized by the might-be-known. The space between them was where she loved to be.

o o o

The SUV was already warm inside, and the coffee and pastries were a pleasant surprise that helped take a little of the edge off the wicked jet lag she was most definitely feeling. It had still been light when she'd tried to close her eyes the night before, and light again when her phone alarm had gone off at 4:30 a.m.. Her brain and her eyelids—hell, pretty much all of her various components—were struggling with that reality.

On the other hand, her driver—to her amazement and mild annoyance—looked as if he'd been up and at it for hours. As he steered them out of the city and onto the highway, she attempted a little small talk, which he apparently wasn't very good at, then rode in warm silence for a while as the coffee kicked in and the landscape changed from rocky seacoast to rugged black-grey-green hills.

"You weren't the easiest person to find, ma'am," he said, finally breaking the silence, "but not the most difficult either."

"Oh? How so?" she asked. *How so? How so? Who talks like that?*

"In some of our cases, it can be a long process to make the right connections. With this one, there was a much greater chance we'd be able to piece it together from official sources and records, and through extended research via other databases and searches. Which, of course, we did, ma'am."

She smiled and nodded. "Ah, right, of course. That makes total sense." Despite what she'd been told about the chance discovery and the potentially long process of forensic verification, she still had no real idea what to expect. And although she'd immediately categorized this expedition as simply another family duty, she hadn't fully admitted to the fact that it was also a convenient excuse to temporarily put some distance between herself and her corporate obligations in Seattle. She took a final sip of her now-lukewarm coffee and stared out of her side window.

"So, if you don't mind me asking, Mr. Wilcox, what got you into this line of work? Oh, and really—just call me Alison."

"And just Scott for me," he said, driving in silence for a moment before answering her question. "Well, I guess you could say it's in my DNA, ma'am. I mean Alison. Ma'am."

And that was it.

For a second she thought she saw another fleeting smile, but she couldn't be sure.

o o o

It had been a little like extracting conversation from some of the ultra-brainiac types at the lab in Redmond, but eventually she'd managed to spark a little more conversation, and had even managed to learn a little bit about Scott Wilcox.

He was ex-military. Maybe the reason, she figured, for the ma'ams and the matter-of-fact-ness. Maybe the reason for the watch thing. *And maybe the scars on his neck?* He'd joined the DHH after his final tour of duty—he hadn't said where he'd served—partly because of his training—he'd never said exactly what he'd trained in—and partly because of his experiences. He hadn't elaborated on those either.

At the end of a secluded road, the SUV crunched to a stop in a small gravel parking lot. As she followed Scott toward a nondescript corrugated metal building, Alison glanced up at the grey sky and shivered as the cold mist touched her face.

"Welcome to Odda, ma'am."

They all shook hands in a cramped, overheated, wood-paneled front office.

"Miss Wiley, Mr. Wilcox, my name is Jonas Lundeen. I'm leading the archaeological team from the University of Bergen. And this is Mathias Eriksen and his son Nils. Nils is the one who found the first piece. Well, actually it was his dog, Laika, truth be told."

Mathias smiled and held out a hand, and Nils was all grin.

With the introductions and small talk completed, Professor Lundeen led them through a metal door and down a short hallway. The building, Alison had noted, was basically a typical low-slung industrial structure, and though she hadn't really thought about what to expect, she wouldn't have been surprised to find that it was actually an auto body shop.

It was almost as cold inside the main part of the building as it was outside, but it was brightly lit by banks of hanging fluorescents. Instead of cars and trucks and engines and transmissions in need of repair, Alison saw what looked to be about a hundred or so random pieces of twisted, corroded, weathered, and aged pieces of metal laid out on a numbered grid that had been taped onto the bare concrete floor.

Scott walked over to the edge of the grid and looked down. "Well, Ma'am. This is it. This is what brought us all here today. This is—or I should say was—a de Havilland Mosquito."

Alison's mind worked to make sense of what she was looking at: this twisted junk had once flown.

These bits and pieces had once been, as Scott had explained on their first call, parts of a stunningly sleek and streamlined and even beautiful war machine. But now they were much more than that, Scott said. "This discovery may help with the resolution of a seventy-four-year-old mystery. We believe these objects to be components of the last known aircraft piloted by Squadron Leader Jack J. Barton of 404 Squadron, Royal Canadian Air Force. Your grandfather, ma'am."

8

Scott walked them all through the story once again. He recounted how Nils and Laika had stumbled on the first piece of wreckage, and how Nils and his father had located more pieces. He talked about the initial Bergen police investigation, and their immediate referral of the case to the Norwegian Ministry of Defence and the Norwegian War Graves Service, which had eventually led to Professor Lundeen and his student archaeologists doing their initial work. Their subsequent discoveries and analysis of the wreckage had led them to various warplane restoration experts in England, Canada, and New Zealand, who had each positively identified one recovered object as a bomb bay door hinge from a de Havilland Mosquito FB Mk VI. That had resulted in a connection to the Commonwealth War Graves Commission, a search of RAF records relating to all aircraft of that type listed as missing in action in that region, and then to the Royal Canadian Air Force and Canada's Department of Heritage and History.

"We analyzed Professor Lundeen's findings further and concluded from various RCAF records and other documents that the aircraft was most likely the one last piloted by Jack Barton," Scott said. "We were able to locate Ms. Wiley by connecting the dots from Squadron Leader Barton to his widow—your grandmother Marie, ma'am—and to her second husband, and from them to your mother and father. And then finally, to you, ma'am."

Alison's father, Paul Wiley, had died suddenly in 2004. Her older brother—Canadian Forces Master Corporal James Andrew Wiley— had been killed in action in Afghanistan in 2005, and her mother, Susan Wiley, had passed away in February. That left her, Alison Todd Wiley, as Squadron Leader Jack J. Barton's only living descendant.

Alison really didn't know what she felt or thought—or what she should feel or think. These corroded and twisted chunks and shards of metal, extracted from the Norwegian snow and ice more than seven decades after they'd been deposited there, were connected to her and to a family that no longer existed.

Professor Lundeen handed Alison a piece of metal. Bent slightly, rectangular, and small enough to fit in her palm, the object had round holes at three of its four corners, but the metal that would have formed its fourth corner had clearly been broken or torn away. Although it was pitted badly, she could still read most of the information engraved into its partially shiny black and silver surface.

MOUNTING CAMERA TYPE 24
Ref.no 14A/774 Serial no 4326
Made by Williamson manf. co. ltd. London and Reading

Scott read aloud from his laptop notes. "Squadron Leader Jack Barton's last known aircraft was a de Havilland Mosquito FB Mk VI. Serial number RF889, coded EO-N. The object you're holding is the serial number plate from an F24 camera mount. We have documented evidence that it was installed in one of the aircraft that 404 Squadron RCAF began flying sometime in early March of 1945."

"A camera?" Alison asked, surprised at the idea.

"Yes. Crews flying with 404 Squadron were assigned to armed reconnaissance and anti-shipping missions, which means they flew over enemy territory to scout and help gather intelligence and, of course, to attack whatever they were assigned or could find to attack. In addition to standard gun cameras, a few of their aircraft carried much larger equipment to document things on the ground or ocean in greater detail."

As she absorbed Scott's words and surveyed the bits and pieces laid out on the floor, Alison could have sworn she felt the tiny metal rectangle in her hands take on an added weight.

A young man—to whom she was related by blood—had been personally connected to this assortment of bent and broken and corroded objects. He'd relied on the machine to which this junk had once belonged to help him do whatever job he'd been assigned to do, to protect him from harm, and to bring him home safely. He'd no doubt experienced fear and exhilaration in it.

And he'd likely died in it.

Gently, she ran her thumb over the pocked and worn surface of the metal plate as Scott read further from his laptop notes.

"We searched the squadron records for any aircraft listed as missing in action after the date it's believed the F24 camera was installed. On April 22, 1945, Squadron Leader Jack J. Barton and his navigator, Flight Lieutenant Robert Vickson, took off from RAF Banff, Scotland, for an anti-shipping strike. They were sent to attack German traffic in the Kattegat. That's the, ah, body of water between Denmark and Sweden. No one saw what happened to them. But they never made it home. Essentially, they vanished without a trace."

Scott looked up.

"Until now."

9

The Mosquito cleared the glistening red and black rooftops of Aarhus at just over 220 knots.

At this speed and altitude the scenery went past like a blur, but glancing over to his right, Jack could see the bombed-out Gestapo headquarters the boys from 140 Wing had hit back in October, a raid that had confirmed for him that Nazi Germany was pretty much done. *Why don't these fools give it up? They don't have a goddamn prayer.* He nudged the twin throttles forward, coaxing a little more speed out of the two Rolls-Royce Merlin engines roaring just feet from him.

Cousineau was head down, glued to his maps and papers as Jack gently worked his stick and pedals to finalize their approach. About two and a half miles ahead and slightly to the left of them, a low-slung black-grey flak ship anchored a few hundred yards out in the harbour lit up like a fistful of sparklers as the sky all around it came dangerously alive.

Almost simultaneously, puffs of black smoke began to appear in the sky, and ribbons of brilliant white tracers from the shore batteries began to arc past the Perspex that separated Jack and his navigator from the freezing morning sky. He knew that for every visible shell trail there were likely four or five invisible standard rounds coming their way, but he never really thought much about that stuff. He just knew that although the shells often seemed to be pulled toward his aircraft by some magnetic force, they'd always be repelled at the last second by some other, more benevolent power. *Better to be goddamn lucky than be good!* he thought. Then immediately, *Shit. I'm turning into my old man.*

As the harbourfront warehouses dead ahead across the basin grew to fill his windscreen, Jack caught sight of the first three anti-flak Mosquitos from 248 coming in from behind the flak ship. Approaching low and fast from the southeast, they climbed slightly before beginning their attack dives, and about six hundred yards out, the lead aircraft let loose with everything it had, the black and white invasion stripes still painted on the underside of its dark grey and green fuselage lighting up as its eight underwing RP-3s fired.

Jesus thundering Christ.

As many times as he'd seen it, as many times as he'd personally unleashed the same massively destructive force, he was spellbound.

The ocean around the German ship erupted into towering geysers and overlapping rings of boiling white foam as the first barrage of 20mm cannon shells and rockets walked across the water toward it. The ship was almost completely obscured by the water and spray thrown up by an explosion triggered by at least one rocket, and brilliant white and red flashes lit up the clouds of smoke and sea mist as the Mosquito's cannon shells struck the vessel's hull, deck, and superstructure. Almost immediately, a massive, roiling column of black and grey smoke, driven rapidly skyward by a ball of angry orange and yellow and red flames, sent jagged pieces of metal of all shapes and sizes spinning crazily, hundreds of feet into the air.

Death from above was absolutely spectacular from this point of view. *Not so great from down there*, he thought.

The lead Mosquito passed to the left of the stricken ship at just above mast height, its pilot, Jack knew, simultaneously clenching his butt cheeks tight and bearing down to push blood into his head in an effort to combat the g-forces trying to crush him, while hoping like hell to avoid his own shrapnel and the sporadic streams of flak somehow still emanating from the burning, smoking mess he'd just created. White vapour trails curled from the plane's wing tips as it flashed by Jack's port side, close enough that he could clearly see the two jokers in its cockpit. He turned his head back just in time to see the second Mosquito rake the ship's hull with cannon shells and rockets before arcing away to the right of the destruction with its own wings almost perpendicular to the ocean.

Jack pulled the stick back to gain a little altitude for his attack dive. He clicked the intercom button on his oxygen mask. "Here we go," he said quietly.

Cousineau, hunched in his armour-plated seat to the right of and slightly behind Jack, glanced sideways for a moment and nodded, the whites of his eyes just a little more visible than usual inside his goggles. He never said much when they finally got to the job site.

Growing larger by the second, the dull, black-grey U-boat was dead ahead, right where 333 Squadron's Norwegian reconnaissance guys had said it would be, snugged up tight alongside a merchant ship in the second harbour basin. Trucks and vans and crates and piles of oil drums crowded the wharf, and a gantry slowly lowered a large pallet of wooden boxes toward the sub's deck as Jack banked ever so slightly right, yawed gently, and dropped his nose to finalize his line of attack. He ignored the arcing streams of tracers and black puffs beginning to come up from the shore batteries in the second basin, focusing instead on the green grinning swordfish emblem painted on the sub's conning tower, and peripherally on the wider scene unfolding beyond his gun sight—the panicked men on the rain-soaked docks beginning to scramble for their lives as they realized what was about to happen.

The Kriegsmarine sailors manning the U-boat's twin-barreled antiaircraft guns, who'd no doubt been stunned and alarmed by the ferocity of the sudden and massive violence inflicted on their comrades in the flak ship out in the harbour, swung their weapon toward Jack's Mosquito and opened fire. Their muzzle flashes and the trails of white phosphorus coming toward him served as a perfect aiming point in Jack's gunsights. *Jesus. You must have known we'd be coming for you, you poor dumb bastards.*

He could taste the rubbery sweat in his oxygen mask and sense the iciness of his always-cold fingers inside his gloves, felt the power and momentum and attitude changes of the aircraft with every bone in his body. But despite the speed of the attack and the potential death in the explosive black puffs and streaking white trails threatening to end him, Jack's world slowed down.

This was never the scary part. He knew the real fear would come later, when he was alone, back in his damp and miserable Nissen hut, after he'd had a chance to actually think about what he'd done. But right now, in this moment, as he caressed the firing button with his thumb, he was dead calm. Just doing his job.

At about six hundred yards distance, Jack fired off a one-second burst from his four cannons to confirm his aim, then immediately triggered his eight rockets. He felt the aircraft shudder and buck slightly, and watched for a split second as the black armour-piercing projectiles dragged their white smoke trails down toward his aiming point just aft of the sub's conning tower. Almost simultaneously, he pressed the cannon button again, firing off a four-second squirt that produced the familiar deafening roar and vibration that always bounced his feet off the rudder pedals. He saw his streams of 20mm shells turn the dark water beside the U-boat to brilliant white before converging into it and then tracking onto the second wharf.

To avoid any shrapnel that might be thrown up by his attack, he banked hard and pulled away, the aircraft lurching up and to the left. Fighting the invisible hand crushing him down into his seat, he caught a quick glimpse of the results of his efforts through his side window. He figured at least three of his rockets must have hit the U-boat below the waterline amidships—wet hits, they called them—their solid metal warheads penetrating the hull and setting off an internal explosion that seemed to lift the entire submarine before sending a massive shockwave outward into the harbour. And while antiaircraft fire continued to come up from the various shore batteries, there were no more tracers coming from the sub's conning tower.

He guessed his other rockets must have hit the supply ship or the wharf or one of the waterfront warehouses. The gantry was no longer there, and he could see a handful of men thrashing around in the icy, foaming water. *Goddamn. That's why I'm up here and not down there.*

○ ○ ○

He'd worked a lobster boat out of Lunenburg for a couple of seasons as a teenager, back and arms aching, hands calloused and raw from struggling to haul the heavy loaded pots out of the freezing water. But when they'd dragged the brilliant white, disgustingly foul-smelling, almost unrecognizably bloated body of a good friend out of Mahone Bay more than a week and a half after he'd gone overboard in a squall, Jack had decided the oceangoing life simply wasn't for him. When the war had shown up a few years later, despite growing up on and around the big water, and in a navy town to boot, he'd somewhat confidently told his beautiful new wife that he planned to aim high. That he'd literally stay above it all.

He'd absolutely loved it when Marie had told him how handsome and dashing he'd looked when he'd finally come home from Trenton with his wings. His parents had been as proud as proud could be, of course, but he'd also been acutely aware of his mother's trepidation about him "doing silly things in aeroplanes," especially after her worst fears had come perilously close to being realized right before her eyes one early autumn afternoon.

Jack knew he'd been lucky to be posted close to home, to RAF Greenwood, for training on high-powered twin-engine aircraft, and he knew he'd been even luckier when he and one of his buddies, a hilarious rookie navigator from Alberta named Gerald Simpson, had convinced their CO to let them take one of the kites up for an "instrument check" one Sunday afternoon. Of course, per Jack's grand plan, they'd made the quick trip over to the South Shore for some aerial showboating. Coming in a little too low and a whole lot too fast up the narrow channel between two islands, Jack had banked hard so that his darling Marie and his parents and grandparents—whom he'd telephoned in advance to be sure they'd be watching from the beach below their house—could see him wave. While those in the gathered crowd had been suitably impressed by the roaring spectacle, they'd not quite realized that Jack's cockiness, combined with his relative lack of experience with the aircraft's handling characteristics, had almost cost him and Simpson everything. They'd come within a few feet of catching a wingtip in the ocean, which was bad enough, but on the way up and out of the channel, Jack had managed to take the very tip-top off an extra-tall Second Peninsula pine tree with his starboard wing—a souvenir he'd had a heart-pounding, sweaty, and sheepish time explaining away back at Greenwood only thirty minutes later. That he'd gotten away with everything had been the most incredible luck of all.

A few months later, as they'd hugged their soggy goodbyes on Pier 21, Jack had looked his mother in the eyes and solemnly agreed with her that, yes, airplanes could be a little tricky. As he'd gently reminded her that life itself could be inherently dangerous, he'd also given her a big squeeze and cockily reminded her that he was inherently lucky. After all, he'd said, his father's entire life had basically been about luck—since he'd had the good fortune to marry such a wonderful woman!—and surely, Jack said, he'd inherited a little bit of that magic. Both his mother and Marie had smiled through their tears at that.

His old man had always worked on and around the water—four years as a harbour tug deckhand before apprenticing as a shipyard welder at eighteen—and Jack had been told over and over again how Bill Barton had benefited from the good graces of lady luck more than once. Seems his father had been making his way down to the wharf one miserably cold Thursday morning when the unthinkable had happened. In the Narrows—the strait that connects Halifax Harbour to Bedford Basin—a French cargo ship loaded with high explosives ultimately bound for the hell of the trenches in Europe had collided with a Norwegian freighter. The resulting detonation—they later said it was the largest man-made explosion in history—devastated the North End of Halifax and killed more than two thousand people. But it didn't kill Bill Barton.

Nope.

Bill, Jack had been told numerous times, had somehow been shielded by a wall or a building or a truck or something, big enough and solid enough that the blast wave had apparently just rolled right over him, leaving him shaken and choking and bloodied for sure, and totally deaf in his left ear, but feeling "luckier than a shithouse rat after Christmas dinner," whatever the hell that meant. And not so long ago, the old boy had almost been taken to the bottom of the harbour along with one of his best shipyard buddies when a few hundred tons of steel had busted loose. He'd dodged a watery fate, his dad had said, simply because he'd stepped away for a piss and a smoke at just the right time.

Immediately after Jack and Bill had somewhat stiffly shaken hands in the sleeting rain that March morning, his father had suddenly and uncharacteristically bear-hugged him. Fiercely gripping his only son by the shoulders, his shiny, red-rimmed eyes had bored into Jack's as he'd firmly but laughingly cautioned him to never, ever skip a piss or a smoke, and he'd repeated for about the hundredth time that he was sure as shit glad that Jack would be "up there with the birds, not down there with the goddamn fishes."

But, Jack had come to understand, the hard, ironic truth was that after more than twenty months with RAF Coastal Command, he, like so many of his friends, would most likely meet his fate in the cold black waters off Norway or Denmark.

o o o

Sixteen more Mosquitos appeared, each rising up in a choreographed aerial ballet before arcing over into their attack dives, each spouting telltale puffs of light grey smoke and streams of bright white tracers as their rockets and cannon shells amplified the annihilation. The harbour became an absolute maelstrom of splashes of all sizes, overlapping white foam circles, towering plumes of water, flashes, explosions, fire, black and grey and white smoke, and whirling chunks of jagged shrapnel, as one by one the aerial predators unleashed their weapons on the U-boat, supply ships, wharves, warehouses, trucks, and other "targets of opportunity."

Truth be told, Jack wasn't really sure how he felt about killing, but as his old man had said, he wouldn't have to be doing anything of the sort "if that little Nazi bastard with the shit-stain on his top lip hadn't made it so goddamned necessary." For now, at least, killing was Jack's job, and he wanted to be good at it. On the other hand, he knew exactly how he felt about living—and he wanted to be especially good at that.

Despite his predisposition toward life, Jack always made sure he was the last to leave any target area, to be sure that all of his boys were on their way home before he personally clocked out. So, at an altitude of less than a hundred and fifty feet, he racked his kite hard around to port one last time, orbiting the harbour and scanning the sky for any threatening black specks.

To Jack, his squadron mates looked like ospreys, the graceful fish hunters he'd loved to watch as a kid out on the island where his grandparents lived, and he counted the aircraft one by one as they burst through the smoke and flak, arcing and twisting and diving in the flat grey skies, heading west at full throttle and leaving chaos in their wake.

Absolute goddamn chaos, Jack thought.

He looked over at Cousineau, head down once again, focused on his charts. "Okay, Cooze. Let's get gone."

In his soft Quebecois accent—the one the local girls all seemed to love so much when he sat down at the Black Thistle's old upright piano—Cousineau replied, cool and calm, as if he did this kind of thing every day, which he pretty much did, "Roger that, Skip. You know I'm going wherever you're going."

Almost three and a quarter hours after they'd left Banff, the attack was over in less than four minutes.

10

Alison savored a second coffee.

"Listen, I just want to thank you again for allowing me to be part of this. I know it's a little unusual, but it was…well…I don't even have the words to describe how I felt yesterday, in the presence of my own family's history. It's all a bit overwhelming, actually."

"I totally understand, ma'am," Scott replied. "I'm glad we could make it happen for you."

"So, what's next?" she asked. "What's the procedure?"

She tried to focus on the now and to keep her uninvited emotions where they belonged, but despite her best efforts, the memories were sneaking up on her.

When her father had died suddenly in his early sixties, she'd been heartbroken. She ached at her own personal loss of course, but her pain had been amplified by the depth of her mother's grief. Still, as she'd been promised she would, Alison had eventually come to view Paul Wiley's passing as an unfortunately premature but basically natural part of the order of life. Her brother's death, on the other hand, had nothing to do with order and there was absolutely nothing natural about it. In the wake of the paralyzing shock and grief and despair had come the poisonous hate for the politicians and military commanders who'd sent him to a pointless place, to fight a pointless war, and to die a pointless death. The cold burning in Alison's heart had never quite gone away, and though she knew there was absolutely no science to prove it, sometimes she actually believed that losing James had ultimately killed her mother.

Now this?

Seventy-four years ago, her grandfather and his crewmate had lost their lives, as so many young men had. Fighting for what? For freedom? For duty? For honour? *Fuck no.* She'd looked it up, done the research. They'd disappeared just a few weeks before Germany had surrendered. *Just like James, they died for absolutely nothing.*

"Well, ma'am," Scott explained, "the RCAF—the government of Canada—technically still owns the wreckage of the aircraft, and they've authorized Professor Lundeen and his team to continue with the crash site investigation for both recovery and teaching purposes. That'll probably go on for a while, I'm guessing. Based on the results from the ground-penetrating radar, Professor Lundeen seems to think the bulk of the aircraft itself may actually be under the ice. That would be a pretty remarkable find for sure."

He glanced up from his laptop, sipped his coffee. "But as far as my immediate responsibilities, there is, ah, something I do need to follow up on. As you know, they found some...some human remains with the wreckage. The small piece of bone, ma'am. That's my priority. The local police had Professor Lundeen take it to the University of Bergen for initial analysis. Once the university rules out the possibility that it may actually be related to a Norwegian citizen, I'll take custody and personally transport the fragment back to Ottawa. We'll do our own DNA analysis there. Ma'am."

Alison put her coffee cup down and turned to face the muted landscape beyond the streaming café window. A two-lane road ran down toward the waterfront, a single car parked on the left shoulder, its rusty shell holding on for dear life in the relentless drizzle. This whole thing was somehow more personal and more real than she'd imagined it would be. "Listen, I... Is it okay if I'm part of that? If I come along? I'm just wanting to make some sense of this, you know? The scientist in me, I guess."

She thought about the young man in the shiny black-and-white photo. She thought about his young wife and his soon-to-be-born baby girl—her grandmother and mother. She thought about the other man, Vickson, who'd disappeared along with her grandfather, and about how many people he might also have left forever grieving, forever wondering.

And she thought about her own parents, about the lives they'd lived, the love they'd felt for each other and for their two children, and the brutally painful losses they'd endured.

And she especially thought about James.

To their friends, and even to their parents, Alison and James were "The Wildees." She'd gone to pretty much all of his hockey games. He'd gone to almost every one of her school plays and tennis matches. For a while at least, their mother had made them both take dance lessons, which they'd both loudly proclaimed to hate but had secretly enjoyed.

Family events had been the greatest times, and the dumb traditions their grandparents had created—and that their parents had perpetuated and built on—had made Halloween and Christmas and the Fourth of July uniquely theirs. And, as she'd grown to the point where some of the boys had started to hang around just a little more than usual, James had made sure that they all measured up and treated her right.

More than anything in the world, she'd loved her big brother and he'd loved her. The three years between them had always made him seem so grown up, and he'd always, always been there for her whenever and wherever she'd needed him.

When James had blurted out during the family's Memorial Day weekend barbeque that he'd decided to take a break from college to enlist in the Canadian military, their mother had quietly cried while their father had tried to be positive and encouraging. Alison had just sat there, completely silent. Completely numb.

James had left them the next month, headed off to some training facility, god knows where, where they'd taught him to do the things that soldiers do. He'd sent the odd note and even called once in a while, but the distance between them had been a constant dull pain for Alison.

She'd departed for the University of Washington in August of the following year, and just a few weeks later, she and the rest of the world had watched, horrified, as two fully loaded airliners were flown into New York's World Trade Center towers.

They hadn't found out until years later that James had been in Afghanistan just a few weeks after 9-11. In fact, he'd been a member of something called JTF2, and he'd been in the first element of special forces troops deployed over there. Where James went and what he did in Afghanistan, they never knew, but his letters and calls became less and less frequent until they became virtually nothing at all. And later, after James himself had become nothing at all, Alison had watched, completely helpless, as her mother had lost even those memories when she'd needed them most.

She tried to ignore the annoying but all-too-familiar swelling in her throat, fought to control her breathing and quell her watering eyes.

"Well," said Scott, "you are Squadron Leader Barton's only living descendant—I'm, ah, very sorry about the recent passing of your mother, ma'am—and you've come all this way. I'm not aware of any prohibitions or rules that would prevent you from accompanying me, if you're up for it. We'll want to get to Bergen by 0900 tomorrow, so an 0630 departure is in order."

Alison turned to the rain-spattered window, the moisture in her eyes and the rivulets on the glass working as one to further diffuse the soft greyness of the town. She simply hadn't expected it, hadn't been fully prepared to feel the sudden and deep loneliness and sense of longing that had enveloped her in the last twenty-four hours. "I just want to be part of this. I...I just want to be there, that's all. I guess I don't really know how to explain it."

In the restaurant window, she saw Scott's laptop-illuminated reflection nod one of those quick, almost imperceptible, affirmative soldier nods. "Yes, ma'am."

As she refocused on the darkening world beyond the glass, she heard him add, a little unexpectedly, "I understand, Alison."

His left hand lay on the table next to his coffee cup. Her right hand lay directly across from it, a full expanse of white linen between them. Without knowing why, without a reason at all really, and without taking her eyes from the rusted-out car and the wet road, she moved her hand just the tiniest bit closer to his.

11

They met, coffee cups in hand, in Doctor Annika Sorensen's bright and sparse office.

"Mr. Wilcox, as per police protocol, we've done a preliminary analysis of the bone fragment, and, ah, unfortunately I'll be unable to release it to you, given what my team confirmed just last evening. Although we'd originally assumed the results might help you with your investigation, I'm, ah, afraid that is simply not the case. There's just no indication that the fragment is related to the crashed aircraft or to your grandfather, Miss Wiley."

"You're already a hundred percent certain of that?"

"Yes, as a matter of fact we are. Of course, we don't have DNA analysis yet, but there is something that we do know about the bone fragment, and we can tell you this with absolute certainty. I'm afraid that the fragment will not be a match with Squadron Leader Barton or with the other missing airman, because whoever that fragment belonged to was somewhere between the ages of eight and nine years old at the time that specific bone ceased its development."

Stunned, Alison glanced over at Scott, then turned back to Dr. Sorensen. "Eight or nine years old? How is that even possible? I mean, how can that possibly be explained…?"

Scott had been listening intently, taking a few notes, absorbing and processing the flow of information. "Well that's, ah, certainly an interesting development, Dr. Sorensen. Are there any other facts or insights that you can share? Anything at all you can tell us about the fragment?"

"Yes, actually," said Dr. Sorensen as she scrolled through the report on her laptop screen. "We asked one of our colleagues in the Department of Osteology to confirm our assessment of the fragment. And it's exactly as we suspected. It's a distal phalanx, one of the small bones of the hand. A fingertip."

o o o

Scott clicked through his notes. "I really don't know what to say, ma'am. I've never run into anything remotely like these circumstances in any previous case. Based on the serial number from the onboard camera, we're almost a hundred percent certain the wreckage the Eriksens found is the last known aircraft flown by your grandfather, but we can't physically place him at the scene. Instead, the forensic evidence indicates that a child might have been involved, which makes no sense.

"My jurisdiction is centered on the investigation of finds that may lead to the identification of Canadian military remains. Given that the remains we thought would be pertinent to this investigation from that perspective are apparently not related, I'm afraid I'm going to have to wrap up my time here in the next few days."

"So, is that it then?" Alison asked, a weight in her chest suddenly making its presence felt. "Do we just give up and go home?"

Scott paused for a moment as he closed his laptop, then looked up. "Well, as I said, I've got a few more days. And giving up is not really my style... ma'am."

And there it was, once again. A hint of a smile.

o o o

The glacier was beautiful, a stunning postcard in a thousand shades of mid-morning blue and white.

Alison had never been on a snowmobile before, but it was clear that Scott had as he maneuvered the rented black and red machine over the snow, slush, and ice as if it was second nature to him. Because it was.

On the three and a quarter-hour drive from Bergen back to Odda, they'd quickly run out of "official" things to talk about. To her mild surprise, Alison had filled the silence by volunteering a little surface-level personal history, talking a bit about her work in biotech. But to her immense surprise, she'd suddenly found herself transitioning to talking about her mother, a subject that had prompted her to immediately switch to question mode, and Scott had haltingly offered up a few more clues about himself. He'd talked a little about his own grandfather, how they'd spent time hunting and fishing in the mountains of south eastern British Columbia. He'd learned to drive a "sled"—a snowmobile—out there. He'd learned how to shoot. How to dress a kill. How to survive the elements. But when she'd asked him about his decision to join the Canadian Forces, he'd deftly changed the subject to the forecast weather conditions up at the glacier. *Message received.* She'd left it alone, and the two of them covered the last twenty minutes of the journey in relative silence.

She hadn't really known what to expect when they arrived, but the crash site was much bigger than she'd imagined. The area had been marked out with perforated fluorescent-orange plastic fencing, the bamboo support poles inserted deep into the snow and ice. The warm weather had already melted down some of the piles the university team had created during their explorations, and a couple of the fence poles had started to lean a little.

Because of the remote and difficult to access location, Professor Lundeen had explained that it had been impossible to use any kind of heavy equipment during the dig. Instead, he and his archaeology team had basically hand-excavated a series of holes of various depths and diameters across an area Alison guessed to be about half as wide and at least as long as a football field. After they'd geolocated and photographed and catalogued every piece of debris they could find, they'd transported it all down to the small metal warehouse near Odda and pieced the clues together as best they could.

Scott parked the snowmobile beside two others up on a small ridge, and they made the short hike down to the flat plateau and the tents and holes and assorted tools and generators scattered inside the orange-ringed area. As they approached the fence, a tent flap flipped open and Professor Lundeen emerged, wearing blue overalls and a fluorescent-yellow high-visibility vest.

"Hello again! Good to see you both. Coffee?"

In the shade of a tent awning, they sat on folding camping chairs drinking surprisingly good instant coffee as Jonas walked them through the progress he and his team had made. He clicked into a diagram on his iPad.

"We've spent the last ten days focusing on an area just to the south and west of the original finds. The ground-penetrating radar told us there was likely a large mass approximately four to six metres below the surface there. That would be a lot of digging up here with no heavy equipment, but the guys are pretty resourceful." He laughed. "They were able to rig up a kind of…a kind of water cannon, I guess you could call it, using a generator, a couple of pumps, some metal barrels, some propane heaters, a few hoses, and some bits and pieces of miscellaneous mechanical junk they got down in town. That made it possible to remove the ice much more efficiently and effectively than by using shovels and the like.

"So we've been able to make a pretty big hole and what we think is a pretty substantial find in the vicinity of the strongest radar hit. Would you care to take a closer look yourselves?"

o o o

The excavation opening was roughly three and a half metres in diameter at the glacier's surface, with slick, tapered, blue-white sides that darkened as they disappeared into the depths. A generator, a few blue plastic barrels, and a couple of pumps sat near its mouth, and various hoses and electrical cords snaked down into the darkness. Jonas motioned to the top of the aluminum ladder poking just above the lip of the opening.

"We're down to a depth of around six and a half metres now. That's about…oh, twenty-one feet, give or take? Now, the opening is not so very wide at the bottom, maybe a metre and a half or so, but once you squeeze through that you'll see we've been able to open up a bit of a low cavern down there, so you should be able to almost stand up. We'll get the lights on for you, and when you get down there, I think you'll agree that we've found what we were all hoping for."

Scott grabbed the ladder and started down first. Alison watched him disappear into the blue-black, the glare from the sunlit snow intensifying the darkness below. And to Alison at least, it took more than a few too many seconds for his voice to reach up to them. *Jesus. What am I getting myself into here?* "Okay, ma'am, come on down."

Swallowing hard and breathing just a little more deeply than normal to try to suppress a tinge of claustrophobia, Alison began her descent just as one of the archaeology students managed to fire up a generator that filled the excavation beyond the bottom of the ladder with brilliant blue-white light.

Despite the comforting presence of the sudden illumination below her, her heart began pounding just a little harder with every step down. Her breath came a little faster, and she shuddered as the sheen of sweat on the back of her neck chilled and the deepening cold cut through her like a thousand needles. The slick floor of the cavern was submerged in about four inches of ice water, and she almost lost her footing as she crouched to squeeze through the narrow opening, but Scott reached out a hand to help her regain her balance. Although Alison could stand, her head grazed the ice, and Scott had to crouch to fit his frame into the confined space. His voice was low, solemn.

"Well, ma'am, it looks like this is the real deal."

As she followed Scott's gaze, Alison forgot all about her claustrophobia, and her first glimpse of Professor Lundeen's latest find took her frozen breath away. Just above the water, part of a twisted spider-web of metal protruded from the ice wall. The clear Perspex panels it had once held were long gone, only a few jagged, badly yellowed fragments still held in place, and its once aerodynamic shape had been subjected to the shifting pressure of tons of ice and snow, but

Alison had seen enough pictures to reach an instant conclusion. Her words came out as a whisper as she turned to Scott. "Is that what I think it is?"

He simply nodded in silence.

They were staring at the crushed, warped, and corroded cockpit canopy framework of a seventy-four-year-old de Havilland Mosquito.

o o o

The previous morning, as she'd sat in Dr. Sorensen's office and absorbed the disappointing and surprising news, Alison's stomach had been in knots. She'd been surprised by the intensity of that response. She'd known that Jack Barton was her grandfather, but she'd really only known him as a character from a distant and almost forgotten childhood story, never as a flesh and blood human being. She'd understood him to be a once-real person, to be sure, but he'd been no more real to her than Marie Curie or George Washington. But when Scott Wilcox had called and explained what had been found on a Norwegian glacier, she'd felt it—connection. And obligation. The grinning young man in that old black-and-white photograph had reminded her of his existence. And his loss.

She'd been pulled to Norway by a familiar and almost irresistible force, but as she'd always been prone to do, she'd wrapped herself in her favourite protective armour: the distance of intellect. She'd convinced herself that the trip would be simply a formality, but she'd also given herself a reason to escape Seattle for a little while, a valid excuse to temporarily take her and her mind away from the stress of board meetings and progress reviews with the always impatient and never satisfied "vulture capitalists." She'd assumed time and distance would have insulated her from the human aspects of the discovery—especially from the personal connection it held—but as she climbed the rattling, frozen aluminum ladder back up to the relative warmth of the late afternoon Norwegian sunlight, her shivers had nothing to do with temperature. A sober realization had come over her.

She'd just been standing in what was more than likely a grave.

More than seven decades ago, a young man who'd left his even younger wife thousands of miles away—pregnant with the daughter he would never know—had been involved in something terrible here. And that young man had been her flesh and blood. His colleague, Flight Lieutenant Vickson, had likely suffered the same fate. There was a good chance they were still entombed somewhere under the ice.

But how did they end up there? What had happened to their plane to cause it to crash? And what about the kid's finger bone?

The questions had begun to pile up, and she knew many more would come.

Questions.

Alison had been asking them her entire life, because they were how she dealt with feelings. Questions were precursors to knowledge, and knowledge was what she craved, because knowledge, she'd always believed, led to certainty, and certainty was safety.

As an athlete, it had never been enough for her to be told by a coach to do something, to hit the ball to a certain place in a certain way. She'd always needed to know why. As a student, it had never been enough for her to just study, to engage in rote memorization in order to pass a test, only to forget the temporarily committed details forever once the moment had passed. From kindergarten through graduate school, her approach had been the same. She'd launched herself into each and every subject, dug and pried and excavated until she'd answered the who, what, where, when, why, or how of it. Until she'd actually *known*. As an adult—especially as a biochemist— those traits had propelled her like rocket fuel. She'd achieved success, at least by standard definitions, much earlier than most others, and at first she'd enjoyed it. Intellectual and career success had seemed like the biggest answer of them all, and she'd simply gone with it, consumed by its heady allure.

But the events of the last few years had ignited another burn in Alison. She'd tried to suppress it, but it was a battle she couldn't win, because the strength of her foe was in her own nature. She simply couldn't ignore the growing heat of the questions beginning to crowd her consciousness: questions about the randomness of life and death, about the almost unbearable pain of love and loss, about the meaning of her work, about herself and her place in the world. They were the kind of questions that she always tried to avoid, because they were questions to which she could never really know the answers.

She'd loved sports and academics and science because they'd always held answers for her. She'd felt safe in those pursuits because she felt safe in answers. But life? People? Family, colleagues, friends? The billions of souls roaming the planet? And most definitely her own self? Too many unknowables to even contemplate. Wherever possible she preferred to avoid asking questions about those things, because she knew from experience that the frustration, pain, and grief to which such lines of inquiry could lead could be crushing. But she also knew that sometimes those questions could be the most insistent. Sometimes she found herself unable to avoid asking them. And this was one of those times.

"You okay, ma'am?"

Alison realized she'd been staring out of her window, lost in silent thought, since Scott had steered them out of the gravel parking lot and onto the road. "Yeah, yeah. I'm fine," she lied, smiling weakly. "Just... thinking, I suppose."

"Let me guess," he said quietly, without taking his eyes from the road. "Every new answer creates a new question."

The pinpoint accuracy of that statement stunned her. She nodded a silent response and turned her eyes to the blurred forest rushing past her window. *That's pretty much my whole goddamn life in one sentence.*

The familiar, hollow feeling in her gut underscored every thought that came into her mind on the trip back down to Odda. It was the same feeling she'd had as a biochemistry student when she'd been faced with the incomprehensible. The same one she'd felt after she'd had to say her devastating forever goodbyes to James. The same one she'd felt as she'd watched, virtually powerless, as her mother had suffered and died from the cancer that had consumed her. The burning need to fill the empty spaces. The need to know.

○ ○ ○

The small restaurant at Odda's Hardanger Hotel was buzzing with the early summer crowd, excited tourists loudly fueling up for the next morning's glacier hikes and kayak expeditions on the fjord.

Scott stared into the blue-white glow of his laptop as Alison picked at her salad.

"This case has really got me stumped." He clicked through the scores of images over and over. "My team firmly believes the wreckage under the ice is the last known aircraft flown by Barton and Vickson. But since the remains we have aren't related to either of them, I'm afraid my official presence here is no longer justified."

Alison struggled to mask her disappointment. Their morning visit to the glacier excavation had hit her harder than she was prepared for, and the thought that there might be no answers to her questions weighed on her.

"But the wreckage under the ice seems so promising," she said. "I mean, there's still a chance something new will turn up, right?"

"Well, sure. But sometimes these things, well…they just fade away," said Scott, giving Alison one of his brief smiles. "Maybe history rhymes with mystery for a reason, you know?"

Alison stared past her own reflection in the darkened window.

"Listen, Professor Lundeen said they've enlarged the cavern since we were down there this morning," Scott said, "and they're working on gaining access to more of what might be in and around the cockpit components we saw. He's hoping that might provide us with a few more answers. So let's plan on regrouping early tomorrow afternoon so we can make an informed decision about what happens next. Okay?"

Alison nodded and smiled just a little as Scott turned his laptop toward her.

"Here's the thing. My official duties in this case may be related to the recovery of human remains, but I can't help thinking about all of the questions here. Like this one, for example."

On a Google satellite image, a triangle of thin, translucent blue lines connected a point in northern Scotland with a point that Alison knew to be the eastern side of Denmark and the point on Folgefonna glacier where the wreckage had been found.

"What's your grandfather's airplane doing almost five hundred kilometres northwest of its last known location at Aarhus, Denmark?"

12

Twenty seconds after he saw the last Mosquito clear the target area, Jack told the rest of the boys to hightail it for home and let them know he'd stay back with the straggler.

Coleman and Wilkinson had either taken a flak hit or gotten punched by shrapnel. It looked to Jack like they'd lost a significant chunk of their port horizontal stabilizer, but they were both okay and they were still airborne, so they formed up on his starboard wing to begin the long run back across Denmark and the North Sea, toward the plates of hot food and glasses of therapeutically essential cold liquids waiting for them at home.

He never liked this part.

Although they'd be following a slightly different course home than the one they'd taken on the way from Scotland to the target, Jack knew they'd be heading over a whole lot of potentially angry Germans occupying the hundred or so miles of darkening Jutland terrain below them. The element of surprise was most definitely gone, and he knew the black-crossed butcher birds could be out looking for them, but with luck, they'd make the North Sea in just under twenty minutes, if Coleman could maintain his stability and speed. *Luck again*, he thought.

"Low as you dare, fast as you care, Jackknife Six," Jack said into his oxygen mask.

"Roger, Jackknife Leader. We're good to go. Let's get the hell out of here," came the reply.

Eleven minutes later, just as Cousineau looked up to call out a new heading, Jack's aircraft suddenly lurched violently, kicked hard by a series of violent bangs that set off an incessant hammering vibration.

He reacted instantly and without thinking, instincts taking over as he simultaneously worked the stick and pedals and scanned his gauges and the deep blue sky all around them for signs of danger. They were down to less than five hundred feet—still in one piece as far as Jack could tell, but buffeting wildly—before he was really able to take a look over at Cousineau. The navigator was writhing in his seat, gloved right hand desperately clutching at the place where his left hand had been. *Fuck!* "Cooze! Hang on, man! Jesus Christ, hang on!" Jack yelled.

There was a jagged, eight-inch long hole in the Mosquito's curved plywood fuselage, just below Cousineau's right knee. Something—a flak shell? a piece of shrapnel? a piece of the Mosquito itself?—had made its way through the laminated wood and metal and found flesh and bone before it exited through the Perspex escape hatch above their heads. Wind whistled and roared through both openings, freezing some of the wood splinters into the blood that had sprayed the cockpit.

Jack grabbed the leather sleeve of Cousineau's flight jacket and shook him hard. "You've gotta get a tourniquet on that!" he yelled, fighting to be heard over the roar of the engines and wind and the relentless hammering noises coming from somewhere to his right. "Cooze!" *Jesus Christ!* "Look at me!" Cousineau slowly turned his head toward Jack, eyes half closed as he fought to stay conscious.

"Cooze! Come on! Stay with it!" *Shit!* Cousineau slumped against his seat back and the side of the cockpit, his right hand slowly falling away from his shattered left wrist as he slipped toward shock and unconsciousness. Jack did the only thing he could think to do. He gripped the control column with his left hand and reached over and grabbed what was left of the navigator's hemorrhaging stump with his right, squeezing as hard as he could.

"Jackknife Leader, this is Jackknife Six. You guys okay? Over," came the squawking in his helmet earphones. Realizing his oxygen mask had come loose, Jack let go of the control stick and quickly snapped it back into place. There was no way he was letting go of Cousineau. The plane veered wildly, shedding even more precious altitude before he was able to get it back under one-handed control with the nose pointed basically in the right direction.

His heart was pounding like a jackhammer, his breath short and sharp, but somehow his voice—his practiced, combat pilot voice—was calm. "Uh, yeah, Jackknife Six, this is Jackknife Leader. I think maybe we took a flak hit or something back there. How do we look? Any idea what happened? Over."

"We didn't see a bloody thing, skipper. Could have been a lone Jerry or maybe some random ground fire. Everything looks basically okay from here, but there's a nasty little hole in your bubble. Over."

Jack breathed deeply, slowly, trying to control his fear, trying to think. He scanned his instruments—everything seemed to be functioning properly—and ran through the various scenarios in his mind.

Given that his gauges all basically read normal, he figured the hammering noises had to indicate some kind of structural damage rather than engine damage, and at this point, they were still flying. But what about Cousineau? He could turn back and hope to find a place to set down in Denmark. If they survived that exercise without getting shot out of the air, that might get Cousineau to a hospital the fastest, but it would be a German hospital. Or he could try to get as much altitude and airspeed as he could out of his now shuddering plywood kite and hope like hell to make it back across the North Sea to Scotland. *Goddammit!*

"Ah, Jackknife Six, this is Jackknife Leader. Cooze is hurt pretty bad. I've got to get him down right now...." Cousineau's gloved hand suddenly grabbed Jack's right forearm and squeezed it like a vise. Eyes shut tight, the navigator slowly shook his head from side to side.

"Yeah, Jackknife Six this is Jackknife Leader. We're gonna chance it. You guys set a course for the emergency strip at Carnaby and I'll follow you in."

One hundred and forty-seven exhausting minutes later, Jack let go of Cousineau's arm just long enough to wrestle the damaged Mosquito safely back to the damp English earth. As his props spun down, the emergency boys converged like hungry flies on his dull grey-green bird, swarming in through the Mosquito's side entrance door and its upper escape hatch. It took them a minute or two to pry Jack's cramped and uncontrollably shaking right hand away from Cousineau's shredded wrist. Jack slumped in his seat, exhausted and sweating and shivering and staring intently at the Mosquito's instrument panel as a medic worked to get a tourniquet on Cousineau's arm, shot him up with morphine, and helped the emergency crew get his friend the hell out of the cockpit.

Coleman and Wilkinson had caught a short ride over from their broken Mosquito. They'd had to land wheels up on the wet grass— on final approach they'd discovered that something had disabled their port landing gear—but both had walked away unscathed. They stared silently as the blood wagon raced Cousineau away and another medic checked Jack out, finding not a single scratch.

Before climbing into the truck to head to debrief, the three of them took a quick walk around Jack's Mosquito. In addition to the holes in the bottom of the cockpit and the top of the canopy, they counted four more in its bomb bay doors and two in its starboard engine nacelle. The trailing edge of its starboard inboard flap had been completely shot away.

Back at Banff a few hours later, alone in his miserable quarters while everyone else was heading off to get drunk and chase WAAFs around a dance floor somewhere, Jack could barely crack the whisky bottle with his still cold, still cramped, and still trembling hands.

As he lay in bed, waiting impatiently for the combination of the brown liquid and Doc McNair's magic little pills to send him into blissful oblivion, he squeezed his eyes shut and tried to picture Marie, but he just couldn't get there. Instead, his brain insisted on replaying the same film over and over—the carnage of Cousineau's mangled stump and the surreal sight of his friend's leather-clad hand lying palm up in the blood and meat and dirt and plywood splinters at the bottom of the Mosquito's green footwell. *Jesus, Cooze. Jesus Christ.* Sweating profusely and chilled to the bone, he tossed and turned, but there was no escape.

Through glassy, burning, drooping eyes, he stared at the pile on the floor at the side of his bed. Cousineau's blood had stained the right arm of his brown sheepskin flight jacket the darkest of reds.

13

They called him "Opa."

At twenty-nine, Günther Graf was an old man, primarily because most men in his line of work didn't survive that long.

He'd read the letter a hundred times since it had arrived in March. He knew she was trying to put on a brave face, to convince him that everything was okay, but he also knew otherwise. He was happy in the belief that they were relatively safe for the time being. He'd been able to get her and Gisele out of Hamburg before the RAF burned it to the ground, but he knew he was running out of places where the bombs and artillery shells might not find them.

They'd transferred the majority of his more experienced comrades back to Germany in late April—it seems the Reichsverteidigung had suddenly taken priority over the fool's errand they'd been sent on out here. Of course, Günther had been left to "lead the men to victory."

Men? They were boys, most of them barely out of their teens and hardly able to fly, let alone fight and win against the seemingly endless supply of Russian planes and pilots. Add in the relentless ground fire they encountered on almost every mission, the unbearable rain and mud and flies and dust and snow, and the rapidly deteriorating condition of their aircraft, and it was easy to understand why life expectancy for "Nachwuchs"—the baby pilots they kept sending him—was less than eleven hours of total flying time. Less than five typical sorties.

His commanding officer, Oberst Werner Marcks, had always tried to protect him—he'd saved Günther's sorry ass more than once over France and England in 1940, and he'd managed to return the favour a few times—but as his disillusionment, disdain, and disgust became harder and harder to conceal, he knew it was all his friend could do to keep him from being grounded or demoted or court-martialed or worse.

But he had a feeling that this time might be the last time.

14

Alison had dragged herself out of bed at about nine—an incredibly late hour for her—and had spent a low-energy morning knee-deep in emails and video calls, attention pulled in a hundred directions by Seattle's requests and demands and problems and challenges. But through it all, over and over again, Jack Barton's grin had pulled her back down into the ice.

Scott was once again focused on his laptop as she walked into the café, and he glanced up with a quick smile as she sat. She ordered a coffee, scrambled egg whites, and toast before turning to him.

"So? Dare I ask?" she said. "Anything meaningful in the last twenty-four hours?"

Scott swung his screen around to face her. "Yeah. Jonas said the dig team was able to remove more of the ice from around the cockpit area and they appear to have, ah, found a couple things that might help us."

The high-res image was crystal clear, but Alison had no idea what she was looking at. Something that resembled a mass of wet, compressed, dark brown and grey cardboard was visible among the twisted pieces of metal and other bits of unidentifiable detritus in the ice and water.

Scott clicked the arrow key and another image appeared, showing an object that Alison interpreted as a flattened, roughly figure-eight-shaped piece of metal. It had been smashed down and embedded into another dark brown, shapeless blob of some kind, from under which protruded what looked to be a kind of crumbled, yellow-grey stone. A curl of thin black rubber tubing was partially visible beneath that. A third image revealed a handful of corroded and bent objects positioned near a tape measure. She had no idea what most of them were, but one appeared to be a small metal toolbox.

"What do you make of all that?"

Scott pointed to the screen with a pen. "Well, Professor Lundeen believes this large dark brown and grey mass to be compressed paper of some kind, or maybe leather. I'm guessing this brown-black area is likely the remains of a flying helmet, which means the figure-eight shaped object could be the lens frames from a pair of goggles. If that's true, the, uh, yellow stone-like material could be…human remains. Possibly a skull. The other objects were found as the archaeology team melted the ice away from the vicinity of the dark mass. Obviously, Professor Lundeen feels this is an important find, so he's personally taking it all to the university for a closer look."

Alison swallowed hard and pushed aside her suddenly unappetizing scrambled eggs. "Wow. Okay. So, could this be it? Could this be what you need to keep your investigation going?"

"Definitely maybe. If these do turn out to be human remains I'll need to get them back to our labs for analysis. I can't imagine remains found that deep in the ice and associated that closely with the aircraft wreckage itself would be related to the finger bone found nearer the surface. The good news is, we've finally been able to locate a next of kin, a younger sister, for Flight Lieutenant Vickson. She's living in a long-term care facility in a suburb of Auckland, New Zealand, and

DNA samples are on the way to both Ottawa and Bergen. So I don't know how you feel about this, ma'am, but Professor Lundeen asked if you'd like to view these new artifacts in person. We could make that trip to the university together. Would you be up for that?"

For about half a second, Alison thought about the insistent knot between her shoulder blades, the one that was clearly growing in direct correlation to the scale of her mounting obligations back in Seattle, but a hundred new questions and thoughts and possibilities quickly pushed all of that out of her mind. *My team can survive without me for another day or two.*

"Well, I've come this far." She smiled. "And I think I want to see this through."

15

Jack hadn't thought much about being called to the special meeting until he arrived at Ops and saw the new guy puffing on a cigarette in the hallway outside the meeting room.

They'd only flown four trips together.

Following his last op with Cousineau, Jack had emerged from the alcohol-bolstered fog of Doc McNair's mandatory three-day leave in Aberdeen to meet his new navigator, freshly arrived in Scotland from someplace or other down south.

Their first two sorties had been to uneventful, no-joy targets off the coast of Norway, the third they'd flown top with the Mustangs while the rest of the boys had hit a minesweeper and its escorts in the Skagerrak Strait, and the fourth they'd taken out a couple of merchant ships and an armed trawler near Bergen.

Jack really didn't know much about Vickson personally, other than the fact that he was single, had sold tractors or harvesters or farm tools or something like that in civvy life, and that he hailed from a place called Swift Current. But he seemed like a stand-up guy, and he was capable enough, navigator-wise. *So why the hell would you be here?* Jack thought as he smiled and nodded. "Hey, Bob. Slumming it?"

Before Vickson could answer, Group Captain Linden had invited

Jack into the room and closed the door, leaving the navigator alone with his cloud of smoke out in the anteroom. *Well, shit. I'm either getting promoted or I'm in the doghouse again.*

Linden had immediately introduced a couple of guys Jack had never seen before. "Squadron Leader Barton, meet Major Ellingson and Captain Hawkes. They'd like to fill you in on a little project they've got you in mind for."

The two officers had commended Jack on his stellar service record, complimented him on his skills as a combat pilot and his reported coolness under pressure, noting with typical British understatement that "Flight Lieutenant Cousineau may have a bit of a long road ahead of him," but that he was "fortunate to be recuperating" in a hospital somewhere near Leeds. *You guys really don't have a goddamn clue, do you?* Finally, they'd gotten around to asking Jack if he was comfortable flying with Vickson, and he'd said yeah, he guessed so. At that point, much to Jack's surprise, Linden had invited Vickson into the room and they'd laid it all out for him.

Vickson wasn't regular RCAF. He was attached to the SOE. And he was somehow connected to the American OSS.

Jack didn't know much about the Special Operations Executive, but he'd heard it referred to by a couple of other names—"Churchill's Secret Army" and "The Ministry of Ungentlemanly Warfare" came to mind. The major and captain had mentioned that they belonged to the "Inter-Service Research Bureau," whatever the hell that was.

They'd asked Jack if he'd be willing to undertake a special mission, unlike any other he'd ever flown. A mission that required the speed, range, and capabilities of a Mosquito in good hands. A mission of vital importance...blah, blah, blah. *Yeah. Okay. Sure. Like I've never heard that before*, Jack thought, glancing over at Vickson as a stream of questions clawed their way to the surface.

Then they'd told him what they'd cooked up.

For the briefest of moments, Jack's intellect had thought soberly about their insane proposal. He'd thought about all of the things he had to live for, all of the things that should have prompted him to say no. But then, of course, like an impulsive, brash, idiotic, identical twin brother he couldn't control, his ego had blurted out a yes.

16

Professor Lundeen removed the corroded object from the laboratory freezer and placed it on a black rubber pad on his workbench.

It was about the size of a small toolbox, although it had been crushed to only eight or nine centimetres high on one end. The few flecks of colour still clinging to it indicated that it might once have been painted a pale, metallic grey-green, and a badly rusted latch on the front side held it closed.

"Since you were still in Norway, Miss Wiley, I thought you might want to be present when we opened this, in case it, uh, holds anything relevant to… Well, it was found in close proximity to the, um, newly found human remains, but of course it may not contain anything at all."

Jonas activated an overhead video camera, then carefully inserted a flat pry bar under the rusty clasp. A moderate amount of force resulted in a grinding metallic pop, and the hinged closure creaked loose. With a gloved hand, he gently but firmly worked the crusted lid open.

The inside of the box was also badly corroded, and a layer of what appeared to be frozen mud or silt coated the bottom. Embedded in the dirty brown ice was an object that Alison immediately took to be a small notebook. Jonas produced a tape measure and called out its measurements and a description for the video record.

"So, what do you think it might be? A diary, maybe? Or a pilot's logbook?" she asked.

"I could be wrong, but I don't think it's a logbook," said Scott. "To the best of my knowledge, pilots never carried their logbooks with them on combat missions, and even if this case was an exception to that general rule, RAF and RCAF logbooks of that era tended to be larger than that and a little more square in format, and most were cloth bound, I believe."

"So what do we do? Do we dare try to open it?" Alison asked.

"No, I think we'll want to be very, very careful with this," Jonas explained. "If we simply try to thaw the artifact out and open it, the materials could simply disintegrate. And of course, if there were any water-based inks used, they could be severely impacted. So actually, the best way to handle this item will be to freeze-dry it. We'll place it in a vacuum chamber and keep the temperature below zero degrees. The materials will be dried by a process called sublimation. Water in solid state—the ice—will be removed in its gaseous state, without ever passing through a liquid state, so there will be no additional wetting to cause any distortion beyond whatever might already have been incurred."

Professor Lundeen summoned a student assistant, who promptly collected the tray and disappeared with it into an adjoining room. "It shouldn't take more than a day to complete the sublimation process," said Jonas. "Let's keep our fingers crossed for some positive results. Meanwhile, there's something else that we've been able to uncover."

The professor opened his laptop and a familiar image appeared on the wall-mounted flat-screen monitor. "Is that what we thought it was?" Scott asked. "Is that a flying helmet? And are those goggles?"

"We were able to identify these particular items, yes," said Jonas. "The dark brown mass appears to be the remains of a British C Type leather flying helmet, issued to Royal Air Force and Commonwealth aircrews in late 1943, early 1944. And the two somewhat angular connected metal rings—this sort of flat figure eight shape—which also appear to hold some leather remnants, are, most likely, the lens holder frames from a pair of Mark Seven goggles, made for the RAF as a standard-issue item in 1941.

"So, although we cannot yet identify the, uh, remains, which Dr. Sorensen's people have indicated are...skull fragments and a few teeth, we can probably assume that whoever they actually belonged to was wearing standard-issue Royal Air Force aircrew kit at the time of their death. There's one thing that has us a little puzzled, though."

Jonas advanced to the next image.

"This object was actually found underneath the mass of crushed skull fragments after we removed them from the ice."

It looked like mottled dull grey metal, roughly half of an oval disk, with a slightly serrated straight edge. Two small holes punched through it near the apex of its rounded edge.

Jonas continued. "It's made of some type of alloy. And as you can see from the tape measure, it's not very large, measuring only sixty-two millimetres long by twenty-two millimetres. But this is actually the back side of it."

He clicked his keyboard and the flat screen revealed a new image.

"And this is the front."

On the object's flip side, beneath the two small holes near its rounded edge, they could see the stamped numbers and letters.

376 92

L.G. K DO X II

"So...what exactly is that? Do we know?" Alison asked.

Jonas looked up. "We do, yes. We've seen objects similar to this before, from time to time, in other Second World War dig sites. It's a military identification disc. Or, I should say, it's half of a military identification disc. This type consisted of two identical stamped halves, with a snap line running across the middle. The rough straight edge at the bottom there is where the snap line would have been. They were designed so that one half of the disc could be left with the, uh, deceased owner, and the other half could be removed and retained as a record of death."

"So, it's what? A dog tag?" Alison asked. "That's got to be good news, right? I mean, I'm assuming we can use the information to help make a definitive identification. Maybe it can help us figure out what happened to my grandfather and his crewmate?"

"Well, yes, Miss Wiley. It is a kind of dog tag," Jonas replied, "but I'm afraid it may not help us much in regard to your grandfather or his friend, specifically."

"I'm sorry, but I'm not sure I understand," said Alison. "How can you be one hundred percent sure of that already?"

As Jonas began to answer, Scott chimed in.

"Because, ma'am, this particular ID tag is German."

17

The sound of the key in the lock terrified her, as it always did, but it was the music that never failed to induce her paralyzing panic.

As the faceless men had ripped away her blanket and clothes, gripped her arms and legs and neck tightly and strapped her to the metal gurney, she'd whimpered and cried out in fear and despair, but only for a short time, because she'd known it was useless. They couldn't understand her, or they pretended not to, and she couldn't understand them. And she knew they would do whatever they would do, and that no one would ever come to save her.

Because her head was usually strapped firmly in place, the most she'd ever been able to see was whatever was directly above her or within her narrow peripheral view—the peeling light green paint on the hallway ceiling, its dangling yellow-white lights, the round windows near the tops of the two doors that burst open when the gurney was forcefully rolled into them, the tops of the cold room's gleaming ceramic tiled walls, its pristine white ceiling, and the huge circular shape with the bright lights that always hurt her eyes, even when she tried to close them as tightly as she could.

And although she could almost always see the white-clad upper bodies and heads of the people who hurt her, she'd rarely seen their faces, mostly just their expressionless eyes exposed between the masks and caps they wore. As they'd strapped her to the frigid metal tables and put the gags into her mouth, as they'd driven the needles deep into her arms and legs and neck and torso, as they'd repeatedly cut her and sewed the excruciating incisions shut, and as her own eyes had filled with so many tears that she could no longer see, she'd often wondered if they cried, or if they ever felt anything at all.

In the cold white room, the music that triggered her dread was always loudest.

She knew it was there to cover the screams.

18

Marcks kept his voice low, his tone intense. And incredulous.

"Disobeying a direct order? Willful dereliction of duty? I can't believe this is true. I never would have guessed it of you, Gunner."

For Günther, it had been the last straw.

They'd taken off just before sunrise, only six serviceable Bf 110s and the eleven remaining Bf 109s. Günther's own battered, mottled grey-green 109—Blue 5—with its weather-beaten Grünherz insignia and yellow wingtips shining dully in the early morning gloom, had been loaded with a single, fuselage-mounted 250-kilogram bomb, which made his thoroughbred handle like an old donkey. He'd been ordered to lead the group to Smolensk, where Schimmel—the widely despised, self-appointed "Gröfaz" who called the shots for what was left of the group—had determined they were to attack and destroy a hospital.

That was it for him.

When he'd joined the Luftwaffe in late 1937, he'd done so for mostly pragmatic reasons firmly rooted in the desire to provide. In the twenty-one months prior, he'd managed to fall in love, start a family, and completely run out of money, an incredible sequence of events that had ultimately forced him to abandon his university chemistry studies at Leipzig. With few promising job options, he had to admit he'd been seduced by the notion of serving as a "knight of the air," with all of the honour and pomp and chivalry that implied.

His mother had cried at the news, and although he'd sensed the essential truth of her admonitions deep in his gut—that the real enemies of any nation were the weak old men who would send its strong young men to kill and maim and die in their places—he'd suppressed any gnawing doubts about his country's militaristic new path, and reassured her that Germany was simply returning to its rightful status in the world, repeating, as he'd been told, that it simply needed to be able to defend itself against any future aggressors. Like most brash young men his age, he hadn't really thought much about what his country might be about to become. Instead, he'd thought mostly about what he, himself, might be able to become.

He'd focused on the pride of personal achievement, and at first, it had been everything he'd been promised it would be. The thrill of learning to fly, the excitement of being assigned to the fighter school, the sharp uniforms, the ceremony, the camaraderie, the commitment to duty. But after twenty-six months of studying and training, reality had suddenly arrived. On a beautiful late spring morning, he'd kissed Karin and Gisele and his mother goodbye and boarded a westbound train, and just forty days later he'd experienced the wildly exhilarating rush of fear and adrenaline that came with entering into and surviving his first aerial combat.

Certainly, he'd killed British pilots in the summer and autumn of 1940 and early 1941, but somehow it hadn't felt that way. Chasing down, shooting at, and destroying a flying machine was impersonal, and he'd detached himself from the flesh-and-blood truth of it all. Like virtually all of his comrades, he'd flown into battle with a misguided sense of honour and nobility, pumped up on methamphetamines—

"Hermann-Göring-Pillen" he and his squadron mates called them—and the glorious, bombastic rhetoric of his commanding officers. And he'd done well, climbing steadily in rank as he'd gained the combat experiences marked by the kill bars painted on the rudders of his aircraft. But now, after experiencing too much reality, he understood that in those days he'd been simply a naive, selfish, impressionable boy—an unquestioning, unthinking believer.

His group had been transferred to Russia in 1941 and it was there, over a surprisingly short time, that his mother's words had risen up to claim him and that he'd come to acknowledge the full, terrible, unforgivable truth. The shine of all of that paper-thin glory had been steadily tarnished by the decisions of those whom he had sworn to obey—the politicians and so-called superior officers whose moral bankruptcy and military stupidity had brought Germany to the brink of total disaster.

Four years after his first combat sortie, he was an old man. He'd witnessed too much horrendous cruelty and seen far, far too many of his friends and comrades perish because of arrogance, and stupidity and callous indifference. And he'd finally come to understand his own place in it all.

The first time he'd actually seen a man he'd killed personally—two men in fact—had been a shock. In early August of 1941, during his first week at the Eastern front, he and his wingman had caught a single damaged and clearly lost Sturmovik—one of the slow and heavily armoured Russian ground attack aircraft the German tank crews and infantry feared and despised—as they'd made their way back to their own base following a ground support strike. Although the Sturmovik's rear gunner had tried to put up a decent fight and the pilot had done his best, Günther had bored in close. It was over in seconds, and the flaming "Zementbomber" had dashed itself to pieces in a scrubby stand of pine trees just a few hundred metres shy of Günther's landing strip.

Despite his protestations, the excited ground crew had insisted Günther and his wingman join them on their expedition to inspect the wreckage. The Russian aeroplane was no longer an aeroplane, reduced instead to widely scattered bits and pieces. Engine here. Red-starred, dark green wing tip there. Unrecognizable chunk of flame-blackened metal there.

One of the young armourers had laughed as he'd shouted out his find, the decapitated rear gunner still strapped into the shattered and shredded and scorched fuselage where he'd breathed his last, the smashed pilot charred beyond recognition just ahead of him. Elated, the men had dragged the gunner's body from the smoking hulk, pulled off a few slimy, red-smeared buttons and badges, and rifled through the man's pockets. One of them had handed Günther a folded leather wallet. Swallowing hard, jaw clenched to conceal his rising emotions as the others crowded around and jubilantly clapped him on the back, Günther had opened it to find only a few scraps of paper and a single tiny photograph. A dour woman stood stone-faced and grim beside a smiling teenage boy, eager and obviously proud in his ill-fitting Red Army uniform. Günther flipped the snapshot over. On the back, in pencil, words he couldn't decipher.

Вернись ко мне

Günther looked away as one of the ground crewmen snatched the photograph from him. The young man's grandmother had been a Russlanddeutsche—a Volga German—forced to flee the goddamned communist purges, he'd said, and she'd taught him enough of the language that he thought he knew what the words said.

"Come back to me."

They'd all burst out laughing at that. All except Günther, who'd simply turned and walked away.

They'd taken root in him from that day on, the gnawing tendencies that were less than desirable in a combat pilot. He simply thought too much, felt too much. Because worst of all, he knew that beyond the willing participants in the shared madness—the pilots and crews of the sixty-six British and Russian aircraft he'd shot down and the countless enemy ground troops he'd annihilated—he'd most certainly killed and maimed untold numbers of innocent civilians. He'd seen the old men fall, seen the mothers, running, screaming for their lives with their babies clutched close and their young children suspended from their outstretched arms as his bombs fell on them in the name of the Fatherland.

He knew deep in his heart that there was absolutely no honour or nobility in anything he was doing. He fought now only to survive, to try to protect his young charges as best he could, and to one day get home to his wife and daughter, if there was still a home to return to. As far as he was concerned, Germany was killing itself right here, although he knew the final coup de grace, the death blow, would be applied by millions of unstoppable American, British, Canadian, and Russian soldiers and sailors and airmen. He was simply along for the ride, a captive participant in the collective insanity, unable to choose the right or forego the wrong.

So when he'd been ordered to take even more lives—possibly hundreds and hundreds of defenceless men and women who were suffering and dying and working in the Smolensk North Military Hospital—he'd decided to set himself free.

He'd led the attack force off course—an "error" he blamed on weather and faulty instruments—and, declaring them to be lost, he'd ordered his young pilots to drop their ordnance in the barren mud fields and head for home. None of them had complained.

Just two days later, on a low-level reconnaissance sortie, his brand-new, baby-faced nineteen-year-old wingman—Günther had barely even known his name—had augured in, lost to a barrage of Soviet ground fire that sheared off his 109's wing at the root. Günther himself had struggled to get back, his own aircraft trailing a white stream of coolant vapour and with a viscous, oily film coating its windshield. Barely able to see the airfield on approach, he'd come down much too hard, collapsing one of his landing gear struts and cartwheeling the aircraft.

Blue 5 had ultimately come to rest inverted, its boxy cockpit canopy prevented from opening by the sucking Russian mud just above Günther's pounding, blood-filled head. He'd hung awkwardly, claustrophobically, from his harness, helpless, anxious, his fear of fire or smoke or explosion rising along with the intensifying stench of his overheated machine, its heavy synthetic oil and fuel smells mixing most unfavourably with the human sourness of his suppressed panic. Eyes closed, he'd focused on slowing his breathing, on trying to get himself to a better place. Fleeting images of pink birthday dresses and dolls and cakes and the smiles of his beautiful girls took him momentarily away as he waited in the seemingly interminable, heat-ticking silence for the welcome sounds of the rescue boys, who finally hacked and cut and pried his dead bird wide open and dragged him away, toward more life. He would not die that day.

Günther's right shoulder had been dislocated, his wrist broken. And, although he hadn't noticed during the intensity of his encounter with the Russian ground fire and his ensuing hard landing, a seven-and-a-half-centimetre-long metal fragment had embedded itself deep in his left calf.

Of course, it hadn't taken long for the story of the aborted hospital attack to get around. An official investigation had been launched, with Schimmel no doubt pushing hard from the top. That miserable bastard had hated Günther since the day he'd arrived at the front just five months prior, no doubt intimidated by his combat record and all the shiny hardware and silk ribbons that came along with it. He was aggravated by Günther's obvious lack of enthusiasm for certain tactical decisions. In Günther's mind, the men making those decisions showed almost total disregard for the lives of the young men he so badly wanted to protect.

In a very short time, it had come to this.

Marcks looked totally exhausted, his deeply lined face drawn and pale, the fibrous burn scars on both of his hands now reduced to a stretched, shiny, lifeless grey instead of the angry red they'd been when he'd been released from the hospital at Abbeville in January of '41. *Shit, Werner. You're making me look young*, Günther thought as his friend hunched forward, elbows on knees, in the chair beside his cot.

Marcks pinched the bridge of his nose, looked up and forced a smile. "Just what you needed, eh? Another wound badge to go with all the others?"

Günther smiled back as Marcks offered him a cigarette.

Marcks got right to it as he extended a flaring match. "You'll be in the infirmary here for a few more days, Günther, then you're gone. The sawbones say your injuries will prevent you from flying for at least two or three months, maybe four. By then, who knows? Between you and me, we may not have anything left to fly even a week from now. You'll take the transport out Friday, assuming it arrives at all."

Günther knew his friend was doing him a favour, getting him out of this hellhole, trying to save whatever was left of his imperilled honour. Maybe even saving what was left of his miserable life.

A year or so before, even Marcks had slipped up and admitted, following a few too many glasses of looted peasant samogon after a particularly difficult day over Leningrad, that he privately wondered what the hell they were all doing in Russia. After all, he'd reminded Günther, it had been less than a decade since he'd done his initial year of training at the Wissenschaftliche Versuchs und Prüfanstalt für Luftfahrzeuge—the so-called Scientific Research and Test Institute for Aircraft that was, in reality, a fighter pilot school—at Lipetsk. The Soviets, "the godless Ruskies themselves!" he'd reminded Günther, had allowed Germany to operate the facility on their soil in order to bypass the terms of the Treaty of Versailles, and the Luftwaffe had employed the training provided there to great effect over Poland, France, England, Italy, North Africa, and now, ironically, Russia.

"You and I both know one thing for sure. This shit world makes absolutely no sense," Marcks said. "And clearly we're not the ones making the big decisions here, but goddammit Gunner, you cannot disobey a direct order."

Günther took a long pull on his cigarette and exhaled slowly. As much as he admired and respected his friend, he disagreed with him on that last point.

"Look, Werner, you already know that my father survived the slaughter at the Somme, and at Vimy?" Günther said. "What I never told you is that only a few years after he returned home, the war took him anyway. He wasn't wounded, Werner. Not physically at least. His injury…his pain was, ah, inside. You understand? Inside. My mother finally told me, years later, when I was about eleven years old. My father had seen and done many, many terrible things. But she said that the one thing that he could never put behind him was that he had…well, that he and his comrades had gunned down British and Canadian prisoners. They'd simply murdered them, Werner, because…

because they'd been ordered to. My father knew the same thing had been done to German boys, but that didn't make it right. Mother said my father could never forgive himself. For not speaking up, for not doing…something. It…ate at him, you understand? For years. Who knows? Maybe speaking up would have been suicide too, huh? Same result in the end, maybe? But without the shame? Without the long pain of guilt?"

Günther took another deep, slow drag on his cigarette, exhaled through his nose, and stared into the unfocused distance as the smoke curled away into nothingness. "But who knows, eh? Maybe just one good act, by one man, can make a difference, even in the face of the most overwhelming odds."

Marcks stared at the floor, not knowing what to say.

Günther stubbed out his cigarette and smiled at his friend. "Well, I do know this. You made a hell of a big difference to me when you chased those two angry Hurricanes off my tail over the Channel."

Marcks looked up, nodding and smiling a little as he inhaled the last of his cigarette.

"Look, you may be right about all of this," he said, voice almost a whisper to prevent any others from overhearing, "but you're in the wrong goddamn place to be idealistic, Gunner. So I'm saving your ass one more time. I've pulled some strings. Secured a transfer for you. I know Karin and Gisele are up around Kiel somewhere, so I managed to get you assigned to a joint military research facility near Rostock. Best I could do."

"A military research facility? What kind of military research? Aeronautics, I hope?" Günther asked, hopefully.

"There'll be no more flying for you, Gunner. It's a laboratory of some kind. Your university studies before the war—and, of course, the lucky fact that you happen to be a wounded, highly decorated and respected officer—helped me persuade Schimmel to approve both the position and the transfer, for convalescent purposes. Of course, I also managed to get him to understand that it really wouldn't look good for the group—and especially for him personally—if an officer of your reputation and Experte status were to be dragged through the mud. Besides"—Marcks smiled—"he'll be glad to be rid of you."

"A laboratory, huh?" Günther smiled wryly. "Science instead of stupidity? Intellect instead of insubordination?"

Marcks crushed his cigarette butt under his boot and put a firm hand on Günther's left shoulder as he stood. He turned and walked toward the tent door, then paused and looked back. "You've served your country and your comrades well. And you've made it this far in spite of yourself. Hell, we both have. But more than anything, Gunner, you've been a damn good friend. I don't want to see you in front of a firing squad. I want to see you waiting for me out in front of a bar in Berlin, with a pocket full of cash and a big smile, ready to buy me a whole lot of drinks."

19

As aircrew, they were treated like royalty, with actual sunny-side ups and real bacon on their plates instead of the powdered eggs and Spam everyone else had to choke down, a small acknowledgement, they all knew, of the odds. Each pilot and navigator knew he could very well be eating what the heavy night bomber crews—whose life expectancy was even lower than that of the members of the Strike Wing crews—morbidly referred to as "The Last Supper."

In a failing effort to smother some rapidly awakening butterflies, Jack stuffed the final bite of a third piece of toast into his mouth and gulped down the last of his lukewarm tea, then joined a steady stream of young men in various layers and combinations of RAF flight gear making their way through the soggy gloom, a few nods and wisecracks sufficing for early morning pleasantries, cigarettes providing the requisite distractions they all needed.

They all stood to attention as Group Captain Linden walked to the front of the room, pulled the canvas cover away from the map board, and turned to face them.

"Good morning, gentlemen. Please, have a seat. Today, we'll be paying another visit to our nautical Nazi friends in the Kattegat."

Fifty-five minutes later, Jack and Vickson climbed the short ladder and wriggled through the Mosquito's hatch into their cramped pea green and black "office," settling into their seats as the ground crew buttoned them up.

The armourers, riggers, and fitters had been busy all night long, prepping the seventeen Mosquitos for the task they were about to undertake. Even now, they buzzed all around the aircraft like overly fussy parents, performing their last-minute duties and double-checks as Jack and Vickson and the rest of the aircrews all strapped in and got to it. Every man in the business had his own way of getting geared up, of getting himself prepared to go and do what he'd been told needed to be done. Every man had his quirks and superstitions and processes. His rituals.

As he always did, Jack closed his eyes, placed his hands and feet on the Mosquito's controls, and sat dead still for a few seconds, calmly breathing in the familiar smells of the cockpit—oil and fuel and sweat and spent ammunition and the pungent, nail-varnish-like aroma he rightly or wrongly attributed to the plane's primarily wooden structure. A final deep inhalation, pushed out hard, was the trigger to begin the next phase—his run through preflight, where he checked off the list that always helped him transition from mostly peaceful terrestrial animal to violent airborne predator. Vickson doubled down on his maps and papers and compass with equal intensity, no doubt his way of crushing butterflies.

Get busy. Get focused. Stop thinking. Start doing.

Five minutes later, checks and runup completed, his six individual propeller blades transformed into two translucent yellow-ringed grey discs as his roaring engines fired perfectly, Jack gave the ground boys a thumbs-up and they pulled his chocks away. With thirty-two other Merlins roaring all around him, he released his brakes and taxied out to wait, first in line.

At the green signal, he shot Vickson a quick nod, quickly rapped the knuckle of his left index finger on the symbol he'd scratched into the paint on his new kite's canopy framework a few days before—a small maple leaf containing a single letter M—then steadily nudged the twin throttles forward, one slightly ahead of the other to combat the plane's somewhat disconcerting tendency to swing on takeoff, and gave the Mosquito exactly what it needed to enable it to do what it was designed to do.

Constructed almost entirely of laminated wood, it was an aircraft unlike any other he'd ever flown. Since they'd switched over from the heavier and slower Beaufighters they'd flown for the last few years, Jack and his squadron mates had quickly become supremely confident in their "wooden wonders." In a very short time, they'd learned from hands-on experience that they could rely on the Mosquitos to get them to the places where they'd need to cause trouble and then get them safely back home, sometimes under the most adverse conditions. Jack had loved the rugged and dependable Beau, but to him, the Mosquito was an absolute dream to fly. *Knock on wood. Literally. Here we go again, lucky one more time*, he thought, as thousands of Rolls-Royce horses steadily pulled the aircraft skyward.

They formed up over Fraserburgh, the Mosquitos joined first by twelve Polish Mustangs from Peterhead, then meeting up with an Air Sea Rescue Warwick out of Wick for the roughly two-hour trip across the North Sea.

Skirting a squall, flying barely fifty feet above the unforgiving ocean, Vickson called out a new heading as they approached the flat Danish coast. As they turned slightly south, the skies ahead of them began to clear to a perfect azure blue, leaving only a few wisps of steel grey clouds to remind everyone that they'd very likely soon be full of actual steel.

20

She was cold. Always cold.

The windowless concrete and brick and iron cell was hard and damp and foul, and the thin blanket under which she huddled did almost nothing to help retain the meagre heat escaping from her damaged body. She knew they'd be coming for her again soon, so she closed her heavy, burning eyes and tried to think of good things.

But there were so few good things to think of.

They'd brought her here some time ago, but she had no way of knowing exactly when. She'd not been outside, not seen sun or rain or clouds since the day they'd come to take her and the others from the squalor of the camp.

From time to time she'd heard them. The others. Sometimes crying out, sometimes whimpering, sometimes just rhythmically knocking on a metal door or a bed frame, trying in some tiny way to confirm that they were still alive, still part of the real world, no matter how horrible it had become. She'd even seen one of them once, glimpsed in a shadowy place she knew neither of them had been meant to see.

But she knew them.

Because they were her, and she was them.

21

The second-floor conference room was large and bright, its windows looking down into a sunlit, park-like courtyard lined with trees and shrubs and benches. Alison leaned against the frame of the floor-to-ceiling glass and sipped her coffee as she watched a couple of young students stroll through the square down below, laughing, hand in hand. *They were just kids, too. No older than you. And they never even got a chance to live.*

"So what now? I guess this is it?" Alison asked. "You take the new remains back to Canada, and if we're lucky, we eventually find out what we came here to find out? But probably not?"

"Well, normally yes, but in this case it seems no," said Scott. "Because of the determination that the first bone fragment actually belonged to a child, I've just been notified that the Norwegian police investigation takes priority when it comes to the newly discovered remains. I personally think it's pretty unlikely that the two sets are related in any way, but they want to officially rule out that possibility before they release the new remains to us. More of a formality, really. But to add another layer of complexity, because of the discovery of the German identity disc with the newly found remains, German War Graves will also need to be involved now."

"Look, I'm no expert in the area of DNA analysis," said Alison, "but I know enough to understand how difficult it's going to be to get any kind of definitive match with my grandfather, given my place in the family tree. Unless there's some new form of analysis I'm not aware of…?"

"Pretty much," said Scott. "Contrary to what Hollywood would have us believe, it's not as simple as pushing a button and getting a perfect DNA match five seconds later. But Dr. Sorensen has the finger bone, she's got your sample, and she'll have the sample from New Zealand in the morning. It's a place to start. We'll know as much as we can know by this time tomorrow."

o o o

The 4:00 a.m. streets of Bergen were quiet and deserted. Well, almost deserted.

She'd done this a hundred times.

Whenever her hyperactive brain, powerless to silence whatever incessant chatter had invaded it, simply wouldn't let her sleep, she'd learned not to just lie there and fight a losing fight, checking her phone every five minutes only to discover that barely five minutes had passed since she'd last checked it.

Get up. Get moving.

Whether she was walking through the early morning streets of New York or London or Paris or Bergen, her escape was always the same. For as long as she could remember, she'd been told and had later insisted that she was simply not a creative person. She preferred to live in a world of facts and logic, not because she thought the world operated that way—she was too logical to arrive at such an overly simplistic conclusion—but more because that was the only way she knew how to operate.

It was on these insomnia-induced excursions that a well-suppressed part of Alison Wiley would flex its tiny, atrophied muscles. There was something about strolling through vacant places that allowed her to imagine. Something about being virtually alone on normally crowded streets, something about the serenity of their beautiful but deserted stores, elegant but unoccupied restaurants, and tasteful but vacant apartment lobbies, that somehow spoke to her. Of potential. Of "what if?" And invariably, whenever she found herself immersed in those curious circumstances, she'd find herself wondering. What if she lived, not in Seattle, but in New York? Or London? Or Paris? Or Bergen?

What if I was someone else?

Of course, she'd seen enough cheesy movies to understand the fanciful concept of a fresh start—where the conflicted protagonist moves to a new town and just starts over. But she'd also lived enough of life to know that everyone drags their life with them wherever they go, that even the fastest boats leave a wake that catches up to them when they stop. But on these pre-dawn excursions, she allowed herself the luxury of imagining. It was almost, she thought, as if the vacant landscapes through which she wandered were movie sets, and that she was simply an actor. *What role might I play?*

She'd allow herself to imagine a new life, but only as a surface exploration. She'd allow herself, for forty-five minutes or an hour, to just ignore the logic and practicality and responsibility and history that she knew would follow her wherever she went.

As she'd known she would, she found it impossible to wander among the three-hundred-year-old red and yellow and blue and white buildings fronting Bryggen's hanseatic wharf, and not be transported away from reality, if only for a few moments. What if she taught at the university here? What if she lived in a beautiful little house near the water? What if she could simply spend her days in one of the town's little cafés or coffee shops, reading or writing or doing nothing at all? How wonderful would that be? To live as the best version of herself and to leave all the stress and sadness and regret and nagging doubt that formed at least a quarter—and maybe more—of her persona out of the picture?

As her new self, she wandered aimlessly until, about forty-five minutes into that imaginary existence, her phone alarm startled her, and she turned back toward the hotel, back toward reality.

A garbage truck emerged loudly from between two buildings. A single car waited at an otherwise empty intersection, its driver looking up at the red light, no real reason to be stopped, but stopped just the same. *Do we all just live by the rules we're taught? By the rules we accept? Do we all just live the lives we've been given? Do we create our lives? Do our lives create us?* She walked on, the streets of Bergen becoming just a little more alive and a lot more real with every step.

And then she saw him.

In black and reflective stripes, the thin white Y of his headphone wires swinging rhythmically as he ran, Scott Wilcox crossed the road about a hundred yards ahead, turning his back to her to follow the same road back to their hotel. Alison ducked into a storefront alcove to watch him, not wanting to be seen, not wanting to fully break the spell that solitude and new surroundings and imagination had put on her. She watched him slow from a sprint to a jog to a walk before he turned left into the hotel. When he'd disappeared from view, she'd covered the last few blocks, thoughts ultimately focusing on the day ahead, but a little surprised by the glimmer of a persistent new "what if" that had suddenly made its presence felt.

○ ○ ○

Dr. Sorensen laid it all out for them.

"Based on a comprehensive suite of tests using the available samples, as we all suspected, we can definitely conclude that the finger bone and the new remains are not directly related—they're simply not from the same person at all—which should be sufficient to officially remove the new remains from the police investigation, given the decidedly military nature of that particular discovery. But unfortunately, the new remains also do not provide enough matching data to associate them with Flight Lieutenant Vickson or Squadron Leader Barton…with your grandfather, Miss Wiley. There is a slim chance that may change with further testing, but at this point that's all I can tell you. I'm…I'm very sorry."

"No, no. Of course, I…I completely understand," said Alison, working to mask her dejection by nodding and glancing over at Scott to gauge his response. "Is there anything at all you can tell us that might help shed some light on any of this?"

"Well, nothing concrete, unfortunately, but I can share this," said Dr. Sorensen. "Determining the potential geographic origin of a deceased person's DNA, especially after an extended period when remains may have been exposed to the elements, is a very difficult and often imprecise science. But, given the samples we have and the tests available to us based on their nature, such as stable isotope analysis, I think we might reasonably conclude that the newly found remains strongly suggest central and western European origins. The child's finger bone strongly suggests northeastern European origins, and your DNA and that of Flight Lieutenant Vickson's sister both suggest strong Celtic and some, but relatively little, central and western

European origins, along with some trace indigenous North American indications. As it can be with testing of this nature, it's all a bit, ah, fuzzy, to say the least." Dr. Sorensen smiled. "So the next steps are really your decision, Mr. Wilcox."

Scott zipped his laptop into his black backpack and stood, and Alison rose as he reached out to shake Dr. Sorensen's hand.

"Thank you for all your efforts here, Dr. Sorensen. This is, as you say, both illuminating and puzzling. Let me get confirmation on the next course of action, but I'm guessing it'll involve getting samples of the new remains to both Canada and Germany for further testing. I'll be in touch as soon as I've verified the protocol and timing."

○ ○ ○

The walk back to the hotel had been quiet. Alison had tried to think of something to say, but the words just hadn't come. She was more disappointed than she'd ever have imagined she would be. The depth of it confused her, maybe even frustrated her. A month ago, she'd had no real connection to Jack Barton, but now she couldn't help but feel she was letting him and his crewmate, Vickson, down. Irrational, but undeniable. And a month ago, she'd had no connection at all to Scott Wilcox. Now, she couldn't help but feel…what?

The waiter delivered drinks as Scott flipped up his laptop screen. "So, I've been thinking, ma'am." He smiled. "Sorry—I mean Alison."

She smiled weakly, wondering why she liked it so much when he called her "ma'am" and even more when he said her name.

"I know you're disappointed. I mean, given the documented records," Scott said, "the physical evidence, and the serial number from the plane's camera, I'm confident we can conclude that the aircraft under the ice is RF889—that it's EO-N. I'm just sorry we haven't been able to place your grandfather or Vickson at the scene. I don't want to get your hopes up about further testing, given what Dr. Sorensen told us."

Alison knew Scott was trying to boost her spirits without giving her false hope. If anything, the past two and a half years with her mother had taught her a lot about that technique. "Scott, listen, I appreciate all you've done. Really. Remember, I insisted on coming over here before you could confirm anything because I...well, I just thought it was the right thing to do, you know? Maybe we'll never know what happened up there. To my grandfather and his friend."

"Maybe," Scott said softly. "And I'm sorry if that turns out to be the case. But this thing has taken a couple of pretty crazy turns, and honestly it's hard to explain." He looked into her eyes and smiled before turning back to his laptop. "Let's just say that this case has really gotten a hold of me. On a professional and, uh, personal level."

Unsure of his meaning, unsure how to react, and not sure she'd be able to get the words out even if she knew what to say, she smiled and turned to the window.

"I've been running through various potential scenarios based on the evidence. I'm guessing you've been doing the same?" Scott said. "We've got two as-of-yet-unidentified sets of human remains recovered. What's more, it seems one of the deceased at the scene may potentially have been a member of the German military, and the other was apparently an eight- or nine-year-old kid. None of that stuff adds up at all. Hopefully the recovered notebook can tell us something meaningful tomorrow, but as you know, barring any significant new developments, at that point I'll have to officially call this one and get back to Ottawa."

The dull weight of a sadness that she couldn't quite understand took what was left of Alison's energy away. She thought of her mother. What would this discovery—this disappointment—have meant to her? More heartbreak? More pain? More loss? Maybe it was for the best that Susan Wiley had passed without ever having to be dragged back into the sorrow of the long-buried past. *But here I am, caught up in some ancient history that'll make no difference to anyone.* She glanced at Scott and nodded. *This thing has really gotten hold of me, too.* For reasons she hadn't completely figured out, and with an irrational intensity that surprised her, she felt compelled to try to solve a seventy-four-year-old family mystery, even if there was no family left to share it with. Maybe, she thought, because so much of her life seemed to be going nowhere, she just didn't want this to be a dead end, too. But given everything that she'd learned, and all that she still hadn't—and maybe never would—she could feel the possibilities slipping away.

They sat quietly for a few minutes, until finally, Scott broke the silence.

"Can I, ah, run a little something past you? Something that's been eating at me?"

Alison smiled a dejected smile and nodded. "Of course, yeah. What's up?"

"Well, there's one thing that's really got me thinking, at least, ah, unofficially, I guess you could say. This."

He spun his laptop to face her, and the half-moon-shaped piece of stamped, oxidized grey alloy filled the screen.

"Look, I know this may be somewhat outside of my area of official responsibility, but there are just so many questions around this. The first two, obviously, are, who did this ID tag belong to, and how did it end up inside a crashed Canadian warplane in Norway? To try to find an answer to the first question, I've contacted my counterparts at the

Deutsche Dienststelle in Berlin. They'll do their own investigation and let me know what they find out. Of course, there may be living descendants who'd want to know what happened to the ID tag's owner. As for the second question? We may never learn the answer to that one. But there's one more question that I just can't stop asking myself: What happened to the other half of the ID tag?"

Alison leaned toward the laptop screen, her exhausted synapses suddenly firing.

"Right..."

"Look," Scott continued, "there are a obviously ton of variables and unknowns here, but I keep coming back to this one piece of metal. We can't be sure the dead man in the plane was actually German yet, but let's run through the facts as we know them. First, those remains were recovered in very close proximity to an RAF aircrew flying helmet and goggles, but with a German ID tag. Of course, it's possible that anyone could have gotten hold of a German ID tag and been wearing it or carrying it for whatever reason, but a Canadian airman who'd never set foot in Europe? I guess he could have traded for it or got it from a dead German found in England, but to me that's quite a stretch. And the German notebook? Very odd. Given all that and the fact that all preliminary indications point strongly to ruling out the possibility that the remains found in the wreck might belong to either your grandfather or his navigator, let's assume for a minute that the dead man was, in fact, German.

"Next, we have to look at timing. Just a ton of unknowns there, too. The man could have died before, during, or after the crash. And if you think about it, he could've died outside the plane and been placed inside of it either before or after the crash. We just have no way of knowing."

"Okay, I'm with you," said Alison, warming to the challenge. "So if he was German, it's possible but highly unlikely that he could've been the one actually flying the plane, or been a passenger, or maybe been a random visitor to the crash site after the fact. And, as you said, he could've died before or after the crash or been placed in the wreck. But since it appears he was likely wearing a flying helmet and goggles, isn't it reasonable to assume he was at least in the plane when he died? I mean really, a random German soldier who came across the wreck afterward wouldn't have been dressed that way, right? And if a dead German soldier was placed there by someone, would they have dressed him that way? Maybe, I guess, but—"

"Well, yeah," said Scott. "A thousand possibilities there."

They sipped their drinks for a few seconds, working to process the complexity.

"Listen," Scott said. "I think you know by now that my world pretty much revolves around forensic science—around facts—but when the facts can't be fully determined, I'm...well, I'm a bit of a proponent of Occam's Razor. I know you're a scientist and all"—he smiled—"so I'm assuming you're familiar with that one?"

Alison smiled back at his subtle and unexpected dig. Yes, science was her world, not supposition. And she followed facts, not feelings. But for once, she too had decided to follow her gut. "Yeah, smart ass," she shot back with a smile. "I get that concept."

Scott grinned and arched his eyebrows above his wine glass. "So? Thoughts? Ideas?"

"Look, I know there's no hard evidence to support this," she said, "but if we assume he was German and that he got into that plane alive and died in it later, then we sort of have to assume that his ID tag would have been whole at the time he died, yes?"

"Makes perfect sense to me," said Scott. "Of course, there could be many other explanations we're not thinking of, but yeah, those assumptions seem entirely reasonable. So you can see where I keep netting out. Since there's no definitive physical evidence placing your grandfather or his navigator in that destroyed two-seat aircraft, and there are no records or even anecdotal stories anywhere that we know of indicating that the wreck was ever found before it got buried in the glacier, my guess is that whoever else was in that plane when it came down was alive immediately after the impact, and that they took the other half of the tag off the dead German and somehow got out of there under their own steam."

Scott closed his laptop and leaned toward her. "So, uh…are you thinking what I'm thinking?"

Alison smiled and leaned her head against the back of her chair. She felt the soft sting as she closed her eyelids, felt her chest tremble slightly as she took a few long, slow, deep breaths and looked over at Scott. She really didn't know what she was thinking, because she was feeling more than thinking. She simply wasn't used to living in the unknown, wasn't used to maybes and what-ifs. But she couldn't keep the hope from rising or the smile from her face. She leaned back toward him, her face feeling just a little warmer than usual.

"Well, I don't know exactly what you might be thinking, but I'm thinking that person just might have been my grandfather."

o o o

Outside the hotel window, the Bergen streets were buzzing in the sparkling early evening, alive with people making their way home from work, heading to bars or restaurants or theatres or concert halls. Alison watched them, emotionally exhausted, but with her suddenly energized brain electrified by thousands of thoughts and questions about Norway, and her grandfather, and a kid's finger bone, and a dead German, and a cryptic notebook, and yes, about Scott Wilcox.

Her eyes tracked the figures rushing by. *What lives have you lived? What lives will you live?* And she couldn't help but think—as she'd done so often in the dark days after her father, her brother, and her mother had each left her forever—how strange it was that the world didn't know or care about her fear or anger or grief or loneliness, how it could just…go on. But how could the world know or care about those things when it had never been given a reason to? She'd simply never shared them with anyone. *Are we all mostly disconnected?* she thought. *Mostly strangers, blissfully oblivious to the pain and happiness and hopes and fears of others?* She glanced at Scott over the rim of her wine glass. *Until maybe one day, we're not?*

22

In name, it was an island, but from the back seat of the staff car, he could see the long causeway that connected it to the mainland. An assortment of low, industrial-looking buildings, a brick chimney, and a water tower seemed to occupy virtually every square metre of its surface, and although the only real military presence he could see from the mainland road was the guardhouse checkpoint on the causeway, Günther knew that the facility would surely be heavily guarded.

His journey had been eye-opening.

They'd patched him up as best they could and strapped him into a Ju-52—a flying, corrugated tin coffin as far as he was concerned— whose young pilots had braved yet another dangerous trip to deliver meagre supplies to the last remnants of Jagdgeschwader 54. *At least these boys are dying delivering toilet paper and tins of beans. My boys are dying for a lot less than that.*

Günther's "boys" had come to see him off, joking and laughing and saluting their venerable Opa with their left hands as the orderlies had shoved him into the back of the transport. He'd saluted them back with his own left hand, feeling a twinge of pain in his right shoulder nonetheless. *Such good spirits. Such naiveté*, he'd thought, fighting the urge to tell them all to run like hell, and instead trying his best to joke and smile back. He knew the odds of any of them surviving even another month were slim to none.

Such bright young lives to be extinguished in the name of stupidity and arrogance.

The flight had been thankfully uneventful, and they'd touched down at a rough airstrip somewhere west of Kaunas a couple of hours later. From there, he'd been driven an hour and a half by truck to a temporary convalescent hospital they'd set up in a mostly intact former school building, where he'd most definitely counted himself among the fortunate.

He'd been surrounded by men who'd been absolutely shredded by war. Missing limbs and eyes and noses and testicles, horrendously burned, deaf, blind, some distraught, some catatonic. He'd tried to speak with a few of them, to find out where they'd been, what they'd seen, what they'd done, to learn what they knew. Most just turned away in silence. Some, like him, had been brought in from the rapidly unfolding disaster in Russia, others had come from Byelorussia and Latvia. From the handful of stories Günther had managed to hear, he'd confirmed for himself what he'd suspected since Stalingrad and Kursk and Smolensk.

They were well past the beginning of the end. The rout was on.

The great idiotic quest for Lebensraum was over, and the so-called subhumans on whom Günther and his comrades had inflicted so much death and pain and misery were coming for them and for everyone they loved. Hitler and his cadre of sycophantic fools had doomed Germany to defeat and ensured the deaths—or worse—of potentially millions of its citizens. For that reason, and for many, many others, Günther worried about Karin and Gisele almost constantly, but in reality, he had absolutely no idea whether he was worrying about flesh and blood or ghosts.

On a drenched and dismal Monday afternoon, a beautiful young nurse with empty eyes had removed his wrist cast, poked at the wound in his calf, and waved his right arm around a little. None of those things had felt particularly pleasant to Günther, but a gaunt, white-haired Wehrmacht doctor had given him a couple of pills and pronounced him good to go. The following morning his travel orders had arrived, with instructions to make his way by air to Danzig, then by train to Rostock, where he was to meet with a Luftwaffe driver who would take him the rest of the way to his new posting.

On the transport hop over Lithuania and East Prussia, Günther saw little, slept as much as he could. But Danzig was rubble, and as Poland slid agonizingly past his westbound train window, his trepidation about what Germany might soon look like grew to an ice ball in the pit of his stomach.

For what seemed like hours, he'd glimpsed nothing but a steady procession of bleak, deserted farm fields, crumbled towns, scorched villages. When they'd passed by a long column of what he'd taken to be hundreds, maybe even thousands, of emaciated prisoners in dull grey and black rags, trudging wearily westward under the watchful eyes of their bedraggled and downcast Wehrmacht guards, the train had slowed momentarily. He'd quickly turned away from his window when an almost skeletal man had summoned the energy to glance up at him, his near-dead eyes burning into Günther's with a thousand unanswerable questions. For a second he'd caught a faint whiff of something almost animal, decayed and fetid, unlike anything he'd ever experienced, and he'd been more than a little thankful when the sad horde had faded into the past behind the slowly advancing train. *What the hell are we doing to each other?*

At one point the train had been forced to stop for resupply, and a wailing air raid siren had prompted its terrified passengers and crew to scramble away in an effort to find shelter from whatever potential death and destruction might be about to rain down on them. Günther had hopped and limped along as fast as he could, struggling just to keep up with the actual Omas und Opas. *Shit. I really am getting old.*

He knew Rostock had also seen its share of war, but the city was a total shock.

He'd spent many happy times there as a boy, visiting with his mother's young cousins and their families. He'd loved the warm cafés and brightly lit shops, and the incredible assortments of sweets and pastries and toys had dazzled him.

And he'd met Karin there in the spring of 1934.

She'd simply been more beautiful and vibrant than any girl he'd ever met, and he'd known almost from first sight that he wanted to spend his life with her. A child of divorce, she'd been a little more cautious, but even still they'd been married less than eight months later, and Gisele had come along not quite nine months after their honeymoon.

He'd felt a profound sense of responsibility when he'd become a husband—a powerful, almost primal drive that had somehow doubled or even quadrupled when he'd become a father. While he'd supposed every new parent must feel that way to some extent, for Günther it had been overwhelming. But compounding his unrelenting anxiety about taking care of his new family was the simple fact that he was completely out of money, so he and Karin had reluctantly decided that his university education would have to wait. Since the newly energized Luftwaffe seemed to offer the kind of immediate opportunity that might provide enough income for them all, despite Karin's initial concerns and his mother's protestations, he'd made the decision. A few short years of military service, then back to his studies, and then on to greater things. Such plans they'd made.

Hitler's war had crushed them all.

And the Royal Air Force had almost totally crushed Rostock. The bomber crews had done their jobs extremely well, devastating the city center in repeated raids, and as he'd passed by the crumbled ruins of St. Nicholas on the way to his assigned overnight lodging, he knew he should have felt something. Anger perhaps? Shame? But instead, he felt almost nothing. *We did this to ourselves.*

The following morning, some eighty-five kilometres east of the devastated city, his driver brought their car to a stop at the causeway guard barrier. A pimply teenage Wehrmacht soldier in an oversized greatcoat sloppily saluted him and quickly scrutinized his papers. As the red-and-white-striped barrier pole pivoted up toward the flat grey skies, the soldier handed Günther his documents and saluted again.

"Welcome to the Institute, Herr Major."

23

The Kattegat was incredibly beautiful in the early afternoon sun. Or it would have been, if Jack and his squadron mates had been there for any other reason than to sink ships and kill people.

With the Mustangs and outriders keeping watch up top, the two waves of Mosquitos came in, ripping up an armed trawler and two merchant freighters caught by surprise on the almost perfectly glassy ocean. The gun crews on the ships fired thousands of antiaircraft rounds toward the buzzing attackers, but the simple reality was that they were outgunned.

In addition to four machine guns with a combined two thousand rounds of ammunition, each of the seventeen Mosquitos carried eight armour-piercing rockets and four 20mm cannons with six hundred total rounds. From a pure firepower point of view, 404 Squadron RCAF was essentially a fleet of airborne battleships, and Jack knew that if even a quarter of his boys were on target today, the sailors floating down there had virtually zero chance of survival.

The blue-black water around the two ships had already erupted into violent white by the time Jack made his approach, as planned, coming in as the lone "tail-end Charlie" from the north. He lined up on the already stricken trawler and, at maximum distance, triggered his eight rockets, watching for a half-second as they streaked toward the ship's black-grey waterline. At 265 knots, his twin Merlins howled as he peeled the Mosquito up and to his left, gaining a little altitude and arcing to the south as Vickson quietly called out the new heading.

"Roger that," Jack replied, banking slightly and pointing the Mosquito's stubby nose down until the aircraft was just forty feet above the water. As he gently nudged the throttles forward to speed Vickson and him south, he looked back and to his right and caught a quick, lonely glimpse of the rest of his boys heading northwest.

I must be out of my goddamned mind.

24

Professor Lundeen clicked the keyboard on his laptop with a white-gloved hand, and an image appeared on the wall-mounted flat screen.

"We were able to remove the moisture, but unfortunately most of the pages in the notebook were too badly damaged to be separated or to reveal anything legible. However, we were able to salvage a small number of them, and I must admit, the contents they reveal are quite interesting."

The yellow-brown, lined paper fragment was badly degraded, with heavy stains encroaching on all of its margins. Dots of mildew spotted its entire surface, completely obscuring the handwritten notes in some places, but a significant portion of the faded purple-blue fountain pen ink was still legible.

A series of rough, hand-sketched diagrams—composed mostly of circular and hexagonal shapes connected by short, straight lines, annotated with what looked like mathematical equations—occupied the center area of the paper, with cursive notations running horizontally and vertically around them in blurred ink. Jonas clicked the button again, and another image appeared on the screen.

The page was torn in half across the middle, its upper section perhaps lost to water and time in the glacier. In the upper center of the surviving material was a portion of another hand-drawn diagram. This one depicted an outline of a human form, from the upper chest down, with what appeared to be the main arteries and veins indicated, along with some notations relating to various locations in the groin, kidney, and upper torso areas.

The handwritten notes surrounding the central diagram were badly degraded, but a few lines of clearly decipherable and beautifully written cursive text nestled near the right upper torso.

1. Oktober 1944.
15:44 B-133404
Verstorbene E. S. M.

"As you can clearly see here," Jonas said, "the notations on these pages are written in German."

25

The pain was unbearable.

They'd cut her again, and she shook uncontrollably under her filthy blanket, sobbing and moaning softly while trying desperately and unsuccessfully to remain motionless. No matter how hard she tried, she just couldn't imagine what she'd done wrong, couldn't understand why she was being punished so harshly.

As she always did on the really bad days, she squeezed her eyes tightly shut and tried to think her way into a dream, tried to remember something good. As always, her good thoughts were weak, so she tried to make them grow before they could be devoured by the bad.

The afternoon sun had been warm on her face, the blanket soft and comforting. The kind, beautiful woman had smiled down at her, stroking her long dark hair gently, and humming softly. A little girl with equally beautiful and long dark curls nestled next to her, dressed exactly as she was, in a cerulean blue satin frock tied with white ribbons.

She'd squeezed the little girl's hand as tightly as she could while the beautiful woman had cried and begged, desperately pleading with the angry men in the dark uniforms and helmets who shouted in a language she couldn't understand. She'd watched, terrified, as the beautiful woman had been dragged away, screaming and shouting, with tears streaming down her face, and she'd tried to be strong for the other little girl as they were taken to the damp, frigid, foul-smelling, dimly lit concrete room where so many other frightened children huddled together. The two of them had clung to each other as long as they could, but the other girl had soon been taken from her too, leaving her to sob, anxious, confused, and lonely, in a huddled crowd of the sobbing, anxious, confused, and lonely.

Today, once again, the unfeeling eyes had looked down on her as she'd begged and cried and whimpered. Rough hands had wrenched her arms above her head, and the straps that had held her tight to the cold metal table had pinched and rubbed her skin raw. Her eyes had been covered, and something had blocked her mouth, and her panic and fear had been almost unbearable, and the singing woman's voice had been so very, very loud as the needles had pierced her frail body.

26

"My name is Generalarzt Doktor Sigmund Morbach, and I am in charge of this facility."

He sat bolt upright behind an ornate walnut desk, sucking on a French cigarette and slurping what to Günther smelled remarkably like actual, real coffee. Günther guessed him to be in his late forties at least, overweight and balding, horn-rimmed half-moon reading glasses perched on the end of a bulbous nose.

When the doctor flipped open the manila file folder lying on his green desk blotter, Günther barely recognized his own upside-down twenty-four-year-old face. Dirty blond hair cropped short, light eyes intensely focused, skin smooth and taut. Confident and proud and self-assured. *Who the hell was that kid?* A paperclip partially obscured the cheek that would be ripped open by a fragment from a British bullet over the English Channel, and the perfectly straight nose was yet to absorb the impact that would bend it permanently sideways, courtesy of the skeletal remnants of a tree it would encounter at the culmination of a bail-out over Kursk. But more than anything, that face projected none of the soul-crushing internal damage that would befall its owner as he slowly descended into his own personal hell of doubt and guilt.

Morbach flipped a few papers nonchalantly. "You appear to have quite an interesting service record, Major...uh, Graf. Some might be inclined to say that we have a war hero in our midst now. But here at the Institute, we too are engaged in tremendous efforts to create significant advantages for the Reich in its battle against the relentless forces of evil. Our weapon, however, is intellect."

Günther smiled faintly. *Arschloch.* He'd met this guy a hundred times before. Arrogant, condescending, and in a position of power. The absolute worst kind of leader.

"Please, Herr Generalarzt. I've simply tried to do my duty, as have so many, many others," Günther replied.

Morbach arched his fat eyebrows and shot Günther the thinnest of crooked smiles. He glanced at the file. "Yes. Quite. It says here that you have at least some minimal chemistry laboratory experience, and I have been informed you are to serve in an administrative capacity with us here while you convalesce from your most recent...incident. Hopefully we can have you on your way back to your more familiar duties at the eastern front very soon."

Morbach closed the file and pressed a black button on his desk, triggering a muffled buzzing in the adjoining room through which Günther had entered. Without looking up, the doctor held out a pale green folder. "Unteroffizier Krueger will show you to your quarters. Study the full contents of this dossier carefully to familiarize yourself with the Institute and its various buildings and facilities. You will report to Building 7 tomorrow morning at 0700 sharp."

Günther clicked his heels out of habit, not respect.

27

The evening view from her Bergen hotel room was spectacular, but for the past two and a half hours Alison had been looking at nothing but her laptop, studying the notebook images Professor Lundeen had provided, Googling various questions and words that had popped into her head, glad to be looking for answers.

She was guessing that the salvaged notebook pages were from some kind of personal lab journal, similar to the kind she'd kept as a student. While she couldn't decipher most of what she was seeing—Google Translate didn't seem to recognize some of her best guesses at the technical language—she had a few thoughts about the circular and hexagonal schematic, and she'd emailed that image to an old friend at the U of W for his opinion.

She really hoped that the origin of the human form drawing and its accompanying notations might have been related to some kind of anatomy class, but she suspected otherwise. She knew exactly what the handwritten date meant. And she'd been able to at least get one word to show up in the online translation.

Verstorbene.

Deceased.

Whatever the truth behind the notebook, whatever unfathomable circumstances might have resulted in it ending up in her grandfather's destroyed aircraft, she knew in her heart the story must be sad and dark.

She also understood that her time in Norway was coming to an end, and that within the next forty-eight hours she'd be immersed once again in the stress-inducing demands of her life back in Seattle.

What she couldn't quite understand was the intensity of her sadness at that thought. She hadn't expected to feel anything of the sort, hadn't really expected a week to change her in any way. But there it was, a fact.

28

Streng geheim!

Nur für den Dienstgebrauch!

The rectangular, red rubber stamp dominated the front of the pale green dossier. Günther had read its entire contents. *What the hell has Marcks gotten me into here?*

The Institute was engaged in scientific and medical research. Under the auspices of the Wehrmacht's Science Section, its team of Wehrmacht, Luftwaffe, and Kriegsmarine scientists and doctors had apparently been working to develop defences against potential biological or chemical weapons that might be deployed against the Reich.

He flipped the folder shut, closed his eyes, and pinched the bridge of his nose. He'd been assigned to Building 7, Dokumentation und Aufzeichnungen, marked in blue on the facility map. *Documentation and Records.* In other words, he was a file clerk. *Not exactly the kind of laboratory work I had in mind.*

Sliding the dossier into his black leather case, he downed the last of his lukewarm Ersatzkaffee and began to limp his way steadily across the drab, virtually lifeless compound toward whatever desk he'd be flying until he was told otherwise.

His natural instincts for reconnaissance kicked in.

The nondescript structures he passed by were no more than two stories in height, mostly red-brown brick, most of them almost completely devoid of windows and more like small factory buildings than what Günther had imagined scientific research facilities might look like. Between the buildings he could see what he'd not been able to see from the mainland road. Partially obscured by a handful of low shrubs and a few sparse trees, a double-fenced barbed wire enclosure surrounded the entire perimeter of the island, complete with periodic skull-and-crossbones-emblazoned signs that sternly warned:

HALT GEFAHR

MINEN!

Are they trying to keep someone from getting in? Or trying to keep me from getting the hell out?

Building 7 was as bad as he expected, and much worse.

A brick, one-story structure, its dimly lit entrance vestibule led to a set of grey doors, in front of which was a grey steel desk, behind which sat an even greyer man. Anselm, Morbach's gaunt adjutant, led Günther down a narrow corridor and into a windowless office. *Spartan would be an understatement.* An unpadded wooden swivel chair sat behind a small metal desk, on which rested a lamp, a couple of pencils, and a telephone. A small paper calendar hung on one wall. There were no other objects in the musty-smelling room.

"You have been assigned here, Herr Major. Your task will be to review official documents prepared by the transcription staff against the original notes provided to them by the Institute's team of medical researchers. The documents will be brought to you for review one set at a time. If there are corrections or alterations required, you will note them in red on the official transcribed document, and you will place your initials and the date in the margin accordingly. Do not mark the original notes. When you have completed each review, you will sign and date the label on the outside of the folder and ring one-one-six-nine-four on the telephone. An orderly will remove the processed documents and provide you with another folder containing a new set for review. Any questions, Herr Major?"

Is this actually a prison cell? "Where do you keep the real coffee?" Günther replied, grinning. Anselm didn't even begin to crack a smile, and he said nothing. He simply nodded and clicked his heels, turned and walked out the door.

Günther had faced the terror of aerial combat hundreds of times. Been shot down twice. Crash landed twice. Been wounded four times. And more times than he cared to remember, he'd been forced to dive into frozen or mud-filled slit trenches as Russian artillery shells and bombs had exploded all around him. But what fresh hell was this? *I do believe they're actually trying to bore me to death.*

Seven and a quarter hours later, Günther had managed to stay awake through the first wave of the interminable flow of documents he feared he might come to see over the next months.

His eyes burned from trying to compare the neatly typed papers provided by the transcribers with the handwritten chicken scratch originals they'd had to work from. He was more exhausted than he could remember being after any combat sortie.

Later, as he slowly trudged back from the mess hall to his drab quarters and his sagging metal cot, despite his best efforts, he couldn't help but think.

He'd once been vibrant, confident, full of piss and vinegar and promise. He'd been so goddamned sure of himself. But he'd been misled and misguided by the people he'd trusted, he'd been lied to, and used for purposes that were at odds with his own sense of self.

Now he was tired and worn down and no longer sure of anything. And he was losing whatever was left of himself. All the years of risking his life, seeing his friends plummet to their deaths or be burned alive or torn apart in their shattered aircraft—and all of the killing and maiming he'd done in pursuit of the wrong things—had taken their toll. He knew he'd continue to decline unless something changed soon. He needed to get back to his wife and daughter.

He needed to stop dying.

29

They sipped their coffees in silence under the high, arched windows of the hotel restaurant.

"Sleep okay?" Scott asked.

Not for a couple of years, really. Alison shook her head and cracked a tired smile. "No, not really. You?"

"Me neither," Scott said. "In fact, I barely slept at all. Like I said, this thing has really gotten hold of me."

He unfolded a paper tourist map, pinned it down with his cup, his laptop, and his mobile phone, and slid his chair around to Alison's side of the table. She studied him for a second as he tapped the paper map with his index finger. He was energized.

"Okay, let me run you through something." On his laptop screen, he zoomed in on a Google Earth image of the area, a red indicator prominent against the white near the ice cap's southwest edge.

"This is the crash site, and I overlaid Professor Lundeen's survey on the satellite image so we can get a little better sense of what we're actually looking at."

He pointed to an area that had been marked out with an irregular translucent yellow shape, clusters of black rectangles tagged with white code numbers scattered randomly inside it.

"This is the location, right here, where we saw the remnants of the crushed cockpit canopy—where they think the bulk of the aircraft might be under the ice. That's where they found the flying helmet and skull fragments, and the metal box with the notebook."

Another, much larger, elongated teardrop shape had been marked out with a translucent pink line, with a handful of black rectangles concentrated near the yellow area and becoming less concentrated near the point of the teardrop enclosure.

"This is the debris field around the main wreck, as far as it's been surveyed. If we assume that some pieces would've likely broken off and scattered behind as the plane slid or cartwheeled forward across the ice during the crash, from this diagram we can pretty much determine the direction the aircraft was travelling when it came down. My guess is it came in roughly from the northeast and landed in a southwesterly direction, in the direction the teardrop seems to indicate."

Three black rectangles clustered almost into one stood alone, just beyond the southwestern leading edge of the elongated pink teardrop.

"Right here is where Nils and his father found the bone fragment and the two metal pieces. Remember? The sharp steel shard and the small piece of brassy metal with the worn red letters? That's what I've been thinking about over and over and over. That crumpled piece of metal. I dug back through my notes and images to find it. At some point it had been speculated that it might've come from the plane's instrument panel or some piece of onboard equipment, but it got back-burnered in light of all the other findings. Well, I think I figured it out at about 0430."

He clicked an open tab and an image appeared. A brassy-yellow tin with red block letters.

"Tubunic ampoules," he said, eyes wide and expectant. "That's morphine. Standard issue to Commonwealth aircrews."

"So…it's from the plane's first aid kit?" said Alison. "But how does that help?"

Scott clicked back to the Google Earth image and pointed to the area at the thin end of the teardrop. "Look, if I'm right, and the aircraft initially made contact with the ice field somewhere back here in this vicinity, and then slid toward the wide end of the marked area, around here, how did a kid's finger bone, an unidentifiable shard of metal, and what appears to be a component of the aircraft's first aid kit end up approximately forty-five metres in front of its final stopping point?"

Alison took another sip of her coffee, captivated but cautious. "Okay, I'll nibble, but I'm not hooked. We agreed, the bone fragment could just be a fluke, right? Just a coincidence? I mean, couldn't some kid have been up on the glacier one day and somehow lost the tip of a finger in that particular location?"

"Possible for sure," Scott replied, "but that bone fragment was found in very close proximity to a couple of pieces of metal debris that we have to assume came from the Mosquito, at approximately the same depth below the current surface as many of the other small pieces from the aircraft. Look, I'm no expert on glacial science, but it seems to me those objects would probably have had to have been deposited on the surface at pretty close to the same time in order for them to have been buried so closely together. So if the kid's bone fragment and the pieces of metal didn't get there during the actual crash, I'm guessing they got there shortly afterward."

"So, what are you thinking?" said Alison, her mood rising along with a few small butterflies in her stomach.

"Well," Scott said, "I don't know about you, but when something keeps me up at night or gets me up in the morning, I pay attention to it. I'm thinking I need to take a couple of vacation days."

Alison could barely contain her grin.

30

Vickson's voice was dead calm. "Okay, Skip. This is the place."

From the SOE briefings, Jack knew that construction on the airfield had been essentially wrapped up by the Luftwaffe early in the spring of 1944, but that it had never been operational. Events on the beaches of Normandy just a few weeks after its completion had suddenly given the Nazis a pressing need to divert significant military resources to western France and Belgium and Holland and Germany, and the spooks were counting on local resistance reports that this part of southern Denmark was currently sparsely populated with armed bad guys.

He also knew there were a handful of pits in the northeast and southeast dispersal areas for fuel and ammunition storage, and that the Jerries had built out a few small aircraft shelters, but there were no real hangars or workshops of any kind. And he knew there was no paved runway, just a levelled and rolled grass surface about fourteen hundred yards in length. Basically it was a flat, empty field just big enough to set a Mosquito down on and, hopefully, to depart from. And most importantly, on this particular spring afternoon, at least they'd been promised, it was temporarily under the control of the Holger Danske—the Danish resistance.

Jack brought the plane in at treetop height, circled around and dropped down at the field's east end, hoping to hell the boys from the Ministry of Ungentlemanly Warfare were right.

That'd damn well better be the good guys, he thought, as four armed men emerged from the trees and ran toward the still-rolling aircraft. One of them waved his arms frantically, signaling for Jack to cut the engines. *Jesus H Christ. I don't think so, buddy.* He throttled down and hit the brakes, but kept the Merlins roaring, RPMs high, ready to get them the hell out of there if things started to go sideways. He looked over as Vickson unbuckled his harness.

"Okay, Bart. Let's get this done."

The small door in the fuselage near Vickson's feet swung outward and almost immediately a man's head appeared in the opening. Silhouetted against the glare of the low afternoon light, Jack thought he could make out a beard, a black knitted cap, and an almost full set of teeth as the man nodded and grinned. Vickson immediately shook off his Mae West, helmet, oxygen mask, and goggles, and scooted feetfirst out through the hatch, the Mosquito's roaring starboard prop just a foot or so from his head.

The next few minutes would feel like the longest of Jack's life.

31

Alison's mind was fully engaged in question mode as Scott navigated the winding road to the foot of the trail.

"So if someone did survive the crash up there, where could they have gone? I mean, it was late April, right? You think maybe the conditions could've been survivable if the weather wasn't too bad?"

"Maybe. But it would've been tough, that's for sure," said Scott. "When I was a kid I spent a lot of time up in the mountains with my grandfather. Even snowshoeing out there for a couple of hours was totally exhausting, so slogging through deep snow in just a pair of boots would have been brutal. And Gramps always warned me about avoiding dehydration, so we carried water at all times. Plus," he said, "when you're wearing sweat-soaked clothing, hypothermia can set in pretty quick once the sun goes down.

"It's possible I guess, but the only way to know for sure if someone could've walked out of there is to try to retrace their likely steps. To try to re-create their journey. And of course there are a ton of unknown variables to consider. Like, were any of the potential survivors injured in the crash? Were they disoriented or did they have some real sense of where they were and which way they might be headed? Were they dressed appropriately? As aircrew in that kind of plane at that time of year, they were almost certainly wearing cold-weather clothing and probably gloves and boots, so at least there's that. But did they have any real survival gear or supplies at all?"

Alison tried her best to hide her trepidation about what they were about to do, but something about Scott's demeanour gave her the distinct impression that he was about to enter his element. *Well, I'm definitely out of mine.*

"And then there's the child," she said. "I just can't get my head around that one."

As the sky above the gravel parking lot steadily progressed from dark to brilliant blue, they pulled their newly purchased gear from the back of the SUV. Down jackets, waterproof pants, hats, gloves, snowshoes, walking poles, and backpacks loaded with first aid supplies, ski goggles, multi-tools, a compass or two, spare gloves, energy bars, matches, a lighter, fire-starter cubes, sunscreen, survival blankets, spare batteries, and water. Geared up, Alison slung her backpack onto her shoulders as Scott activated his GPS and waited for the screen to come to life. *Man, we're a hell of a lot more ready for a long hike in the snow than anyone would have been in 1945.*

"Okay. No snowmobile today. You ready?" Scott said.

Not at all! "I guess so. I mean, I've got all this shiny new gear, so I might as well give it a whirl."

Just under four hours later, they topped the small rise that led to the flat plain, revealing the orange-fenced crash site spread out below them. They made their way down to the barrier and Scott walked its perimeter three times, squinting at his GPS in the midmorning sun. He finally stopped at the spot labeled 100916-65, where the bone fragment had been found.

He turned to Alison. "Well, that was a long walk, and we knew where we were going. I don't know about you, but if I was a survivor, and I had some sense of where I was, I think I'd probably take the line of least resistance to get myself down from here."

"Yeah, I totally agree," said Alison. "If the weather was bad, or I was hurt, or I was with someone who was, I think I'd want to get to a lower altitude and find some shelter as quickly as possible."

Scott cupped his hand to shade the GPS.

"From this spot we're about fourteen kilometres, give or take, from the parking lot where we left the SUV. That's not so bad in the late spring of 2019, but it probably would have been a heck of a hike in the spring of 1945, especially after surviving an emergency landing in a possibly damaged warplane. There's a town called Rosendal about seven kilometres to the west of here. That's about half the distance we covered getting here. Now, it may be around seven thousand metres as the crow flies, but who knows how far it really is and how long it might take us once we factor in altitude changes and degree of terrain difficulty. There's risk in this, of course, but I let the Odda police know what we'd be up to, so if we don't check in within a day or so, I'm sure they'll eventually send someone to look for us."

Scott had smiled his crooked little smile as he'd delivered that. She smiled back, took another bite of a chocolate-sawdust energy bar, washed it down with a swig of water, and wiped the moisture from her lips. The heat of the morning sun in the crisp air felt good. Being up on a brilliant white glacier felt good. The energy bar even tasted good. There was no denying that this little adventure was getting crazier and crazier by the minute, but Alison hadn't felt this energized—this alive—since she couldn't remember when. *I'm way, way out of my element here, but I think I'm all in.* She slipped the water bottle back into the mesh pouch on the side of her pack and turned to Scott.

"Ha! Well, it might not be possible, especially for me, but there's only one way to know for sure, right?"

32

The terror was always the same. The sudden metallic jangling of the keys in the lock, the rough hands, the cold, hard gurney, her panic rising in unison with the volume of the music as the faceless people rolled her toward the antiseptic stink of the frigid white room.

But today, the gurney's relentless roll had stopped suddenly as a massive booming sound had jarred the world, sending the faceless people into a panic. They'd hurled themselves to the floor as clouds of fine white dust shook loose from the gently swaying lights, the individual powder puffs combining to fill the air like a fog that drifted down onto everyone and everything. For a brief moment, her panic had subsided, and she'd strained to turn her head. From the corner of her eye, she'd seen her.

Or at least she thought she had.

The little girl from her dream ran down the hallway, naked. And screaming. Her long, beautiful hair was gone, replaced by dark, patchy stubble. Her thin neck accentuated her bulbous head, and her terrified eyes were wide open. Thin tubes trailed from her arms and legs, and her pale rib cage was slick with dark red blood. She scrambled down a short corridor toward a door, desperately clawing at its locked handle as some of the faceless people shouted and moved haltingly toward her.

As she turned to face her pursuers, for a brief moment the dream girl's horrified eyes locked onto hers, and something—a memory perhaps?—passed between them.

The faceless people stopped dead in their tracks, suddenly unsure what to do. They continued to bark their overlapping, unintelligible demands at the tops of their lungs, but for the first time in forever, the girl heard words that she actually understood.

"Nie możesz mnie pokonać!"

"Nie możesz mnie pokonać!"

"Nie możesz mnie pokonać!"

Over and over and over, the dream girl screamed out her defiance, revealing an incredible inner ferocity that belied her emaciated frame.

"You cannot defeat me!"

In the dream girl's tiny clenched fist, a flat metal object reflected the glare from the gently swinging light bulb above her, glinting like lightning through the haze as she brought its polished silver blade quickly and violently and repeatedly to her own throat.

Three of the faceless people called out almost as one and ran, hands outstretched toward the now fallen child, sliding on their knees across the dark liquid floor to reach for her.

From the gurney, heart pounding, chest heaving, eyes welling up with uncontrollable tears, the girl felt something she really had no words to describe.

Hope.

33

The letter, postmarked Kiel, 1 Oktober 1944, was delivered to him along with yet another brown file folder and its incomprehensible contents.

Günther had written to her six times in the four months since his arrival at the Institute. Although he hadn't been able to tell her exactly where he was or what his new duties entailed, he'd at least been able to let her know that he was back in Germany, closer to them. He hadn't mentioned his injuries or the reasons for his reassignment—he dearly hoped there would be plenty of time for all of that later. He'd only wanted her to know that he was safe and that he loved her. And he so desperately wanted to hear the same from her.

He tore open the envelope, anxiety gripping his throat like a fist.

Bedauern zu informieren…
Regret to inform…

The words stopped him ice cold.

On July 24, the RAF had hit Kiel again, just because they could. He'd thought they'd be safe out there, in a mean-nothing little town some five kilometres west of the city's docks and naval base. But somehow, through incompetence or fear or equipment malfunction, a single aircraft had dropped a stick of high explosive bombs that had taken out virtually an entire block of the town, including a crowded air-raid shelter in the basement of a school.

There were no survivors.

Günther stared at the paper in his hands, paralyzed, empty, and unable to draw a breath, his heart ripped out by the shocking violence of those two words.

No survivors.

As he had feared it would—had known it would—his life had finally come to this. No honour. No glory. Only anguish. And regret. And guilt.

Devastation.

The terror, pain, death, misery, and destruction that he and his fellow countrymen had inflicted on so many innocent others had been returned to him in spades. He had ended the tomorrows of thousands of people. Now someone had ended all of his.

He wished with all his heart that it could have been him instead of them, but he understood why it was not. Instead of simply taking him, the fates had punished him far more severely by leaving him to suffer the deaths of those he'd held most dear. His mother had died alone, of hunger and some terrible wasting disease or another sometime in early 1943, and now the only other people who'd really meant anything to him at all were gone.

Tears flowing uncontrollably, he sent a silent, agonized scream toward the dismal grey ceiling, and crushed the letter as it had crushed him.

No survivors, indeed.

34

Two and a half hours in, they were about halfway to Rosendal.

Far from "as the crow flies," the terrain had proven to be somewhat challenging, but they'd managed to traverse the western edge of the ice field and were making their way down toward the upper edge of a forest of pine trees that dotted the steep rock face on which the glacier sat.

Scott stopped and looked back up at Alison.

"Hey, are you doing okay? For sure this is proving to be a little more difficult than the longer route, but you can imagine how any survivors of the crash might have felt. And once you're committed to something like this, it's not as if you're going to climb back up and try the other direction. I've got a pretty good hunch this is the right way."

Alison looked down at him, brain going a hundred miles an hour, heart going even faster.

Gotta be the altitude and the exertion, right? He was standing in the sun on a large rock about twenty metres below her.

"Hey, listen! I'm a trained, professional scientist, remember? I don't do hunches. You're the ex Canadian Forces combat medic slash investigator tough guy."

He laughed a little laugh and turned to continue down the slope.

"I'll buy you a cappuccino in town in less than three hours," he yelled. "Trust me!"

She laughed right back at that and forced her feet to move.

I guess I kinda do.

35

For his first four and a half months on the island, Günther's days had been filled with endless brown folders. Each folder contained an original document of some kind, typically a carefully cut fragment or portion of a larger whole. The information on the original documents tended to be written or drawn in blue fountain pen ink or pencil or a combination of those things. Along with each original was a draft of an official typed transcription that he assumed would ultimately be filed and stored somewhere for posterity. *We Germans certainly excel at detailed record-keeping, if not much else.*

At first, he hadn't paid much attention to the actual content of the documents. Rather, he'd simply compared each individual word—or more accurately, each set of consecutive letters—from the original notes with whatever the transcriber had typed. It was monotonous, mind-numbing work, and he'd struggled to generate the energy to face each day.

But since he'd received the devastating news about Karin and Gisele almost three weeks ago, he'd sunken deep into the abyss.

For the first two weeks, he'd been almost unable to move, the grief overwhelming him, reminding him, with its relentless, paralyzing pain, of what he had lost. And of what he had taken.

Every second of every minute of every day.

No survivors.

Even now, weeks later, he rarely ate and slept even less. He barely glanced at the documents they brought him, but more often than not found himself simply staring into empty space for twenty or thirty minutes before passing each folder along without a thought. And he'd taken to wandering around the Institute's grounds whenever possible, rather than toss and turn in the bleak nothingness of his quarters. As he walked, he challenged himself—often unsuccessfully—not to think, because thinking leads to feeling, but he always seemed to end up at the same spot by the skull and crossbones sign on the inner fence, wondering how difficult it would be to climb the wire and end his miserable, pointless existence.

On a meaningless Tuesday morning just like every other meaningless Tuesday morning, an orderly brought Günther yet another brown folder. But inside this one, paperclipped to the standard set of documents, was something out of the ordinary. The pale blue envelope was marked *Empfindlich*.

Sensitive.

That got his attention.

Inside it, he found a document unlike any he'd seen so far. A small rectangle, complete rather than an obvious fragment of a larger whole, the paper was much thicker than the typical notepaper he normally dealt with. A handwritten blue-ink notation filled the top left corner:

31 Oktober 1944

A-122349

Lymphadenektomie und Vollständige Transplantation

Überlebte 1 Stunden 11 Minuten

Dr.med. E.S.M.

He turned it over. The glossy black-and-white image made his throat tighten.

A young boy, who looked to be no older than his beautiful Gisele had been, was splayed out, faceup and naked, on a stainless steel table. His arms, legs, torso, and head were held in place by thick straps. His shaved head looked much too large for his bony, emaciated body, and there were bloody, open incisions visible on his neck and his chest, near his arms. A series of tubes trailed from the boy's arms and thighs, connecting him to bottles that hung from thin metal poles. His mouth was gagged, and his lifeless, staring eyes were wide open.

Günther dropped the photograph onto his desk and recoiled in absolute horror.

He'd seen and caused his own fair share of death. Machine gun bullets, cannon shells, high explosives, and shrapnel can completely shred human bodies. Fire consumes living flesh in the most horrendous ways. And skin, muscle, sinew, and bone are absolutely no match for the forces of gravity and momentum, especially when they meet the sharp metal and glass of a broken aeroplane or impact the unforgiving, immovable earth.

This was no enemy fighter pilot, no willing participant in the chest-thumping insanity of aerial combat. This was no heavily armed soldier willing to shoot it out with another. This was a child. And he knew that Morbach—E.S.M.—had been involved in whatever had happened to him.

He felt a prickly heat rise around his collar as his breathing became shallow. For a brief moment he felt nauseous, feverish almost, the fear—or more accurately the knowledge—that he'd caused the deaths of children himself absolutely panicking him, filling him with revulsion and self-hatred.

He shoved the photograph back into its envelope and left his office, barking at the miserable Anselm as he passed by the adjutant's desk without pausing.

"Getting some air."

He quickly made his way to the skull and crossbones sign, hands cold and clammy, mind screaming with unanswerable questions. He tried to rationalize what he had done from the air, and what he had just seen. Morbach wasn't a combat pilot caught up in a senseless war, fighting more for personal survival and the lives of his comrades than to carry out the murderous orders of his superiors. No, Morbach was a doctor. A doctor! Maybe he'd been trying to save the boy? Maybe the boy had died elsewhere from the "lymphadenectomy and complete transplantation" described on the back of the photo? Maybe Morbach had been conducting an autopsy? *Maybe.*

He was no physician, but he couldn't imagine why the subject of an autopsy would need to be gagged, would need to have their head and torso and limbs forcibly restrained. With trembling hands he grabbed the fence and tried to steady himself as he squeezed his eyes shut tight, but that only brought him flashing mental images of the boy, of Gisele, and a parade of Russian memories he wanted so badly to erase.

What the hell is this place? What the fuck is going on here?

As he hung on the wire, staring unseeing into the distance and working to control his breathing, Günther made a promise to himself. He would find out.

36

Scott had been right.

They'd found a trail that wound down through the pine forest—
a well-worn track no doubt created by thousands and thousands of
hiking boots—that showed them the way.

The trailhead emptied into a small gravel parking lot, where a
carved wooden sign bore a sun-bleached map that proclaimed Du er
Her—You Are Here.

"Okay. So we know it's possible." Scott said, grinning at Alison
as she slumped against a short wooden fence. "Let's get that coffee and
take a little look around the town."

Twenty-five minutes later, they sat in the early afternoon sun at
a small table outside a small café, directly across from the town's main
wharf.

Man, this guy's really making me look bad, Alison thought, leaning
back in her chair and closing her eyes as she smiled to herself and
groaned. Her legs burned as if she'd just walked fifty miles uphill,
and Scott looked as if he'd just taken a Sunday afternoon stroll through
Pike Place Market. He laughed as she admitted as much.

"I think I might need more than coffee. I've lived right next to
a whole lot of mountains for about fourteen years, but I haven't done

anything even remotely like that in all that time. I mean, I ride the elevator up two floors to my office, for crying out loud!"

A young server brought them water and coffee and sandwiches, and Alison found herself immersed in it all—the warmth of the sun on her face, the smell of the salt air, the texture and taste of the fresh crusty bread and smoked salmon, and hell, even the burning sensation in her legs. She felt alive.

And beneath it all, she felt something else.

Purpose.

She'd thought about that word, that concept, a lot over the last few months. She'd known all along that her purpose as a scientist was as much personal as it was professional, so much so that she feared that her burning desire to find a way to kill the thing that had killed her mother might be clouding her judgement. She so badly wanted to get the new drug to FDA approval but the massive effort involved in the work-up to the clinical trials was taking much longer and burning much more cash than she'd anticipated. The company had enough funding to go another year, maybe, but drug development is an expensive business, and she was definitely feeling the pressure. She desperately wanted a win, for everyone in the world who might face a devastating cancer diagnosis, and of course for everyone on her team. She'd learned from past experience that approval would simply be the end of the beginning, and that the soul-destroying process of satisfying investors by selling a life-saving medicine at the highest possible price would be the final act. Her original purpose—to help people—had been sold to the investors because there was simply no other way to bring it to life, and although they claimed to be in her corner, she was under no illusion that their ultimate goals fully aligned with hers. She wrestled with that every day. On the other hand, she simply didn't know what she'd do if she failed. What if she couldn't even achieve what she thought her original purpose was? To come this far and fall short would be devastating.

Her mother's pain and suffering and death had already taken its toll on her emotionally. Seeing someone you love decline and vanish before your eyes while you're powerless to do anything about it is absolutely brutal, and she'd thought of James and her father often as she'd sat on her mother's bed, stroking what was left of her hair, holding her frail hand. *What's worse? To be alive and present and basically useless as a loved one is slowly taken from you, or to be oblivious to their departure until the sudden, sharp agony of their loss is dropped on you like a bucket of ice water?*

Purpose.

What the hell had James's purpose been? What possible good could he have done—could any of them have done?—in a godforsaken place like Afghanistan? What the hell was any of it for? And now this.

A phone call from out of the blue had her halfway around the world, meeting with government investigators and university archaeologists and walking over mountains and glaciers in pursuit of clues about the disappearance of a long-dead relative she'd never met. *Why does this whole thing feel so weirdly right? So absolutely necessary? Why do I feel so compelled to follow it as far as I can? And why does he?*

"Listen," she said. "I, uh, just want to thank you for doing this. For coming out here, I mean. I know it's above and beyond and, well, I just really appreciate it, you know?"

Scott leaned back and clasped his hands behind his head, stretched his legs out and smiled into the sun. "Uh, I'm on vacation, ma'am. Remember?"

She smiled right back. "Oh, right, right. I forgot. Well...then thanks for letting me tag along."

They sat in the warm silence for a few minutes, and Alison found herself wondering if his eyes, hidden behind sunglasses, might be open or closed. She found herself wondering what he might be thinking.

Wondering.

As she glanced over at him, the realization suddenly dawned on her. She hadn't noticed herself actually wondering about any of the men she'd spent time with in recent memory. They just hadn't spurred her to want to know any more than they'd all been so overly eager to tell her. They'd all seemed so ready to provide her with an almost continuous flow of information that they hadn't sparked any questions for her to ask.

She hadn't thought about the difference until that very moment, but other than information pertinent to the investigation, Scott Wilcox had been more or less a closed book. Professional, of course, and polite, and clearly intelligent. But also something more. She'd seen glimpses, sensed a kind of depth in him, an underlying strength and intensity and caring warmth that made her want to know more. The questions had simply presented themselves.

What's your story? What's your purpose?

So she took a breath, and she asked.

37

Each day since the blue envelope, Günther had awakened at 0445.

He'd begun to do recruit calisthenics in his quarters, working to try to regain a little of his lost muscle tone. He'd started to take early morning walks, even working up enough of an appetite to consume more of the powdered eggs and black bread and watery porridge they substituted for real food at the mess hall. And he'd begun to take much more frequent breaks from his office duties, glaring intensely at the stone-faced Anselm as he strutted silently past him, daring the miserable bastard to say something.

At first, he'd hobbled around the compound as best he could, but he'd gradually worked his way up to a stroll, and eventually to a brisk walk. His eyes, he'd accidentally noticed as he shaved one morning, were still sunken and empty, so he rarely looked in their direction anymore. But he could feel himself growing physically stronger.

He'd begun to keep records of his own in a small black notebook he'd pilfered from the supply office. Which buildings experienced the most activity and at what times? What kinds of people came and went from those buildings? What did they wear? Were they medical or scientific types? Civilian? Military? What kinds of vehicles frequented the compound and when?

And he'd also started to meticulously copy the contents of every folder that came into his possession, regardless of whether he could decipher and understand them or not. Over a period of a few weeks, he'd begun to get a sense of what he thought was happening.

Since he was only ever given a fragment of any particular note or diagram or schematic, he'd guessed that he was likely one of many such proofreaders in the employ of the Institute, and it had become increasingly clear that the compartmentalized system he was part of had been designed to ensure that very few people knew and understood the totality of what was going on. The scope and scale and reality of the Institute's activities were being deliberately masked.

For the first time in too many years, Günther was on a mission he actually wanted to be on. He wasn't flying into combat, pumped up on lies, methamphetamines, and adrenaline. This was something much more powerful and compelling.

A dead boy had brought him back to life.

38

"So, mister glacier-hiking action investigator," said Alison. "Tell me something. About Afghanistan. How did you get from there to here?"

Scott took a sip of water, took off his sunglasses, and smiled a squinty little smile. "What can I tell you about Afghanistan? Hmm. Let me think. Well, it was hot. And cold."

"Oh, come on," Alison said, smiling. "I know you can do better than that. My brother was there, but he…well, he never talked about it at all. He…he never really got a chance to."

Scott turned to look out at the perfect sparkling blue of the harbour. "I know he was there. And…I'm really sorry for your loss."

He paused for a couple of breaths.

"I guess I joined up for my own reasons, but they were probably the same reasons a lot of people did. Most of us enlisted because we wanted to serve our country, you know? A few people were there because they just needed a paycheck or someplace to go, but I think most of us were there to, you know, maybe try to do something bigger in life. To make some kind of difference.

"Personally, well, I've always wanted to help people," he said, "so I wanted to serve as a medical technician. A combat medic. Like I said before"—he smiled—"it's pretty much in my DNA."

She smiled back at him and silently sipped her coffee as more questions formed.

"And let's just say I've seen Afghanistan in all of its glory," he said. "The best of it and the absolute worst of it. We spent half of our time at the base just trying to survive the boredom—playing sand hockey and reading and working out and listening to The Hip—and the other half humping through some absolutely stunning landscape while a handful of people we didn't know tried to kill us and we tried to kill them. Today's little walk was basically the equivalent of any typical day on patrol in Kandahar. Minus the periodic shooting and explosions, of course."

He squinted into the glare coming off the water. "To tell you the truth, I still don't know exactly what we were supposed to accomplish over there. I just tried to look after my people, you know? To do what I was trained to do." He focused his gaze on a seagull circling the harbourfront. "As for this job? I never really thought about it until now, but I guess this is about helping people too."

He paused before turning to her.

"The one thing I learned for sure from war is that it's only the people who go on living who feel pain." He smiled softly and looked back out at the sunlit water. "At least, that's what I'm going with, because nobody who died ever told me any different."

Alison smiled back, but the old feelings were beginning to rise, and she fought hard to keep them below the surface. *Only the people who go on living feel pain? Goddamn right they do.* "I think that pretty much applies to all of life Scott. Not just war."

She closed her eyes and turned her face back to the sun, let the warm silence envelop her for a few moments.

"Tell me about JTS2," she said.

"Ah, you mean JTF2?"

Alison opened her eyes and felt a pleasant something as Scott leaned a little closer, peered over his sunglasses, and whispered with mock-intensity, "You're actually asking me about Joint Task Force Two? If I told you, I'd, ah, have to kill you. Ma'am."

She smiled at that.

"In all seriousness, though," he said, pulling back, "I really can't tell you much more than what you can read on Wikipedia. That's a pretty secretive group."

Alison suddenly wished she hadn't brought that subject up, but somehow the words had made themselves heard. "I never knew what James was doing over there. None of us did. I mean, they told us he was killed in action by a roadside bomb or an IED or whatever they called it. You know, doing the job he'd signed up to do and all that official-sounding crap. But nobody ever told us exactly what happened. Nobody ever told us why it happened."

She went silent for a moment, sipping her water to buy a little time. *Keep it together. Don't go there.* All these years and she still welled up at the thought. "He looked so peaceful when we finally...when they brought him home."

She paused again to try to collect herself, to blink her eyes clear and to will the tightening in her throat and chest to subside. She looked away, focused on the boats rocking in the harbour, and tried her very best, but the thoughts and feelings were unstoppable. And, as she knew they would, the next words caught in her throat. "You're right, though. James was the one who died"—her voice dropped to a whisper—"but it was us who were destroyed."

Scott reached out and put his hand on her forearm, then quickly withdrew it, despite Alison's sad smile.

"I'm sorry, ma'am. I...I didn't mean to overstep. It's just that... well...I guess I'm just used to trying to heal the wounded."

39

Günther heard it before he saw it.

Quickly scanning the afternoon sky, he guessed it to be coming from the southeast, but his view was partially blocked by the mess hall behind him. With the sound bouncing off all of the brick and concrete surfaces, he just couldn't be sure. When it suddenly appeared, deafeningly low overhead, he ducked instinctively.

A big silver bird was going down.

With one of its four engines on fire and trailing a plume of dense black smoke, another engine stopped completely, the giant roared past in a gently curving arc no more than thirty metres above him. The entire nose of the aircraft was missing, leaving a gaping, chaotic mess of shredded shiny aluminum skin and pea green and black framework and wiring and tubing where its flight crew had once been.

A hatch in the belly just forward of the port wing appeared to be open—*looks as if someone got out?*—and he could see a single black bomb dangling awkwardly from its rack inside the open bay. White stars on dark blue circles dotted the bomber's fuselage and wing, and a massive black square containing a white letter *A* adorned what was left of its vertical stabilizer, most of which had been lost to flak or cannon fire or some other destructive impact.

In a split second, the doomed B-17 flashed out of Günther's field of view and almost immediately a massive explosion rocked the earth beneath his feet, sending a huge ball of fire and smoke into the skies beyond the buildings.

He began to move toward the impact area as quickly as he could, as groups of people—some in civilian clothes, some in lab coats, some in uniform—poured out of various buildings to see what had happened, frantically babbling and shouting to each other in panic and confusion. As he rounded the corner of Building 4, Günther remembered seeing a narrow space between it and Building 5 that he hoped might give him a more direct route to the spot where he guessed the bird might have hit.

He squeezed sideways between the two brick walls.

About halfway down the claustrophobic passageway, he stopped dead in his tracks. For a brief moment, he thought he heard the faint sound of a child's incessant, unintelligible screaming, and angry but muffled deeper voices echoing off the bricks. The subdued cacophony seemed to be coming from behind a door in the otherwise featureless back wall of the building directly across the walkway at the far end of the space he was squeezing through, but he couldn't be sure.

Building 8 was a squat, redbrick structure that had been clearly marked on his facility orientation map as a file storage warehouse. A short set of crumbling concrete steps led up to the handle-less door, and he gripped the rusted iron railing to steady himself as he climbed. Pressing his ear to the peeling, brown-painted wood, he strained to listen above the echoing sounds of the panicked voices and alarm bells, and the horns and sirens of the emergency vehicles making their way toward the pall of black smoke far to his left.

There were no high-pitched screams to be heard, no deep, angry shouts. He began to wonder if he'd completely imagined all of that, to wonder if it might have been some kind of cruel trick of the mind played on his still-grieving soul. But there was no mistaking what he did hear.

Somewhere deep inside the nondescript file storage warehouse, a woman was singing, her powerful Italian voice mournfully lamenting the death of her mother.

o o o

The grey-haired driver backed his old black truck up to Building 4, as he did every Thursday morning at 0600. Günther lit another cigarette and leaned against the wall in his now preferred solitary smoking spot, beneath the green metal awning outside the mess hall loading bay.

"Guten Morgen, mein Herr." Günther nodded.

He'd noticed the man a few weeks prior, overheard him interact with the kitchen staff. He'd asked one of the cooks about him, casually but pointedly inquiring about the man's "strange accent" as if he was mildly suspicious more than just curious.

"Oh, that's just old Henrik. He's totally harmless," he'd been told.

Henrik had been delivering food and supplies to the Institute for more than three years. He was somewhere in his late fifties, a Dane who'd apparently been living in the area since just after the war. He was a civilian. With a vehicle. And access. Exactly the kind of man who might know things, and exactly the kind of man Günther figured he might need to know.

"Moin," came the wary reply.

"Zigarette?"

The man looked at Günther, sizing him up in the dawn light. This morning, Günther had intentionally neglected to shave to his usual standards. His tunic was unbuttoned at the top, his hair a little less tightly groomed than he'd once again begun to keep it.

Henrik reached out a calloused hand and took the offer. "Vielen Dank."

"I think I see you here two or three times every week. I hope you don't mind me saying this, but I'm counting on getting the hell out of this place long before I'm your age." Günther laughed a little, one eye on Henrik as he scraped a match to life and held it out. Henrik said nothing, but nodded and cracked a little smile as he leaned over and drew the flame to his cigarette.

"I'm here as a kind of punishment," Günther continued as he lit his own smoke and tossed the still-burning match to the ground. "I guess you could say I, uh, broke a few rules."

Henrik arched a bushy eyebrow slightly, his gaze focused on the spot in the wet gravel where the match had fizzled out.

"But what the hell are you doing here?" Günther said. "A man of your stature and impressive bearing? You look like you should be at least a field marshal or a general or something!"

Henrik chuckled audibly at that one, looked up.

"No, sir. Not me," he said quietly. "I just want to do my job. And to go home to my family every night."

"That's a noble pursuit, my friend," said Günther. "A truly noble pursuit." He dropped his cigarette butt and crushed it under his boot, calling out over his shoulder as he walked away.

"See you next time."

40

"Hallo, there. My name is Anders Strevik. I'm the publisher here. What can I do for you today?"

The offices of *Heralden*, Rosendal's local newspaper, were on the second floor of a gabled beige and red-brown two-storey building on the town's main street. "Thanks for agreeing to meet with us on such short notice Mr. Strevik," said Alison as she shook his hand. "This might be a bit of an odd one."

Twenty minutes later, the look on the publisher's face said it all. "Well, that is just an amazing story," he said. "Absolutely fascinating. And of course I'm very happy to check our archives for you, but the newspaper has only been published here since 1952. My father bought it from the original owner and I took it over in 1992. And I'm afraid the war was a very long time ago."

As the publisher spoke, Alison's gaze wandered to the various framed pictures on the wall behind his paper-strewn desk.

Cruise ships.

Monuments.

A very large cow.

People in dark business suits posing in front of buildings.

Kids playing soccer.

Everyday, normal life, she thought. And now we show up.

"Anything you might be able to do would be much appreciated, Mr. Strevik," she said. "We know it's a long shot, but we thought this might be as good a place to start as any."

As Alison and Scott stood to leave, the publisher handed them business cards. "Of course," he said. "I can't say we do a lot of investigative journalism here—our stories are mostly local interest stuff and the like—but I can do a little asking around and see what I might be able to come up with. I don't really know what else to suggest. Maybe you could try the local library? It'll be on your way out of town."

They walked to their newly rented car. "So, where do we go from here?" said Alison.

"Gee, I don't know," Scott deadpanned. "How about the local library?"

She laughed out loud.

○ ○ ○

They'd stopped in at the Rosendal public library and told their story to a couple of women there, then made the fifty-five minute drive back to the parking lot where they'd left the SUV some eighteen hours earlier.

The Norwegian skies were still lit by the glow of the sun, low on the horizon at 9:49 p.m., and virtually every cell in Alison's body cried out for sleep as she followed Scott around the last few turns on the road back to the hotel in Odda, but she knew the flood of thoughts and questions and emotions sloshing around in her head would play like a late night movie on the inside of her eyelids.

As they walked into the hotel lobby, Scott looked up from his phone. "Hey. I got an email from the Deutsche Dienststelle. Looks like they may have a hit on the identity tag found in the wreckage. They're going to do some more cross checking, but they hope to be sending details in the next few days. Oh, and there's one more thing. Jonas left a voicemail. He's got something he wants us to see and he sent a video conference link for 0900 tomorrow. You up for that after our little adventure today?"

Alison stopped and smiled at him, hands on hips. "Look, action man. I may be an out of shape thirtysomething biotech executive who just walked ten hours over the top of a glacier and down a mountainside to prove that it might have been done by someone much younger than me seventy-four years ago, but video conferences at nine in the morning are totally my thing."

He laughed his quiet laugh. "Well played, ma'am. Well played."

41

They'd almost become friends.

Over the weeks, they'd burned a lot of cigarettes, traded a few stories, and begun to hint at their mutual disdain for the pack of idiots who were making the real decisions. Günther had regaled Henrik with tales of aerial daring, stupidity, and pure dumb luck, and he'd almost gotten around to explaining the actual circumstances under which he'd come to be at the Institute. And eventually, when the inevitable but in wartime potentially risky subject of family had finally come up, he'd told Henrik about the constant, gnawing grief he felt after learning of the deaths of his wife and daughter.

Henrik had divulged a few things about himself, too.

He was a Dane, but he'd been compelled to serve in the German infantry in 1917, risking his neck in the mud and shit and blood of Belgium because of some idiotic nineteenth-century political agreement. He'd come back to southern Denmark after the war to try to build a new life, but of course a new war had come along, and he'd needed to put bread on the table. So here he was, working for his old German bosses again, this time out of necessity.

As for his own family, Henrik had finally let on to Günther that not so long ago, his sixteen-year-old son had gotten himself into a little trouble up near Copenhagen. Apparently the boy had always been a little headstrong, and he'd been somewhat "unhappy" with the situation the last few years. He'd been arrested and imprisoned by the Gestapo, and Henrik was constantly worried that they would eventually execute him, as they'd done with so many others.

"You mean he didn't like us moving into his house?" Günther asked. "Who could blame him, huh? The reality is, we Germans are going to have a few million unwanted houseguests ourselves, not so long from now."

At that, Henrik's eyes had come up under his bushy eyebrows.

"I know I don't have to tell you this, Henrik, but wars don't just end. They don't just stop. They linger and fester and cause pain and suffering long after the shooting has ceased and the papers have been signed. Germany is heading toward another bad ending, Henrik, and it will be a long, long time before there can be a new beginning. Such an ending can't be avoided. Hell, we're already in it, we just can't see or feel it here. But when it becomes visible to us, when it finally begins to deliver to us the confusion and turmoil and pain and death that we've earned, that will be the most dangerous time for everyone."

Günther's eyes focused on a wet cigarette butt as he lit up again. "It seems neither of us has ended up where we wanted to be. We're both…on the fringes, Henrik. We're both…used up. And hell, the powers that be won't save us. Shit, they can't even save themselves."

They smoked in silence for a few minutes.

"I'm afraid," said Henrik, his voice low, "that the time you speak of has already arrived for me. I'm hoping you won't, Herr Major, but I'm afraid that my family and me, well, we're going to need a miracle to survive the long ending. My grandson—my oldest daughter's boy— he is only thirteen. But he's German. They, uh, they just put a rifle in his hands and sent him east. And I'm Volkssturm now."

Günther looked up, stunned. "What? They're sending children to die now? And you? Volkssturm? A soldier? You did your part in the last war, Henrik."

"It seems someone at the top thinks that a bunch of babies and old men will be able to win the war for them now. They already took the boy. And I, ah, I report for weapons and tactics training down near Rostock in a few weeks. After that, who knows."

Günther stared out at the placid blue water beyond the buildings and the fences, familiar anger beginning its rise. *Is this what it's all come down to? Is this the last gasp of the thousand year Reich?*

"That's craziness, Henrik. The Allies are in France, Belgium. Holland. Their bombers and fighters are over Berlin and Hamburg and Dresden, killing my family and hundreds of thousands of other families at will. The Russians are charging through the Ukraine. They may already be in Poland. Soon they'll be in Berlin. We're virtually powerless to stop any of them. You and I both know what that means."

Günther looked at Henrik, saw the stoic desperation in his eyes. "I have no family to return to," said Günther. "They've already been taken from me by this pointless fucking war. Now yours is to be taken from you? And maybe you'll be taken away forever? For what, Henrik? For what?"

With a low, exasperated sigh, Günther dropped his cigarette to the ground, where it joined the countless others that had been crushed under their bootheels.

"The politicians, the generals, they see us no differently. We're of no more value to them than…these goddamn cigarette butts. We're just to be used up and discarded. And there's no one we can look to for salvation, Henrik. We can only look to each other."

Henrik was resigned. "Ja, Herr Major. Ja."

"Henrik," said Günther. "My friends call me Gunner."

○ ○ ○

Filled with meticulously copied notes and diagrams, Günther's secret notebooks had become an obsession. Each night, alone in his quarters, he pored over their contents. He'd had to give up his university chemistry studies after only two years, so his ability to interpret what he'd gathered was limited, but there were things to understand other than what was written.

He'd realized early on that the parade of document fragments was not provided to him in chronological order, and that clearly they did not originate from a single source. Where possible, he'd noted any dates and his interpretations of subject matter, and he'd begun to catalog the various paper types, ink colours, or pencil used by their authors. And soon after he'd begun his "study," he'd assigned code numbers to individual styles of handwriting, as he'd come to recognize and remember certain characteristics.

He'd begun to suspect that the strings of codes he'd see from time to time were actually references to individual study cases. It was one such alphanumeric cipher—A-122349—written on the back of the horrifying photograph that he was sure he'd never been meant to see, that had prompted his personal investigation. There were many others.

T-268345
H-369025
H-872360
B-133404
C-114329
J-773210
R-81810

He'd also begun to compile a list of certain technical words he did recognize, along with a record of the frequency with which they appeared in the documents.

11 Ablation

17 Chloroform

3 Sulfonamid

9 Abszess

19 Adrenalin

2 Isotop

56 Lymphknoten

39 Knochenmark

17 Rückenmarksflüssigkeit

22 Phenol

8 Adenine

36 Leukämie

27 Verstorbene

Patterns were emerging, random words beginning to paint a picture for him. But most troubling to Günther were the drawings, their cryptic indicators tending to point to the same areas of the various illustrated human forms. He needed to know more than he could recall from his Reifezeugnis anatomy studies so many years ago.

○ ○ ○

The white-coated Wehrmacht doctor peered over his clipboard. "Herr Major, I understand that you have joined us from an active

Luftwaffe unit? Perhaps that explains all of these scars, yes? Now tell me again about your concerns?"

Günther smiled weakly. He was in his underwear, perched on a high padded table in a cold, virtually featureless pale green room. He'd been measured, weighed, prodded, poked, and intimately explored for the last fifteen minutes.

"I was assigned here to recover from my most recent adventures with our Russian friends. My leg wound and other injuries seem to be healing just fine, but I can't seem to shake a kind of general malaise. A kind of, ah, overall fatigue I guess you might say."

"Yes, well, fatigue is extremely common in times of war, Herr Major, but surely your duties here are not nearly as taxing as those of your previous assignments? It's possible that you are experiencing the psychological effects of being removed from what must have been a chronic high-stress condition and are reacting to finding yourself now in a place of significantly less...excitement. Your vital signs certainly indicate no cause for concern at this time."

Günther brought his hand up to his armpit and then to his neck. "Sometimes I feel a sort of odd sensation, here and here. Should I be worried about any of that?"

The doctor pressed his ice-cold fingers to Günther's skin. "Hmm. All seems completely normal at this time. Swelling in those areas can usually be associated with the body fighting an infection of some kind. The lymph nodes are important for the proper functioning of the immune system. But not to worry, only very rarely is swelling in them an indication of more serious issues."

"Uh, what kind of more serious issues, Herr Doctor?"

"Well, cancer would be the most serious, but that, of course, is extremely rare, Herr Major."

"I see," said Günther, continuing his informal education. "My father died of cancer. If my, ah, lymph nodes were to suddenly stop working for some reason, could you start them up again with some pills or something?" He laughed. "Or just take them out? Or perhaps give me someone else's?"

The doctor scribbled a few notes on his clipboard. "I'm afraid not, Herr Major. Should a person experience a serious malfunction of the lymphatic system, their life expectancy would be severely impacted."

He nodded toward Günther's uniform draped over a chair in the corner. "I think we can get you back to work now. And not to worry. For the time being, just keep an eye on your symptoms. I know the food is less than stellar here, but please do try to eat more, and get as much rest and exercise as you can. If the fatigue persists for more than a few weeks, or if the swelling returns, come back and see me, ja?"

The doctor clicked his heels, pivoted smartly, and left the room.

42

She'd heard bells and sirens and distant booming before, but she had no idea what the sounds meant. She knew only that the people would come for her, as they always did when those noises got too loud, too close.

They hauled her from her mattress, but this time there was no metal gurney, no straps. They simply lifted her, rough hands excruciatingly close to the wounds under her arms, and half walked, half dragged her along the corridor and down the stairs.

She huddled on the cold concrete floor, the pain in her armpits and chest excruciating, but still she wrapped her skeletal arms around her scarred legs to try to ward off the chill.

She felt almost no fear, but she could tell that the people were all terrified.

For her, this was a far, far better place than the white room, the bells and sirens and booming noises so much more comforting than the loudly singing lady. The single dim light bulb flickered once or twice in its cage on the wall above the door, but it somehow managed to remain on, lighting up the gathering of pale and anxious faces as their owners stood silently, eyes nervously darting from one another to the low concrete ceiling, and back again.

As her vision adjusted to the dim light, she noticed something she'd never seen before.

Across the room, through the fence of legs partially blocking her view, in a shadowy area near the far concrete wall, were two other children. Their identical heads had been shorn, like hers, and their scabby, exposed arms and legs were so thin that their elbow and knee joints looked like knots on pieces of rope. They sat back to back on the floor, gently rocking in unison, staring expressionlessly at her as she did at them. And then she realized. They moved as one because they had to. Because they were one.

They were joined together at the spine.

43

When the first one hit, Günther thought it might have been an accidental release.

He knew from personal experience that pilots sometimes strayed off course, panicked or ran out of time, and simply jettisoned their bomb loads to expedite a safe trip home. He looked up from his notebook with a wry smile. *Hell, I know for a fact that some pilots intentionally drop their bombs where they shouldn't.* The second and third and fourth detonations told him otherwise. They were hitting the small docks across the bay for some reason. *Nothing of any importance there, boys. Nothing worth destroying. We're right over here! I'm right here!*

He shoved his notebook into his case, leaving the file folder and the documents he'd been surreptitiously copying on his desk as per protocol, grabbed his tunic and cap, and began to make his way toward the air raid shelter. Sirens from the outside and alarm bells from the inside wailed continuously as he glanced up and down the corridor. Anselm's desk was abandoned.

First to run, chickenshit?

He walked out of the building, looking up at the gently curving streams of flak seeking the bombers in the beautiful late-afternoon sky. The central compound was already virtually deserted, just a few guards still at their posts, their attention divided between the bomber contrails and fireworks overhead and the last few people running for the shelters.

Günther made a snap decision. Instead of heading for the shallow concrete basement in Building 4 that passed for the Institute's air raid shelter, he turned and squeezed through the narrow brick passageway. He moved quickly toward the peeling brown wooden door on the back side of Building 8, then worked his way around to the structure's front facade. A single door was cracked slightly open.

He climbed the brick stairs, pulled the door open a little further, and peered inside. Across a small, dimly lit vestibule were two more doors, and on his right, a staircase that led down to what he assumed must be a basement level. *Okay. Here goes.*

He jerked the main entrance door wide open and limp-strutted through the vestibule with as much commanding Luftwaffe demeanour as he could muster, but no one challenged him. Past the two inner doors, he entered a virtually windowless corridor illuminated by six yellow-white hanging lights. The place smelled strongly of antiseptic chemicals—*odd for a document storage warehouse*—and a light haze of dust floated in the air.

The rumbling of another not-so-distant bomb impact shook the building, and Günther could hear the muffled sirens and alarm bells and the dull staccato sound of the flak batteries across the water, but nothing else. No movement. No talking. No shouts. The building appeared to be abandoned.

Rows of heavy doors lined each side of the corridor's thirty-metre length, five on each side. Each door bore a nonsequential alphanumeric code chalked onto a sliding access panel. *Same type of code I keep seeing in the documents.* Günther inched toward the first door on his left and tried the latch. Locked. *Very odd*, he thought, *for a document storage facility to require metal doors with sliding access panels built into them.* He pressed an ear to the door, trying to ignore the ongoing cacophony and detect any new sounds. Nothing.

The fifth latch he tried was unlocked, and the metal door creaked open as he stepped into its threshold. A caged, grime-covered light bulb barely lit the room. The windowless space was about two metres wide and three metres long, empty except for a rusted and dented white metal cot pushed up against the concrete wall on one side, its badly stained grey mattress and a single blanket lying partially on the filthy concrete. A foul-smelling hole in the far corner of the floor made Günther gag.

He recoiled, backing out. *What the hell is this?* He moved farther down the hallway, finding another door already open, revealing the same kind of dank, stinking, barren cell.

At the end of the hallway, a short corridor led off to his left, toward a single brown wooden door at its terminus. Directly ahead of him were two pale green doors, each with a dented and scratched stainless steel kick panel on its lower face and a porthole window in its upper half. Locked. He strained to see inside. Whatever was on the other side of the round windows was mostly cloaked in darkness, but there, partially illuminated by the diffused circles of yellow-white light projected into the room by the ever so slightly swinging light bulb hanging above his head, was a stainless steel table equipped with what looked like thick brown leather straps.

He'd seen enough.

Ninety seconds later, he made his way across the cobblestones and down the short flight of stairs to the air raid shelter. He hunkered down, gripped his black leather bag tightly, and worked to control his breathing and his racing mind as he waited with the others for the all-clear.

44

The first image appeared on Scott's laptop screen, a high-resolution photograph as sharp as a tack, and Professor Lundeen walked them through the details.

"We've been able to extract a significant portion of the cockpit canopy framework you both saw firsthand in the ice during your recent visit. This piece, found a few days ago, would have been located, we believe, somewhere near or on the bottom left edge, basically beside the pilot's left shoulder."

A second image appeared. A close-up detail.

"After cleaning up the fragment a little, we thought it might bear more scrutiny. It's a bit difficult to see, given the level of corrosion and surface degradation, but if you look closely, you can just make out the faint outline of what looks to be a leaf, and what might have been a letter *M* scratched into what's left of the paint."

Alison's breath caught in her throat as she locked eyes with Scott.

"That's a maple leaf. And a letter *M*! My god!" she gasped. "My grandmother's name was Marie."

Jonas continued. "As for next steps at the site, we believe we've located one of the aircraft's armour-plated seat components and what appears to be part of a propeller hub assembly, so we're going to keep looking for more bits and pieces for a little while. But we're guessing that the larger metal objects like the engines and landing gear and possibly the weapons the aircraft might have carried may have been dispersed and separated by the movement of the ice over time, as the aircraft's structure broke down. That would, of course, likely apply to the majority of any…uh, potential human remains also. We will, of course, continue to do what we can in that regard, but in the meantime, we have some very curious findings related to the notebook that was recovered from the metal box."

The image changed again.

"You're now looking at a composite of the seventeen notebook pages or page fragments that we've been able to recover successfully. I took the liberty of sharing them with a few of my colleagues in the departments of science and history, and it took some time for the translators to decipher some of the more damaged content, but Dr. Sundstrom in biochemistry believes the notes on the pages that we have labeled three, five, seven, ten, eleven, and thirteen are most likely related to some form of medical research. Given your area of expertise, I thought you might find that particularly interesting, Miss Wiley."

Alison was all ears. "Medical research?" *Now we're in my world.* "That's exactly what I suspected when I saw the first few notes. What do you make of it?"

"From what we can tell," said Jonas, "and as you may be able to see here, most of this seems to be focused primarily on some form of cancer research. The notations most definitely reference the human lymphatic system, leukemia, bone marrow, tumors and malignancies, for example. And there are terms that appear to indicate the, uh, demise of certain study 'subjects.' It seems, however, that the nature of the research may not be exactly what we might naturally assume it to be. It may not be…positive."

Cancer research? Not positive? What the hell does that mean? Alison was confused. She'd spent the last six and a half years of her life fully immersed in cancer research, launching and building a company that was committed to finding ways to trigger the body's own immune system to attack and destroy cancerous cells.

"What kind of cancer research could be anything other than positive?" she asked as the image on the screen changed. Labeled *17*, the photograph showed a badly damaged page fragment, its surface stained and degraded by the elements and its time entombed beneath the glacier.

"As you can see, the notes written on this fragment are mostly indecipherable, but it's this word that got our attention."

An enlarged portion of the image appeared on the screen. Alison read the purple-blue script, barely legible on the stained, mildewed surface.

"Blitzableiter."

"Yes," said Jonas. "It translates to 'Lightning Rod.' Blitzableiter was the Nazi biological warfare program. Our best guess here is that these notes relate to their efforts to weaponize disease. In this case, we are surmising, cancer."

45

The rumors had been flying around the Institute for weeks. As much as he'd kept to himself, the rumblings he'd heard at the mess hall echoed what he'd heard from Henrik. In the east, the Wehrmacht was in complete disarray, and the Russians were steadily killing, looting, burning, and raping their way westward. *No different than what we did to them.* They'd be in Berlin by summer, if not sooner.

The official notification had arrived on his desk via memo the day before, confirming the gossip and his own suspicions.

Apparently it was time to get out.

Although the memo mentioned nothing of the sort, Günther guessed that the relentless Russian advance had consumed East Prussia and he had no doubt that Poland would soon be overrun by vengeful Soviet hordes. And in the west, he'd heard, the Americans, British, and Canadians were pushing hard and fast through France, Belgium, and Holland toward the Rhine. Unstoppable.

Although not explicitly stated in the orders, the implication was clear. Germany's fate, although still to be determined in detail, was imminent. Günther and the rest of the Institute staff were to prepare for evacuation—to move toward the west, obviously away from the advancing Soviets.

Henrik lit his cigarette and puffed slowly in silence, his mood as grey as the gravel.

"What's going on today, my friend?" Günther asked.

Henrik's eyes never left the soggy ground and he struggled to force the words past the lump in his throat. "Nothing good, Herr Major. Nothing good," he said. "My... my beautiful grandson is... missing. They, ah, they don't.... They don't know where he is."

Günther put a hand on Henrik's arm. "He'll turn up. Not to worry." But he knew what Henrik knew. The boy would probably never turn up.

"What will you do, Henrik? You're leaving soon yourself, for god knows where."

Henrik finally looked up, his grey-blue eyes rimmed with red. "I don't know why, Herr Major...Gunner, but I trust you. I...feel I can trust you."

Günther nodded in silence.

"We both know the war is lost. Your family is... Well, I'm so very sorry about your family. My son is... And now my grandson? Who is next? It's just more madness. And I've seen too much madness already, Herr Major," said Henrik. "I won't be going."

Günther stayed silent. He knew that when a quiet man started to talk, it was best to let him continue.

Henrik took a last pull on his cigarette, dropped the butt, and stomped it into the mud. "I've seen too much. And I know too much, Herr Major. I know what goes on here, and...and I know the war will not be long now, and that certain, ah, arrangements have been made."

"What kinds of arrangements, Henrik?" said Günther, eyebrows arched. "What exactly do you mean?"

Henrik glanced around cautiously and moved half a step closer to Günther before continuing in a hushed tone. "Of course there are many who understand the war is lost. The only question now is which of us will die and who will capture those of us who survive. No one wants to be taken by the Russians, so those who have power—or those who have something of value to trade, perhaps—they're making arrangements."

Henrik paused and took another look around.

"Morbach is getting out."

Günther tried to process what he was hearing. "Getting out? What does that mean Henrik? Can you be more specific?"

"He's going to be taken to the west. To the British. With the help of the resistance. And... I, ah, I can trust you, yes?"

"Of course you can trust me, Henrik. There's nothing left for me to care about in this world except my own pathetic skin, and yours."

Henrik paused for a brief moment before looking up. "I helped make the arrangements for him."

46

Scott's phone buzzed just as he clicked out of the video conference.

"Yes, hello? Good morning. Is that Mr. Wilcox? My name is Inga Nygård. I was given your name and telephone number by my friend Mrs. Jaborg, down at the library. She said that you and a nice young woman were there looking for some information. Asking something about the war? Something about escaping airmen?"

"Yes, yes!" Scott said. "Hello, ma'am. I'm Scott Wilcox. Do you mind if I put you on speakerphone? That, ah, nice young woman," he said, as he arched his eyebrows and smiled toward Alison, "is actually here with me now. Miss Wiley."

"Oh, of course, not at all, not at all. Hello, Miss Wiley. Now, I don't know if this is of any help to you at all, but my father was involved in the Milorg during the war. That was the resistance, you know. He's…oh, he's long dead now, but when I was a girl, many times my mother told us the story of a young man who came down from the mountain and how my father had helped him. I remember it quite vividly because she told us that the man had a child with him. We always thought she made it all up—you know, to entertain us, but also to help us remember our brave pappa."

Alison's mouth dropped open and her eyes bored into Scott's

as the instant chill rippled up her spine. Scott scribbled a few notes as he replied. "Actually, yes. Yes, Mrs. Nygård, that's potentially very helpful to us. Is there any way that we could come and see you? We're only about an hour or so away. We'd love to learn whatever we can."

"Why, of course!" came the cheerful reply. "Why don't you both come for tea?"

47

Günther had been instructed to report to Building 11 at 0625 sharp.

The structure was typical of the Institute. Brick. Two storeys. Few windows or doors. He was directed into a small, overheated, windowless meeting room where he waited as nine others eventually joined him. A mix of men and women, mostly civilian but a few in uniform, they eyed each other silently, nervously, nodding and smiling weakly. The anxiety in the room was palpable.

At 0635, the door suddenly opened, and much to Günther's surprise, an SS officer strutted in. An Oberführer. He was stuffed into a uniform that might have fit him at one point in time, but it was abundantly clear that the hardships of war had passed him by. He was accompanied by three other men. Two wore civilian clothing. The third wore a lab coat and stood at the back of the room with his arms folded—the man in charge. Morbach.

The fleshy SS officer's surprisingly high-pitched, nasal voice got everyone's attention. "Guten Morgen. I am Oberführer Erich Vogt. My responsibility is to ensure that the Institute's most valuable assets are carefully protected and preserved during this operation. You will be assisting with preparation, packaging, and transportation, and you will work in assigned teams under the direction of these gentlemen.

The preparation and packaging phases of this operation must be fully completed within forty-eight hours. When your name is called, you will report to your assigned unit leader. And please be advised that this operation is of the highest personal importance to the Führer himself and it must be executed with precision and urgency. Clear? Gut."

The SS officer clicked his heels, and he and Morbach strutted out.

Fifteen minutes later, Günther found himself—along with two middle-aged civilian men and a young military nurse—in the now familiar corridor of Building 8. They gathered outside the two doors with the round windows as a short, balding man addressed them. Morbach and an SS guard stood off to the side.

Personal attention here? Interesting.

"You will be engaged in preparations of materials that are of vital importance to Generalarzt Doktor Morbach and, of course, to the Reich," said the balding man as Morbach, who acted as if he had no recollection of Günther at all, stepped forward to address them.

"You will assist with the collection and packaging of various critical assets contained within this room and its adjoining storage facilities. Because of their importance, I will be transporting a number of these high-value materials personally by staff car. Anything and everything you might see during the process of this action is to be considered most secret. Am I clear?"

They all nodded, except Günther. He simply stood and glared at Morbach, thinking only of Henrik's recent revelations. *So this is how it begins? The grand escape plan?*

"You will follow all instructions provided by my staff," said Morbach. "They will direct you to your specific tasks. Heil Hitler!"

You piece of shit. Heil Hitler? Now? Here? Günther suppressed a sudden, violent urge, and remained motionless as Morbach spun on his heel and pushed the doors of the operating theatre open.

The brightly lit room was cold and antiseptic and hard. It was dominated by three stainless steel tables, each contoured in a way that was reminiscent of a shallow sink, with drains at their deep points near one end. Each table was equipped with a set of thick leather straps, and each was located beneath a large, circular, ceiling-mounted light fixture. Benches and work surfaces and glass-fronted cabinets crowded with an assortment of trays, cloths, bottles, tubes, pliers, forceps, saws, scalpels, stethoscopes, and other medical paraphernalia lined the room's white-tiled exterior walls. The place reeked of chemical disinfectant, and something metallic and sour that Günther recognized but couldn't quite place.

The short, balding man signaled for Günther and the young nurse to follow him as he walked toward a set of doors at the far end of the operating room. Beyond the doors was a small, windowless office with a wooden desk at its center. The room was ringed with banks of five-drawer filing cabinets, and a pile of flat, unconstructed cardboard boxes occupied the floor in one corner.

The balding man got right to the point. "Working sequentially, you will transfer the contents of each filing cabinet drawer into the boxes provided, and label each box precisely, according to the code numbers on the drawers in which the materials were originally stored. You will record each box by code number range on this manifest. And you will not, in any way, attempt to view the contents of any of the folders, dossiers, or envelopes contained within the cabinets. Clear?"

The nurse nodded and replied in the affirmative, but Günther did nothing, said nothing. As the balding man turned and walked out of the room, Günther draped his coat over the pile of flat boxes as an SS guard stepped through the door and took up a position facing them.

○ ○ ○

They'd worked in silence for just over two hours.

Günther had stuffed twenty-two boxes with brown file folders, his coworker had managed twenty-five, all under the not-so-watchful eyes of the bored young guard. Günther had about had enough when the door suddenly swung open and Anselm's skeletal form appeared. Without saying a word, the adjutant looked down at his clipboard, then scanned the room. He pointed to two boxes labeled with identical code numbers. "These cartons are to be set aside, over there. They will be taken to a specific location in due time." And with that, he turned and walked out.

Ten minutes later, the short balding man popped his head into the room, announced that it was time to take a break, and indicated that Günther and the nurse should follow him. As he led them back through the operating room toward the double doors and the long hallway, Günther noticed something he hadn't seen before, something that seemed oddly out of place in what he took to be a medical facility.

A gramophone and a stack of records sat on one of the cabinets.

Thirty-six minutes later, as they walked back to resume their duties, Günther noticed something else. Written in chalk on a rusted panel next to the now closed dark grey-green steel door he'd found open during his brief air-raid-enabled exploration was the code number he'd made a mental note of earlier.

T-268345.

The exact same code was marked on the two boxes Anselm had demanded be set aside from all the others.

48

The house was painted in brilliant azure blue, perfectly trimmed in crisp, sparkling white. From the wrought iron gate at the front of its neatly manicured front garden, obviously tended by loving hands, Mrs. Nygård greeted them warmly.

"Milk, honey, or lemon? Please help yourselves." She poured tea into her finest bone china as she told them what she remembered. "So, you see, my father worked in a bank during the war. He was the manager, you know. And, well, he certainly looked like he worked in a bank. Not at all like he'd be running around in the forest with guns and hand grenades and things like that, sabotaging the Germans or whatever it was that he and his friends did."

She'd been sent to live in England a few years after the war, to attend school and to learn to speak her almost-perfect English. Love, she said, had brought her home—love for Norway, of course, but mostly for a boy she'd been sweet on since she'd been a little girl. They'd married and raised a family together in this very house, she told them—the one she'd grown up in—but her two adult children were both living near Oslo with their families and her husband had, unfortunately, passed a few years back.

"My father was taken away by the Germans in the spring of

1945," she said. "It was terrible, just terrible. Only a few days, really, before the war ended. I was only about eleven years old. My mother and I never saw him again. Let me show you."

She walked to a walnut china cabinet and opened the bottom drawer, returning with a small, well-worn, silver-trimmed wooden box. Piece by piece, one by one, she began to lay its contents out on the white lace tablecloth. A photo of a smiling woman sitting on a blanket on a rocky beach, hand shielding her eyes from the bright sun lighting up her blond hair and the snowcapped mountains far behind her. Another with a baby girl in a white christening dress, cradled in a happy young woman's arms. One showed a young boy on skis, squinting and grinning widely in the brilliant snow glare as he leaned forward on his poles, while the last image featured two men in suits and ties, proudly standing in front of a dark, shiny new 1930s car.

"That one there is my wonderful, handsome pappa," she said, pointing to a tall, slender, man with a thin black moustache and round, steel-rimmed glasses. "He was always so very gentle, so very loving and kind…"

Mrs. Nygård dug deeper into the box. A few folded letters, some greeting cards. Her father's favourite pipe. More photographs of boats and mountains and houses and dogs and unsmiling old ladies and laughing children.

"That's me as a four-year-old, I think, with some of my cousins," she said, setting down a small photograph with white, scalloped edges. "Of course I didn't know what was coming. None of us did."

She quickly shuffled through another batch of loose photographs, giving them each a cursory glance before placing the pile on the table with the others. "I really don't know who most of those people might have been. Friends of my parents, maybe?" she said.

Alison immediately picked up one of the discarded photographs and turned it to face her, the goosebumps rising on her arms as the hairs on the back of her neck stood to full attention.

A young man with dark hair, piercing eyes, and an I-don't-give-a-shit grin stood in front of what appeared to be a log cabin. He wore dark trousers, a dark open-collar shirt, and a heavy jacket. His left hand held the right hand of a tiny young girl who wore a midlength coat over a flower-print frock. Strikingly, she had almost no hair and bore virtually no expression.

Her left hand was only partially visible behind her blurry, wind-blown dress, but it appeared to be covered by a white bandage.

49

Günther grabbed a thick handful of brown folders from the file cabinet drawer and moved toward the two identically labeled boxes that Anselm had instructed them to separate from the others. Without stopping or looking up, he casually opened one of the boxes and withdrew an almost identical handful of its folders, then quickly replaced them with his substitute set. Neither the disinterested SS guard nor Günther's diligent coworker paid the slightest bit of attention as he walked to the pile of flat, unassembled cardboard boxes and slid the folders underneath his coat, then casually returned to the table with another flat box and began to assemble it.

Four hours and forty-two boxes later, the balding man announced that they were done for the day, and he and the guard escorted them from the room. Günther made sure his limp slowed him just enough that he was last in line as they walked. A few steps into the operating room, he stopped.

"Damn it. I left my greatcoat back there. Can I go and get it?"

"Ja, ja. Schnell. Time to eat. And time to sleep," said the balding man, clearly impatient.

"Okay, sorry," said Günther. "I'll be right back."

Günther turned and hobbled back toward the office. As soon as he'd entered and closed the door behind himself, he darted across the room and retrieved the hidden folders, taking just a second or two to carefully arrange his overcoat over his arm so as to totally cover them. A few moments later, he was back in the darkened laboratory, nodding at the guard and slowly limping his way past the stainless steel tables.

On this trip, he noted that all of the cabinets along the side wall had been virtually cleaned out—the scalpels and forceps and pliers and stethoscopes were gone.

But the gramophone and the records were still there.

50

Mrs. Nygård had been completely stunned by Alison's revelation. The grinning young man in the small photograph was most definitely Squadron Leader Jack Barton.

"Well, I think we can officially conclude," said Scott with a wide grin, "that the wreckage under the ice is most definitely your grandfather's aircraft."

Alison was incredibly energized, the questions piling up faster than she could process them. "Mrs. Nygård, are you quite sure you don't recognize the young girl in the picture? A neighbor, maybe? A distant cousin?"

Mrs. Nygård shook her head as Scott turned the glossy print over and over.

"How about these numbers on the back? 47-905143?" said Alison. "Would you have any idea what they might be?"

Mrs. Nygård was equally excited. "I just don't know, my dear. Let me try to think for a minute."

"Let's, ah, maybe try breaking the numbers up in a few different ways and see if that helps at all," said Scott. Mrs. Nygård walked to her kitchen counter and returned with a yellow legal pad and a pen. Scott wrote out the code.

4

7

9

0

5

1

4

3

He held up the notepad. "Anything there?"

Mrs. Nygård pursed her lips and focused. "Unfortunately no."

47

90

51

43

"How about now?" Scott asked.

Hand on her chin, Mrs. Nygård peered intently through her reading glasses, slowly shaking her head. "I'm sorry, but I just don't see anything that means anything to me."

"Okay, let's try one more classic investigator trick. I think I learned this from an old TV show my dad used to watch when I was a kid. *Columbo*, maybe." Scott tore the page from the pad and walked over to a mirror that hung near the home's front door. He held the paper up, numbers facing out and away from him.

"Well they don't magically spell out a secret code word in the mirror, that's for sure. What if we just reverse them? What would that do?" he said. Alison wrote the numbers down on the yellow pad as Scott called them out loud.

74

09

15

34

"Oh, my! Oh, my! Oh, my!" Mrs Nygård gasped and put her hand to her mouth to catch her breath. "I think I see it now! Yes! Yes! Oh-nine. One-five. Three-four."

She had tears in her eyes. "September 15, 1934. Why that's my birthday!"

Alison squeezed her hand. "What about the other numbers, Mrs. Nygård? Seven four. Do you have any idea what those might mean?"

"Unfortunately, no, I'm afraid I don't," she replied, "but now of course I really, really, really want to know!"

Alison's mind was racing. *Why would a bank manager who was a Norwegian resistance member write a cryptic code like that on the back of a photograph of a disguised, escaping Canadian airman? Why his daughter's birth date? What could the remaining numbers mean? And who was the girl?* An idea clicked. *Banks. Numbers. Dates.*

"Mrs. Nygård, you said your father worked at a bank, yes?"

"That's right, yes. He was the manager."

"Was that bank local?" said Alison. "Like, near here somewhere?"

"Well, yes, as a matter of fact, it still is. It's just down on the main road in town. On the waterfront. And it's still my bank!"

Scott's eyes tracked from Alison's raised-eyebrow grin over to Mrs. Nygård's quizzical smile. "Would you, uh, like to take a short drive with us, ma'am?"

Mrs. Nygård's shiny blue eyes lit up, and she smiled a huge smile as she reached out and squeezed Scott's and Alison's hands. "Of course I would, my dears! I haven't had this much excitement in forever."

51

Günther had them all laid out on the floor of his quarters. Inside each large folder, he'd found multiple smaller folders—the kind he'd been receiving for months. But he'd never seen a full, sequential set of documents together at one time, only the randomized individual fragments he'd been provided for proofing.

He was feeling...what? Shame? Guilt? Revulsion? Rage?

All of the above.

T-268345 was a human being. A child, from what he could tell. He didn't understand everything he'd been reading or seeing, but his best guess was that Morbach and his team of researchers had been conducting some kind of medical procedure or experiment on the child, and most likely on many others.

The notes referenced "Total blood transfusion with T-268346," "Injection with 0.5 mg compound DS-411," "Bone marrow transplant T-268346," "Injection 0.5 mg compound DS-412," "Lymphectomy," "Lymphatic fluid transfusion," "Nodal transplantation attempt." "Bone marrow extraction." And the most final of words: *Beendigung.* Termination.

Other pages clearly referenced T-268346.

Günther didn't understand most of the terminology, but he could deduce that this particular subject was somehow different from the others, and that whatever horrors that person might have endured, Morbach and the others had taken a most special interest in them, and had singled them out for even more extensive study.

A blue envelope lay unopened on his bed. He had an inkling of what he might find sealed inside, so he braced himself, but nothing could have prepared him for what he saw when he tore it open.

The child—a girl of no more than seven—had clearly suffered terribly. She stood, naked and exposed, her sad, dark, black-ringed eyes averted from the camera. Bright lights provided a clinical view of her horrendous wounds. Massive, lumpy scars covered her misshapen calves, thighs, upper chest, and biceps. Tiny round marks dotted her neck and chest, a few of them larger and darker than the others.

At first glance, the small piece of white paper to which the image was clipped appeared to be a medical order form, a prescription of some kind. The words he read chilled him to his core.

Dated November 30, 1944, and initialed by E. S. M.—*E. Sigmund Morbach*—the handwritten order called for Subjekt T-268345 to be given an injection of two grams of phenol directly to the heart.

He knew without a doubt what that meant. The paper was not a medical treatment prescription.

It was an execution order.

52

Mrs. Nygård had led the way.

"Hallo. Vi er her for å se Mr. Arnesen, vær så snill."

They'd been ushered into a small, wood-paneled office, where Scott and Alison had watched the bank manager's thin eyebrows arch up more than a few times as Mrs. Nygård told their story and shared the black-and-white photograph with him.

The two Norwegians had conversed for a few more minutes, with Mr. Arnesen smiling quizzically at Scott and Alison from time to time and scratching his head a whole lot. Abruptly, he'd picked up his desk phone, and a few seconds later, a petite, white-haired lady had entered the room.

"Mr. Arnesen has been manager here for only five months," said Mrs. Nygård. "He was transferred in from Bergen. But this is Mrs. Karlsen. She's been working here since 1985. Mr. Arnesen thought she might be able to help us."

Mrs. Karlsen listened and nodded as Mrs. Nygård recounted the story once again and shared the cryptic code with her. She studied the numbers for a minute or two, asked a few more questions, then nodded, stood up, and gestured toward the door.

"Jeg er ikke sikker, men jeg kan ha en ide. Vil du følge meg?"

Single file, they followed Mrs. Karlsen through the bank lobby to a door marked *Oppbevaring*, then down a narrow, dimly lit staircase. At the foot of the stairs, she produced a key, opened a heavy metal door, and felt around in the near darkness for an obviously familiar light switch.

When the ceiling-mounted fluorescents finally flickered on, they illuminated a long, narrow, concrete room—a tunnel really—not quite high enough for Scott to stand straight up in, and lined along both sides with banks of mismatched filing cabinets. Piles of over-stuffed cardboard boxes holding dusty old adding machines, staplers, black rotary telephones, umbrellas, and other assorted oddities claimed the space between them. A convoluted array of cast iron pipes, dull silver electrical conduits, fluorescent lights, and drooping telephone wires jammed the apex of the slightly arched ceiling.

Mrs. Nygård interpreted as Mrs. Karlsen led them in, warning them all to watch their heads and to be careful of spiders. "Mrs. Karlsen absolutely hates spiders," Mrs. Nygård informed them, then continued to translate for the other woman. "As you can see, this is the old storage basement. She says no one really uses it anymore, because of the new computers, you know? But apparently this is where they used to keep the records. In the old days."

Carefully navigating them through the cramped, musty aisle, Mrs. Karlsen stopped at a spot near the far end of the tunnel. She pointed to the bottom drawer of a grey-brown, four-drawer cabinet, and Scott used his phone's flashlight to take a closer look. A yellowed index card had been inserted into a metal holder on the front of the drawer. The inscription, although typed long ago, was crystal clear:

Juni 1934---September 1934

Mrs. Karlsen pointed at Scott and motioned for him to follow her. The two of them made their way back to the storage room entrance, and Mrs. Karlsen opened a dust-caked galvanized silver-grey metal cabinet located on the wall just inside the door. It was almost completely filled with small keys that hung on rows of individual hooks. She trailed her right index finger over a line of numbers that ran along the top row, stopping at the number seven. Trailing her left index finger down a column of numbers that ran vertically down the left side of the cabinet, she stopped at the number four, then brought both fingers together to converge at the brass key hanging on the hook where they met.

"Og her går vi!"

Scott grinned from ear to ear. "Seven. Four. Zero. Nine. One. Five. Three. Four."

"Key 74. September 15, 1934."

53

They were leaning against the wall in their usual spot, outside the mess hall loading bay, a few months' worth of crushed cigarette butts littering the muddy wet gravel beneath their feet.

"There are things going on in this place that do not sit well with me, Henrik. I've seen some very, very disturbing evidence with my own eyes, but I...I need to know more. I need to know what you know."

Henrik looked at the ground for a few seconds. "Okay, Herr Major. Okay.

"The trucks and the vans, they, ah, they come in from time to time," said Henrik. "They drive to Building 8, and the, ah, the people are taken inside. When the trucks and vans leave the island, they are always empty. No one ever leaves. Do you understand what I'm telling you, Herr Major?"

"I think so. But what people, Henrik? Who is in the vans?"

Henrik looked up with sad eyes. He spoke under his breath, almost afraid to say the words. "Children, Gunner. The vans bring mostly children."

Günther was chilled, his worst fears confirmed.

"Tell me about Morbach. His arrangements."

Henrik spat into the mud. "It seems that somehow, a while back, he found out that my boy was connected to the Holger Danske. The, ah…the resistance. Of course I was very concerned, but Morbach is not stupid. He knew that someday he might need a connection, you know, when the war went the wrong way for Germany, and for him. So not so long ago, in exchange for a promise to get my son released from prison, he requested that I, ah, ask the resistance to contact the British on his behalf. To make a deal."

"A deal? With the British?" Günther exclaimed, eyes wide. "What kind of a deal?"

"Ja, a deal, Herr Major. The Engländers must think he's worth something. Or maybe that whatever he told them he knows is worth something. Or that he possesses something of value. I don't know. But it seems they're coming to collect him in a couple of weeks or so. To, ah, keep him safe from the Russians. To fly him from Denmark to England."

Günther stood in silence for a few moments, burning another cigarette down to its stub, his mind racing, eyes boring a hole in the ground. He turned to Henrik. "That son of bitch. That's just not going to happen, Henrik."

Henrik looked up at Günther, wide eyed, a little alarmed by his menacing tone. Sensing his friend's fear, Günther put a reassuring hand on his shoulder and smiled. "Don't you worry, my friend. I don't know much, but I do know this. You're a good man. And your secrets are safe with me. And I don't know exactly how just yet, but I can absolutely promise you this," Günther said. "Morbach is never leaving this place. But I'm going to need to know what you know, Henrik. I'm going to need your help."

54

"So what should we be looking for?" said Alison.

Scott looked at the contents of the filing cabinet drawer spread out across the floor and table in the bank's small meeting room. "I don't know, exactly. But my guess is we'll know it when we see it."

They'd been carefully sorting through the various folders and papers for more than twenty minutes when Mrs. Nygård found it. It was exactly as Scott had predicted it would be. Just like everything else, but not quite the same. She handed the brown file folder to Scott and he laid it down carefully on the meeting room table.

Inside the file folder, a fat sheaf of papers sandwiched a small leather-bound notebook. Despite seventy-plus years in the musty concrete basement of a Norwegian bank, everything looked as if it had all been deposited there just yesterday.

Alison leafed through the loose pages, carefully handing them to Scott as she assessed each one. "These appear to contain the same kind of handwritten notes and diagrams—in German—as the pages from the frozen notebook," she said. "But the different inks and writing styles in the individual documents seem to indicate that they were created by more than one person."

She opened the notebook gingerly. The handwriting and ink on its pages appeared to be consistent with those they'd seen on the page fragments that Professor Lundeen's team had been able to salvage. *The same author?* Alison thought she could decipher what appeared to be dates, but as she carefully turned the pages one by one, it became clear to her that the notes were not in chronological order.

"Yeah," said Scott. "This sure looks like more of the same stuff Professor Lundeen showed us. We need to get this copied, translated, and in front of some people who might know what they're looking at. Sorry…" He smiled sheepishly at Alison. "No offense."

"None taken," Alison replied. "And I agree. It looks like more lab journal stuff. Again, some kind of surgical or medical or pharmacological notes, if I had to hazard a guess."

She'd gotten about a third of the way through the rest of the loose documents when she found the unsealed blue envelope. Its contents absolutely horrified her. A thin, stubble-haired young girl no more than seven years old stood forlorn, passive, naked, and terribly vulnerable, her eyes averted from the camera. The clinical lighting clearly showed terrible scars on her calves, thighs, upper chest, and biceps, and tiny round marks that dotted her neck and chest.

Alison gasped and dropped the photograph in revulsion. "Oh, my god, Scott! Is this what I think it is?" He picked up the image, turned it over, and read the blue handwritten notation.

30. November 1944.

S. Morbach.

Subjekt T-268345.

2 g Phenol.

Vorbereitung für die Präparation.

"I'm afraid it looks that way."

55

On this day, everything had been different.

They'd taken her to a room she'd never seen before, given her a little more food than normal, dressed her in warm, oversize clothes, and even given her some boots. When they'd brought her back to her room they'd sat her down on the edge of her cot and spoken to her in their mystery voices, but of course she'd had no real idea what they were saying.

When they'd departed, she could tell from the absence of the familiar second metallic clunk that they'd not locked her door, only latched it.

And later, when she'd heard the terrible noises, felt the whole world shake, and seen her light bulb flicker and then go out, she'd not known what to do. So she'd done nothing. She'd simply wrapped her blanket around herself and, to keep out the darkness, closed her eyes as tightly as she could.

56

Their instructions were clear. Günther and the others were back in Building 8, and they'd been told in no uncertain terms that they were expected to complete all document packing and be fully prepared for relocation by the end of the day.

About an hour in, the short, balding man thrust his head into the room and motioned for Günther to step outside. He handed him a typewritten document.

"You are to transport the items indicated here to the personal staff car of Generalarzt Doktor Morbach, located immediately in front of this building. He will be departing momentarily, likely within the hour, once another important additional…item has been prepared for transportation. Clear?"

Suppressing a wry smile, Günther turned and walked back into the room without saying a word.

Günther had delivered the first box of brown files to the black Mercedes and was on his way back toward the main entrance doors with the second when he caught sight of them. In the long corridor that led to the main laboratory, Anselm watched like a hawk as two burly orderlies dragged a tiny figure toward one of the cells. It was clearly a child, dressed in baggy dark grey pajamas and heavy black boots, and it was almost totally limp and completely silent. Günther watched, stunned, not knowing what to do as they all disappeared through the metal door.

Children. The vans bring mostly children. And no one ever leaves.

Henrik's chilling words echoed in his mind. He'd read the notes about the insertion of fragments of wood and crushed glass into incisions in limbs. He'd seen diagrams referencing transfusion and transplantation. He'd seen documents calling for phenol injections—absolutely fatal when introduced to the bloodstream. He'd seen the horrifying photographs. And with his fountain pen, in his elegant hand, he'd written the word *verstorbene* twenty-seven times in his two notebooks.

He checked his watch.

It's time.

He walked as briskly as he could to the staff car, dropped the cardboard box into the back seat, then quickly made his way to his quarters in Building 2. He was on his way back to the laboratory, black briefcase in hand, when the shock wave knocked him flat.

Hearing nothing but a smothering, muffled roar, grit and dirt and dust filling his eyes and ears and mouth, Günther managed to get to his hands and knees. Coughing and spitting, fighting to clear the thick fog in his head, he tried to focus. As he raised his stinging, watery eyes, through a long, dark tunnel he caught a glimpse of three sleek single-engine British fighter-bombers flashing through the sun directly overhead, the red, white, and blue roundels on the undersides of their bomb-laden black-and-white-striped wings no more than twenty-five metres above the rooftops. Turning slowly, he saw that a massive explosion had almost totally destroyed the mess hall behind him. A split second later, another series of explosions toppled the water tower behind Building 8, but Günther felt more than heard that impact, the combination of dull roaring and high-pitched whining in his ears drowning out virtually all external sounds.

Struggling to his feet, he staggered toward Building 8.

Chaos had taken over.

A dull cacophony of sirens and alarm bells and panicked voices slowly filled his ears as the sounds inside his head began to subside.

Stunned and terrified orderlies, nurses, and uniformed personnel staggered and ran in every direction, some bleeding, some limping, almost all of them ghostlike, choking on the pale grey and red dust and grit that had enveloped them. A small green van spouting red and orange flames sent thick black smoke into the morning sky.

Two more explosions shook the ground, and Günther crouched down and instinctively held the black case over his head to try to protect himself from the smothering cloud of choking powder and the hail of dirt, rocks, bricks, and glass that rained down on him.

Both front doors to Building 8 had been blown wide open and what looked like a combination of smoke and dust billowed out. Adrenaline pumping, Günther took the stairs two at a time and burst through the inner doors. The long corridor, filled with an almost impenetrable white haze, was cluttered with debris, eerily illuminated only by the diffused daylight filtering through the shattered round windows in the laboratory doors at the far end.

With one outstretched hand waving at the dust in front of him, he charged almost blindly down the corridor and pushed hard on the swinging doors, plowing through the thick layer of debris and dust that covered the room's green linoleum floor. Inside the laboratory, the stainless steel tables were helter-skelter, knocked from their places either by panicked people running for their lives or by the force of the exploding British bombs or both. To his left, a spray of water from a broken main caught a ray of sunlight through the haze, its muted rainbow totally out of place in the destruction. *Beautiful,* he thought as he paused in stunned amazement, *like something from a dream.* He stumbled forward through the mud and shattered bricks and splintered wood, broken glass crunching under his boots.

The wall between the laboratory and the room where he, the young nurse, and the bored SS guard had spent the last two days was completely gone, a mess of bricks and plaster and crushed filing cabinets and scattered papers in its place. There was no sign of his coworker or the guard, but he could see blue sky and smoke and hear the sounds of panic and alarm bells coming in through the gaping hole in the building's side wall.

As he turned, he heard a voice, muffled and faint.

"Help me…"

"Hello?" Günther yelled. "Hello? Who is it? Where are you?"

He clambered over the rubble toward the anguished, guttural groans that emanated from behind one of the overturned stainless steel tables, near what used to be the laboratory's side wall.

Morbach was lying face up, buried to his sternum in splintered wood, shattered white ceramic tiles, and crumbled bricks. His left arm was twisted grotesquely, obviously broken above the elbow, and its hand and forearm were pinned awkwardly beneath his torso.

Because the thumb on his right hand had been completely torn away, with his index and middle fingers he pulled desperately but unsuccessfully at one of the long shards of glass that protruded from his blood-and-dirt-encrusted right cheek. A few metres away, Günther could see the short, balding man's upper body lying facedown in a dark pool of blood, a shattered gramophone and a jumble of broken records near his crushed skull, a jarring look of almost delighted surprise on his completely untouched face. His pelvis and legs were nowhere to be seen.

Morbach blinked rapidly as he tried desperately to get the dirt and splinters out of his watering eyes. Sensing Günther's presence, he screamed out in agony. "Who's there? Who is it? Help me!"

Günther stood over the doctor, completely silent as Morbach finally managed to focus one eye on him.

"Graf! Graf! Help me! Please, help me!"

Günther looked down at Morbach, but didn't see him. He saw Gisele. He saw Karin. He saw the shiny black-and-white images of the emaciated, scarred little girl, and the gaping mouth of a dead boy strapped to a metal table. He saw the old men and the women and children, screaming as they ran from his bombs.

The doctor's escalating screams and moans and demands faded, until Günther heard nothing but the sound of his own breathing and the low whoosh of his own blood pumping furiously through his veins. He dropped his leather case—he'd forgotten he was even carrying it—and crouched down, eliciting a high-pitched scream as his knee crushed Morbach's lacerated free hand into the jagged debris on the floor. As he lowered his face close to the red pulp of Morbach's mashed and partly severed ear, Günther put his right hand firmly over the doctor's mouth, forcing the needle-sharp slivers of glass deeper into the man's puffy flesh.

Günther felt his eyes watering, his throat constricting, his heart pounding. But he heard himself speak in a calm, clear voice.

"I know only a little of what you've done here. But I know about the pain and suffering you've inflicted, about the horrible deaths for which you are responsible. And I know about your deal with the British. Your plan to exchange your terrible knowledge for your pathetic life. Well, that's not going to happen. You are not a hero. You are nothing. Just a stain that needs to be removed."

Günther let his words sink in, staring into Morbach's widening eyes as the terrified doctor grunted and jerked his head frantically from side to side—a futile attempt to dislodge the firm hand covering his bloodied mouth and driving the excruciating splinters of wood of glass deep into his flesh.

"You will never see England. In fact, I'm the last thing you will ever see."

As he spoke, Günther calmly placed his left hand over Morbach's nose and squeezed his nostrils hard shut. For thirty-seven long seconds, the doctor bucked and heaved violently, desperately, his terrified, dirt-filled eyes bulging as Günther stared into them, his muffled screams escalating with his unbearable panic.

Then, except for the soft hissing of the water spraying from the broken main, the alarm bells, and the sounds of distant confusion, silence.

57

To steady himself as he picked his way back through the corridor, Günther ran a shaking, bloodied hand along the wall. About halfway back to the building's main entrance, he noticed it through the haze: the metal door to the cell into which he'd seen Anselm and the two orderlies dragging the child was closed and latched, but its lock had been left open.

T-268346

The chalked number was the same as the one marked on the two boxes Morbach had wanted placed in his personal car. Günther slid the bolt from its latch.

It took a few moments for his vision to adjust to the gloom, but there, sitting calmly on the edge of a filthy mattress on a rusted white metal cot, was a small child. He couldn't tell if it was a boy or a girl, but it sat completely still in the beam of dim light coming from the dust-filled corridor, a dirty blanket over its shoulders, feet on the floor, eyes closed, hands in its lap, as if it was simply waiting for someone to come and take it somewhere.

"Are you...okay?" Günther said, as he took a half step forward, almost gagging on the cell's rancid stench. He stopped in his tracks as the child opened its eyes and instantly recoiled in fear, scooting as far back into the darkness as it could possibly get. Günther suddenly realized how he must look, menacing and huge, a frightening, filthy, ghostlike silhouette, backlit by the dusty chaos outside the doorway. *This child is absolutely terrified of me.* He knelt down—as he'd done so many times when he'd wanted to soothe his darling little Gisele— and reached out a bloody hand. And despite his anxiety and fear, his racing pulse, and his shortness of breath, he managed to make his voice quiet and soft.

"Hey. It's okay now. It's okay. My name is Günther. I'm Günther. Do you want to leave this place? Do you want to come with me?"

Dark, glassy eyes stared at him from the deep shadows against the back wall of the cell, their owner frozen in terror, completely motionless. But when another muffled explosion rocked the building, to Günther's immense surprise, the child suddenly moved to the edge of the bed, swung its feet to the floor, and shuffled toward him. He wrapped the filthy blanket around its shoulders and scooped it up.

Trying hard not to stumble and fall on the debris in the corridor, Günther moved as quickly as he could toward the building's front door. Morbach's staff car was still outside, its windshield shattered, a few crumbled pieces of brick resting on its now dented and dust-covered hood and roof. He quickly opened the back passenger-side door, placed the blanket-wrapped child on the floor, and tossed his black briefcase onto the back seat beside the two cardboard boxes. Then he slammed the door hard and turned to make his way around the back of the car toward the driver's side.

Anselm was standing beside the driver's door.

His dark grey uniform covered in whitish grey dust, his face and hair and hands caked in the same powder, his ghostly pallor sharply contrasted the rivulet of dark red blood that ran from his forehead down over his thin nose and onto his tunic.

"Going somewhere, Herr Major? Where is Generalarzt Doktor Morbach?" he rasped. He was clearly trying to sound commanding, to project authority, but to Günther, Anselm sounded hollow and shaky, like someone who'd never really experienced fear before.

With his left hand, the adjutant drew a short-barreled pistol from his holster, and Günther fixed his focus on Anselm's rapidly blinking and darting eyes as he began to move gradually toward him. *War is much less enjoyable when others inflict it on you, huh? You piece of shit.* As he continued to inch forward, Günther cocked his head back over his shoulder, toward Building 8. *Take control.* "Morbach is still in there. Inside. And he won't be coming out. Ever. Whatever was happening here is over. It ends today."

"What are you talking about, Graf? Nothing will be over until the Führer declares our final victory and ensures the eternal greatness of Germany!" Anselm snarled, his tremulous voice belying his attempt to hide the shock and uncertainty consuming him.

Günther continued to move slowly toward the adjutant. *Keep him off balance.* "Victory? Greatness? What do you know of either?"

Anselm blinked nervously and shuffled backward, pistol waving carelessly as he stumbled on the shattered bricks beneath his boots.

"Nothing about this place has anything whatsoever to do with greatness," said Günther as he inched forward. He felt no fear. Instead he felt something he thought he might have remembered from long ago. From another life.

He felt true. And right. And sure.

He felt the good in himself.

"Not much of what I've done in the last few years has been for good," said Günther. "But what I'm doing today is. I'm taking this child away from here. This one child. It may mean less than nothing to you, but to me, right here and right now, it's everything."

Anselm cocked the pistol, struggling to sound composed as his voice quickened and rose slightly in pitch. "The affairs of this institute are none of your concern. And this child is none of your concern. You will be…you will be tried and executed…for gross insubordination. And…and…as a traitor to the Reich."

Günther looked calmly into Anselm's twitchy eyes and spoke quietly, slowly. "No. I won't. Because there is no Reich. And you will never stop me."

As Günther's left hand touched the driver's door handle, Anselm raised the pistol and took a tentative half step forward. Günther swung the door open as hard as he could, catching the adjutant in the shoulder and knocking him off balance. A shot cracked out, shattering the left rear passenger window of the car as Günther's left foot swung around, kicking Anselm hard on the outside of his right knee, collapsing the adjutant's leg. Anselm instinctively dropped his right hand to the muddy gravel to try to break his fall, then quickly tried to bring the pistol in his left hand to bear on Günther. Too late. Günther's left knee caught the adjutant in the solar plexus, doubling him over, and as the pistol came up weakly, Günther grabbed the stubby barrel and twisted it hard.

The single bullet went up through the soft flesh at the center of Anselm's lower jaw, exiting just below his right ear.

Günther ripped the pistol away and tossed it into the rubble. Breathing hard, he looked down at the dying man, feeling virtually nothing as he watched his miserable life literally flow out onto the ground. Anselm's eyes were round with fear and panic as he writhed in the dirt and debris, emitting terrified keening and gurgling animal noises, his hands clutching desperately in a futile attempt to stop the deep red flood pulsing from the ragged hole where his tongue, teeth, upper jaw, cheekbone, and ear had been.

Without a second thought, Günther stepped over the adjutant's quivering form and climbed into the driver's seat. He reached back to make sure that the child was okay, then jammed the vehicle into gear and gunned it over and through the rubble and debris, blasting the car's horn continuously to scatter the panicked people who got in his way.

He didn't look back.

No one paid the slightest bit of attention as Günther drove with both right wheels partway down the gravel embankment in order to avoid the large crater that had replaced the guard gate. And he didn't bother to slow down to help the dazed young Wehrmacht guard who was staggering haphazardly along the rubble-strewn causeway away from the island, carrying part of his severed left arm in his bloody right hand.

When the causeway met the mainland waterfront road, Günther turned right—to the west—and pressed down hard on the accelerator, spinning the car's back wheels in the wet gravel until they eventually found the pavement.

58

At first, the strange feeling of motion in her stomach had frightened her. But when the shouting and banging and terrifying swerving had subsided and been replaced by the steady droning of the car's wheels on the paved road and the whistle-roar sound of the wind through its shattered window, she worked up the courage to get to her knees.

With the blanket still hooded over her head, she peered out of the window in absolute amazement.

A brilliant blue sky, marked periodically with plumes of black and grey and white smoke, stretched above a rapidly changing sunlit landscape of sparkling water, tangled wire fences, piles of red brick rubble, broken concrete, rusted metal, splintered timbers, and burned-out trucks and cars that quickly gave way to forests of skeletal trees and lifeless fields of brown-grey, muddy ruts.

As the car gained speed, she closed her eyes and breathed, slowly, deeply. She marvelled at the smells—leather and carpeting and cigarette smoke and the faintest hint of exhaust—and at the wind rushing through the shattered window to envelop her in the rich earthiness of the dirt and trees and clouds and smoke, all of it somehow deeply familiar but also completely new, completely exhilarating.

Eventually, the steady hum of the car's engine and the droning rumble of its tires on the road lulled her, and she curled up on the floor, warm and safe beneath her blanket, and closed her exhausted eyes in spite of herself.

When she awoke, jolted airborne as the car had rolled up and over something immovable in the road, she resolved to stay huddled in the warm pitch-blackness beneath her blanket as the vehicle continued to bump and roar along. Not long after, it abruptly slowed and turned sharply, first tossing her sideways against the door and then pressing her firmly against the back of the front seat as its wheels eventually crunched to a stop and the engine cut off. In the suddenly deafening silence, she felt the vehicle rock gently, heard one of its doors thunk solidly closed. When she sensed the door above her being opened and heard urgent voices speak in a language she couldn't understand, her fear returned instantly, so she made herself small and burrowed farther down into the safety of her woolen nest, one eye peeking out surreptitiously through a fold.

In the gloom she could barely make the man out, but his smiling, ruddy face, with its shock of light grey hair and wild bushy eyebrows, calmed her. He reached out a stubby-fingered hand and spoke words that she couldn't understand, but in a soft, kind tone that she could.

"Moin, mein Schatz, ich bin Henrik. Wir werden dich jetzt an einen warmen Platz bringen."

59

They'd been in the barn for more than two weeks, and she'd felt herself gaining strength daily, thanks in large part to the kind-faced woman who'd fed her an almost continuous stream of smørrebrød, potato soup, goat cheese, salt cod, and eggs.

She'd stood, silent and still, as the woman had bathed her with wonderfully soothing warm water, gently dressed her incisions, and helped her into soft, warm, sweet-smelling clothes. She hadn't understood why they'd all gathered around her as the woman had rolled up her sleeve and showed the men the blue markings on her arm. She'd only understood that no one was hurting her in that place.

The man in the grey uniform had been incredibly kind to her, continuously bringing her food and milk and water and making sure she was tucked into her blankets and covered with a thick layer of hay to help keep her warm. When she went to sleep he was there. When she awoke, sometimes crying out and shaking and terrified in the dense blackness, he was there. He held her hand gently and smiled down at her whenever they walked in the barnyard. And he kneeled down and talked to her. A lot. And while she had absolutely no idea what he was saying, his voice was always soft. Always gentle.

It made her feel warm.

Safe.

It made her feel good.

She thought she might have once known a man like that. Or had dreamed him. Kind and caring and warm and smiling. He'd sat on the bed and told exciting tales of elves and trolls and princesses and knights and dragons, and she and her sister—her sweet, wonderful twin sister—had wished the stories would never end.

But of course they had.

The beautiful woman had cried for a long, long time after she'd learned that the dark grey men had taken the kind man away. And it hadn't been long before the dark grey men had come for them all.

The uniformed man studied the books and papers from the boxes and his black case every day, and today she'd watched him place one of the books and some of the papers into a small, green, metal box. Some new men had come into the barn, and spoken in hushed, urgent voices, and she'd watched quietly and warily and with a growing sense of foreboding as they'd put all of the boxes and some more blankets into a black truck.

Later, as the truck had lurched and bumped wildly over a rutted road, the uniformed man had quietly spoken his unintelligible but soothing words, and cradled her safely in his arms. But as the vehicle had made its way through a thicket of pine scrub and rolled out onto the edge of a field, a terrifyingly deep roaring sound had filled her ears, and heavy vibrations had resonated through her body. Keeping her bundled tightly in her blankets, the uniformed man had picked her up, jumped down from the truck, and run with her, and she'd cautiously looked out through the folds to try to get a glimpse of the source of the deafening terror.

A fearsome, dark shape had loomed ahead, silhouetted against the afternoon sky. The thing had at first looked like a winged monster, like some enormous dragon from a long-ago story, but she'd sensed its heavy mechanical pulse deep inside her lungs and heart and ears, and she'd known instinctively that it was a machine. As they'd drawn ever nearer to its earsplitting roar, despite her fear she'd been awestruck by its raw energy, and had tried unsuccessfully to make sense of the strange arrangement of concentric red, white, blue, and yellow circles, and dull grey markings on its side—E O N.

But she'd not been afraid.

She'd come to understand that there was something so much more powerful than fear in the feeling of the uniformed man's arms wrapped tightly around her. She'd not understood how or why, but despite the threatening intensity of the breathtaking power that the terrifying machine projected into every part of her being, she knew she was safe.

She hoped he'd never let her go.

60

Jack's adrenaline was pumping wildly.

In the waning afternoon light, a beaten-up old black truck had emerged from the treeline and rolled up fast, lurching to an abrupt stop on the grass about thirty yards in front of the roaring Mosquito.

A young man dressed head to toe in black jumped out of the truck's passenger-side door, a German MP-40 submachine gun in one of his hands. In his other hand, he gripped the handles of a dirty black leather briefcase and what looked to Jack to be a small, flat, metal toolbox. Vickson immediately ran up to the man and took the leather case and toolbox from him, as a white-haired man climbed down from the truck's driver's seat and walked quickly to its back end. The old man dropped the tailgate, and, in spite of what Jack had been told at the final pre-op briefing, he couldn't help but be moderately alarmed when he saw a man in a dark grey Luftwaffe uniform emerge from the truck bed.

Jack watched in amazement as the Luftwaffe officer hugged the white-haired man and shook his hand, then picked up a dark bundle and cradled it carefully in both arms—the "package," Jack assumed, that they were risking their necks to retrieve—as Vickson moved to guide him toward the rear of the aircraft.

Leaning into the prop wash, the two of them disappeared from Jack's field of view as they ducked below the starboard wing. Just a few seconds later, the German—now wearing Vickson's sheepskin flight jacket and parachute harness over his grey uniform—worked his way up into the Mosquito's cockpit through its entrance hatch. He looked Jack right in the eyes and nodded curtly before taking Vickson's spot in the navigator's seat, then reached down to carefully accept the wool-wrapped bundle being boosted up through the open hatchway.

Head on a continuous swivel, Jack's eyes nervously scanned the field and the treeline as Vickson tossed two small cardboard boxes, the black briefcase, and the metal toolbox onto the cockpit floor at the German's feet. Then Vickson stuck his head and torso through the entrance hatch, reached up, and squeezed Jack's hand. Grinning like an idiot Cheshire cat, he cupped his left hand to his face, and yelled at the top of his lungs to try to be heard over the roar of the engines. Jack could barely make it out, but he knew the words weren't English.

"Bis später Kumpel, viel Glück!"

And with that, Vickson snapped a sloppy salute and ducked out of sight, and as the hatch slammed shut, Jack's hyperactive brain entertained two simultaneous thoughts: *Well, whaddya know? That crazy bastard speaks German.* And *Let's get the fuck out of here!* Following one extremely quick scan of his gauges, Jack eased both throttles forward until his engines were almost screaming and released his brakes. The Mosquito immediately began a bumpy roll, picking up speed rapidly as its tail came up, and Jack worked the throttles and rudder pedals to keep her on a line toward the thicket of trees that he knew marked the far end of his available runway space.

At 120 miles per hour—barely fast enough, Jack knew, for the Mosquito's broad plywood wings to take advantage of Bernoulli's invisible magic—he pulled the stick back and almost simultaneously retracted the aircraft's undercarriage. As the power of the two Merlins dragged the airplane forward and up, over the trees and into the Danish sky, Jack sucked in a few deep breaths, tapped his lucky maple leaf again, and relished the beautifully reassuring sensation of rock-solid lift he loved to feel deep in the pit of his stomach.

He'd been so intensely focused on getting them off the ground and on their way home—and especially on not getting himself killed or captured—that the Mosquito had reached an altitude of fifteen hundred feet and an airspeed of more than two hundred knots before Jack glanced over to his right.

The German looked straight at him and nodded again. That was strange enough. But stranger still, from the depths of the blanket bundle cradled in the German's arms, the dark eyes of a child glared back into Jack's stunned stare.

61

They were over water.

Their egress route had been carefully planned to get them away from southern Denmark as quickly as possible. Fourteen minutes after takeoff, they were almost over Sylt, headed west-northwest, with some four hundred and forty miles of North Sea between them and Scotland, according to Vickson's detailed navigation instructions.

That crazy, crazy sonofabitch! Jack thought. He just couldn't stop thinking about Vickson, and about the insane choice he'd made. Jack had admittedly made some pretty questionable decisions in his own short life—*landing a perfectly good airplane in occupied goddamn Denmark is now one of them*—but he knew it took a special kind of crazy to do what Vickson had just done.

At the second mission briefing, to Jack's stunned amazement, the Ungentlemanly types had revealed that once the "package" had been acquired, Vickson would be staying behind in Denmark. The brass, they said, figured the war was winding down, and with the Russians charging hard from the east they knew the race would be on. Vickson would stay and work with the resistance in advance of an operation that had been created after Swedish intelligence had reported that Stalin planned to violate the territorial terms he'd only just agreed to at the February conference in Yalta. To give the Russian navy greater access to the Atlantic, Stalin wanted Denmark, and, the Ungentlemanly types stressed vehemently, the western allies sure as hell didn't want that.

But there was another objective for the operation.

Apparently a whole lot of SOE and OSS types like Vickson would be working hard to secure Nazi "science and research assets" before the Soviets could get to them. Jack had just never clued in that an asset might actually be a human being.

Over the course of about fifteen minutes, Jack figured he must have glanced over at his two passengers more than twenty times in disbelief.

So who the hell is this guy?

And more to the point, who the hell is this kid?

62

"So I guess this is it?" Alison said. "I guess we've done about all we can do?"

They'd thanked Mrs. Nygård, Mrs. Karlsen, and Mr. Arnesen for all of their help, and they'd promised to stay in touch regarding any future findings or developments. They'd made digital and physical copies of every paper and photograph and page of the notes they'd found in the filing cabinet, and Mr. Arnesen had arranged to have the originals FedEx'd directly to Alison's attorneys back in Seattle. And they'd contacted the university to inform Professor Lundeen and Dr. Sorensen of their latest discovery, and to thank them and their students for all they'd done. And finally, Scott had made arrangements for the most recently found human remains to be released to German custody. Mrs. Nygård's photograph had proved definitively that they didn't belong to Jack Barton, and Dr. Sorensen's tests had confirmed that they didn't belong to Robert Vickson.

But now, in spite of everything they'd accomplished, in spite of everything they'd been able to discover, Alison couldn't shake a feeling of immense sadness as she drove them toward Oslo.

She'd be heading back to Seattle the following day, and Scott would be returning to Ottawa, but too many unanswered questions still gnawed at her. They still had no real idea what had happened to her grandfather or his navigator. Squadron Leader Jack Barton had made it to Rosendal, Norway, that was for sure, but without Robert Vickson? And with what appeared to be a dead German man and a live little girl in tow instead? What had happened to her grandfather after that? What happened to Vickson? What was the story behind the notebooks and documents? Who was the German? And, of course, who was the girl and what had happened to her?

Alison drove on in somber silence, caught up in her own swirling thoughts. From time to time, she glanced over at Scott, who seemed equally lost in his own head, his gaze seemingly fixed somewhere on the distant horizon.

There were just so many other questions she wanted to ask, and she wished the road to Oslo would just go on forever.

63

Goddammit! He'd let down his guard for only a few seconds, a rookie mistake.

The fighter must have come up from below his starboard wing, but Jack had no idea it was there until he heard the bang and saw white tracers flashing past his canopy.

His instincts had taken over. Kicking the rudder hard to port, then hard to starboard, he'd pushed the throttles to the stops to coax as much speed out the plane as he could, simultaneously pushing the stick forward and to the left to put them into a banking power dive. All the while, he'd rubbernecked wildly, desperately trying to see where the enemy aircraft might be, but in seconds they were in clouds and he'd seen nothing. He'd continued to jink the Mosquito around violently for another fifteen seconds, pushing it to its limit to try to put some distance between them and whoever or whatever had been trying to do them harm. When the Mosquito dropped below the wispy grey-white ceiling, he pulled back on the stick hard and let the Merlins do their thing, finally leveling out as they reached the upper edge of the cloudbank at about eight thousand feet—as high as he dared go without oxygen for his extra passenger—reasonably sure he'd escaped the worst.

He was wrong.

He felt it before he knew it, but that was how it always went.

The Mosquito had begun to shudder ever so slightly. Within a few seconds, Jack could see he was starting to lose oil pressure in his starboard engine, and he watched the gauges closely for indications that the Merlin might be starting to heat up. *Goddammit!*

He immediately ran down the options in his head. *North Sea? Give or take four hundred miles to cover. If I need to shut one engine down, I can make maybe 165, 170 knots. That's 190, 195 miles per hour. About two hours minimum flight time, not accounting for any headwinds or course corrections. And the North Sea is both goddamn cold and goddamn deep. What's Plan B?*

The Ministry of Ungentlemanly Conduct had been crystal clear. The brass had decided that the package and its escort were important enough to risk an SOE agent, a highly trained combat pilot, and a Mosquito for. Vickson had done his part. He'd gotten the package and its handler into the airplane. Now Jack had to do his part.

Plan B presented two options. He could risk trying to make it to an airfield in Allied-controlled western France, which would mean flying close to the heavily defended German territory in the northern Netherlands, or he could divert to a place he was pretty familiar with.

The Norwegian coast was less than two hundred miles from his present location, and though Norway, too, was still occupied, they'd been told that the bad guys were a little more sparsely dotted around that country than in other places, and Jack and his Coastal Command Strike Wing mates had been briefed many times on potential landing spots and escape routes should they be forced down there.

He scanned the control panel instruments again. The starboard engine temperature was beginning to move toward the red, and to compound things, he seemed to be losing juice from the wing tank on that side a little more rapidly than he should be. The indicators made the decision for him. He immediately shut down the starboard engine, closed off its fuel supply, and feathered its prop. Throttling back slightly to conserve fuel and combat the effects of torque created by his single good engine, but being careful to maintain enough airspeed that the aircraft would continue to respond to its controls, he periodically adjusted the aircraft's trims to reduce its new tendency to yaw to starboard, and banked a little to steer them onto what he reckoned was a direct heading for the southern Norwegian coastline, all the while keeping a watch for any more black-crossed vultures.

Only when they'd entered another cloud bank did he think to glance over at the German. And the package.

From inside the bundle of blankets, now crumpled down among the instruments and the jumble of boxes in the shadows of the footwell below the German's feet, the child stared up at him, wide-eyed. Jack thought he could see a little vomit on the blanket, no doubt a result of the violent evasive action he'd been forced to take. He reached a hand down, but the tiny figure pulled back from him and burrowed deeper into its woolen armour.

The German was slumped forward against the navigator's seat harness, his head bent down toward his chest. Jack reached over to give him a shake, and the man slowly turned to face him. He was bleeding from a cut above his right eyebrow, and he seemed a little dazed.

Jack pointed to the earpiece of his own flying helmet, then to the German's head. He pulled his own oxygen mask up to his face—he'd neglected to clip it on in all the excitement—then pointed to the German's face. A look of understanding flashed in the man's eyes, and he nodded and began to slowly root around the cockpit. A few seconds later, he'd managed to locate and pull on Vickson's flying helmet and oxygen mask.

Jack clicked the intercom button. "You speak English? English?"

The German squinted hard and shook his head a little, obviously trying to clear some cobwebs, then turned to look at Jack.

"Englisch? Ah, Englisch? Ja...ja ein bisschen. A little."

A little? thought Jack as he glanced back at his instruments. *Well, lord thunderin' Jesus, man. I got a whole lot of questions for you.*

Jack clicked the intercom button. "What's your name?"

The groggy German looked at him quizzically. "Was?"

"Your name? Name? What's your name?"

"Ah, name? Graf. Major Günther Graf."

"I'm Jack Barton."

The German struggled to reach down and pick up the blanket-bundle off the cockpit floor. He cradled the almost invisible child in his arms as if it were a newborn.

"Sorry about the excitement back there. I think one of your buddies thought he'd gotten lucky."

The German gave Jack another confused look.

Maybe your buddy did get lucky. Jack pointed to his instrument panel, and to the feathered starboard engine right outside the canopy. "We've lost our starboard engine, so the plan's changed. If we're gonna make it, we've got to get to Norway." Jack stabbed a finger dead ahead. "Norway!"

"Norwegen?" Günther replied, his eyes widening a little before closing again.

Yeah, got to admit I'm a little concerned about that myself.

They flew without speaking for about nine minutes, Jack constantly checking his compass, watch, and gauges to try to determine direction, estimated landfall time, and whether or not the Mosquito would actually stay in the air long enough to get them there. He knew the kite would want to veer to starboard under power solely from its port engine, and he'd lost enough fuel that it was definitely becoming a concern should they be off course to any significant degree. *Shit. Not a whole lot of room for error here.*

The German kept the child carefully under wraps, and from time to time he pulled back the blankets to make sure it was okay. Jack had no idea why it was on board, or even whether it was a boy or girl.

"Your kid?" Jack asked. "Uh, your kinder?"

"Mein Kind? Das könntest du sagen," came the slow reply. "Ah, nein. Nein. Aber sie sollte nicht sterben. Sie ist einzigartig." Günther struggled to find the words. "No. Not mine."

Jack glanced at the child and thought of the letter he'd received from Marie back in November. They'd shipped him over to Halifax for a stretch, back last summer, ostensibly to be the Local Boy Makes Good in their efforts to flog more war bonds, but he knew different. In reality, he knew they needed him to recover from what the boys called "the goddamn heebie jeebies" but what the docs had called "combat stress." He'd noticed he'd developed a few unwanted tics— and what had started to become a dangerous inability to sleep—on the heels of one particularly rough stretch. They'd flown a whole lot of ops in support of the big day in early June, tasked with keeping German naval threats from the Bay of Biscay and south of France away from the invasion. The days and weeks had dragged on, and Jack's mission count had piled up until its weight had become almost unbearable for him. By early July, he'd simply flown too many sorties in too short a time, and he'd lost two crews in a week. When he and Cousineau had both had to be hospitalized after he'd brought their shredded Beaufighter in for a hard no-wheels landing, the doc had figured it was time for a break.

It had just been so goddamned good to see Marie, and at the same time so goddamned hard to hide himself from her. In the end, he simply hadn't been able to, and that had turned out to be what he'd needed most of all.

Of course, as much as hello had been wonderful, goodbye had been absolute agony for both of them, with the long, boring, and dangerous boat ride back to England doing nothing but exacerbating his sense of separation.

In his absence, the squadron had been relocated again, this time from Cornwall to Banff, in the cold, wet wilds of the northern Scottish coast. But Jack had quickly settled in. After all, he'd figured, they'd been moved around so much he should be used to it, and he especially figured a guy from "New Scotland" should be able to do just fine in old Scotland. And he'd literally jumped for joy—and bought a whole lot of rounds—when he'd read Marie's powerful and somewhat daunting words: "You may know how to fly an aeroplane, but now you're going to have to learn something really difficult. You're going to have to learn how to change a diaper!"

Ever since that revelation, in his quiet moments he'd thought about his impending fatherhood almost constantly, but given the distance between him and Marie and the stress of his daily existence, the concept still felt totally surreal to him.

All he knew, as he stared at his tiny passenger, was that he sure as hell couldn't imagine his own child wrapped up in a dirty, vomit-encrusted blanket, riding a crippled airplane toward an uncertain fate in an occupied country, in the care of two strangers who'd normally be trying to kill each other.

Jack glanced over and reached back with his gloved right hand, and the German nodded and shook it firmly. *Well shit, that's certainly a first.* When he brought his hand back to the control stick, he noticed something he didn't like.

His glove was smeared with blood.

o o o

Something was up.

Jack had checked and double-checked, but by his reckoning he figured they should've crossed the Norwegian coast at least six or seven minutes ago. Breaks in the overcast told him different. *Still over water. That's not good.*

The only logical answers were that he'd been correcting a little too much to port to compensate for the single engine, or that the wind was pushing them to the west, or maybe both. That would have put them out over the North Sea.

He needed to make a decision. Now.

Banking the plane gently to the right, he dropped the nose, shedding altitude to try to get below the sporadic cloud cover. The sky grew darker as the Mosquito descended, what was left of the daylight diminished by the clouds and the reduction in altitude. At about five thousand feet, they dropped through the ceiling.

To his left, nothing but black-grey ocean.

To his right, the dappled dark green and black of land.

A little of the weight lifted from his back. *Okay, that's a damn good start. Now where the hell are we?* He knew they had to get down soon. The kite was a little rough, still stable and still moving forward, but his fuel situation was on the verge of becoming a fuel problem. He throttled back a little further to make the most of whatever was left.

Jack and his squadron mates had visited the west coast of Norway many times over the previous seven months, so he was counting on spotting something he recognized down there. Up ahead and slightly to his right, an expansive fjord dotted with islands punctured the almost solid coastline.

Two and a half minutes later, they passed over a distinctive point of land at the southern entrance to the broad inlet. Jack felt a massive wave of relief as the darkened wharves and docks of a town nestled on the eastern side of the peninsula appeared in a break in the clouds. *Stavanger! We've shot this place up a few times before.* By sheer luck he'd somehow skirted the heavy antiaircraft batteries that he knew dotted the coastline south of the town, and he hoped like hell the Luftwaffe boys down at Sola had already settled in for the evening with a bottle or three of schnapps.

He glanced to his right. The German was slumped forward, head resting on the bundled child cradled in his lap, and his eyes appeared to be closed. Jack couldn't see the child at all.

Okay, let's get the hell away from here. Got to get down. Think.

They'd made a few runs near Bergen in recent months. Estimating the port town to be about sixty miles ahead, he racked his brain as best he could. *Come on. Come on!* They'd been briefed constantly on potential emergency landing sites and escape procedures for their trips to Norway, but he'd never in a million years thought any of that would ever mean anything to him. That stuff was for unlucky guys. *Well, you dumb bastard, it means something to you now. Think!*

And then he saw it. Ahead, slightly to the east, through scattered clouds, a blue-white expanse stood out, eerily luminescent above the dark terrain on which it sat. They'd been told about it once or twice— a likely unoccupied, reasonably flat spot in an otherwise hostile and pretty lumpy country. And he and Cousineau had flown over it once before, on a brilliant October morning, as he'd brought them around to make a run on a flotilla of merchant ships and escort vessels hiding in the Bjørnafjorden. He made the instant decision. *We're going there.*

Jack reached over and shook Günther's arm, hard. "Hey! Hey, buddy! You okay?"

The German looked up slowly, eyes obviously heavy. He wasn't okay, wasn't all there.

"We're going to have to set down rough. I can't risk landing at any airfield around here. Your friends sure as hell won't like that and it probably wouldn't be good for any of us." Jack pointed ahead at the blue-white mass, barely visible through a small cloud break. The darkening sky was going to make the next few minutes even more interesting.

The German nodded weakly, eyes closed. As his head flopped back against the green seat back, the blankets he held in his arms parted. An expressionless face stared at Jack, two wide open, intensely dark eyes locked on his.

Jack didn't know who this kid was or why a whole bunch of people had risked their lives for it. He sure as hell didn't know why one of those people was a Luftwaffe officer. So he did the only thing he could think to do.

He winked.

64

Violent turbulence tossed the Mosquito like a leaf as it cleared the bottom of the cloud bank, the luminous blue-white glacier just visible in the deepening gloom less than a thousand feet below. Glancing at his gauges, Jack knew he'd only get one chance at this. He shook the German again, trying to get him to understand what was about to happen.

"I've got to put her down! Down!" he yelled, pointing his finger at the floor of the cockpit. "Wheels up!"

Günther looked over at him, his eyelids droopy above his oxygen mask, voice hoarse and low. "Okay. Nicht mein erstes mal... Uh... Not first time. For me."

Jack nodded. He worked the controls to bank the Mosquito as gently as he could to port. He hoped to circle at least once before they lost the last of the remaining light, to try to get a better sense of the surface of the ice before he committed them.

As the plane began its lean, the German suddenly came alive. He gingerly placed the blanket-wrapped child among the boxes on the cockpit floor, then reached up to his chest to unclasp his seat harness. Awkwardly working his way to his feet in the incredibly cramped space, he strained as he wrestled the bundled child carefully into the navigator's seat, rewrapping the blankets as best he could before securing the harness. The child's boots barely extended past the seat front, and its eyes never left the German's face as he brought a shaky hand up to gently touch its cheek.

Although his attention was focused intensely on guiding the plane safely to the ice, Jack couldn't believe what he was seeing, and as the German hunched over and faced the back of the cockpit to strap the child in, his right side came into Jack's view. In the gloom, Jack almost missed it, but just below the bottom of Vickson's sheepskin jacket, the German's bloused grey trouser leg was moist and almost black. "What the hell are you doing?" he yelled. "You're hurt! Looks like you're hurt!" He pointed to the dark stain.

Günther put his hand on Jack's arm and shook his head. "Nein. Nein. Sie muss sicher sein!" he yelled, then crouched and folded himself gingerly, awkwardly, among the sharp-edged equipment and boxes crowding the tiny footwell, his back jammed against the Mosquito's drift sight, fuselage, and forward bulkhead.

Jesus thundering Christ.

The luminescent plateau was coming up fast.

Jack had picked his spot, and this was it.

o o o

"Okay, guys, here we go."

At 110 knots, Jack lowered his flaps, cut the port engine's fuel supply and shut off its mag switches, feathered its propeller, and put the airplane down.

The momentary roaring whistle of the Mosquito's last airborne seconds was suddenly shattered by a thundering scraping and grinding noise as a blizzard of ice and snow thrown up by the aircraft's impact billowed around the cockpit canopy and obscured everything outside the Perspex greenhouse.

The plane slid smoothly for a few seconds, then began to tip up on its nose, its tail lifting skyward, before violently spinning almost three hundred and sixty degrees to its left as its port engine nacelle and wing smashed through a hump of ice and snow. Seconds later, after sliding for another seventy-five yards or so, the plane came to rest on its belly, essentially facing in its original landing direction, and mostly in one piece.

The last few clumps of snow and ice rolled to a stop, and the rolling cloud that had followed the Mosquito finally caught up to it and drifted softly down, dusting its grey and green camouflaged upper surfaces with a thin white film as the last glimmer of daylight in the winter sky faded to purple-black.

And then, dead silence.

o o o

Jack had no idea where he was.

All he knew was that his head was pounding like hell, that he was freezing, and that he couldn't see his hand in front of his face.

Reality came back to him slowly. The glacier, the belly landing. *Okay. Okay. I'm still in the kite. And I must be alive.* A brief moment of panic quickly subsided as he realized that if anything was going to explode or catch fire it probably would've done so already. Then he remembered his passengers.

Unbuckling his seat harness, he called out into the pitch black. "Hey! Hey! Everybody okay?"

No answer. In fact, no sounds at all.

He took off his gloves and reached over toward the navigator's seat, his freezing cold hand immediately contacting the armour-plated bulkhead on which it sat, then its leather seat cushion, then the webbing and buckles of the harness securing the bundle of blankets. Finding an opening in the wool, he first noticed warmth, then breath, then subtle movement. The kid was alive, but he had no idea if it was injured, or unconscious, or sleeping, or staring wide-eyed into the blackness like him.

He moved his hand to the ridge at the top of the instrument panel in front of the navigator's seat, then blindly felt his way down toward the floor of the aircraft. He found the leather of Vickson's sheepskin jacket. It too was moving ever so slightly. The German was jammed into the tiny space down there, no doubt folded like a piece of paper, but still breathing.

"Hey! You okay, buddy? You okay?" He reached down and tugged on the jacket's leather collar but got no response, and instead tried unsuccessfully to move the man into what he thought might be a more comfortable position. His pounding head made a second attempt impossible. Jack sat back and tried to think. *Well, we're alive. But what the hell do we do now?* He looked at his watch, barely able to see the luminescent hands and markings around its dial. It was 9:59 p.m. Banff time, as best he could tell. There was really nothing left to do but wait out the night and try to come up with a new plan when it got light.

Jack grabbed his parachute pack and yanked the ripcord. Silk billowed out into the cockpit, and he did his best to cover the kid, the German, and himself, then tried to get comfortable. *That's not going to help much, but it's no worse in here than a Lunenburg lobster boat in January,* he told himself as he wiggled his perpetually ice-cold fingers back into his gloves.

Yeah. Right.

○ ○ ○

The pain jolted him back to reality.

Dull and throbbing, sharp and piercing, his head, shoulders, back—hell, his entire body was screaming at him. Forcing his heavy eyelids open, Jack took a look around the dimly lit, frozen cockpit. A blanket of snow covered the canopy, lending an intense, smothering silence to the already claustrophobic interior of the aircraft, but he could tell they weren't buried because of the soft glow beginning to illuminate their little green cave. His breath fogged in front of him as he rubbed his eyes and tried to focus on the rivulets of condensation frozen on the inside of the windshield.

The kid was moving. It had gotten itself buried about as far as it could into the blankets and the parachute silk draped over it, but he thought he could see wisps of breath emerging from a fold.

"Mornin'," Jack croaked quietly, his mouth sticky and foul. "Boy, I could sure use a cup of coffee. How about you?"

He reached over and gently lifted the silk, forming a dimly lit tunnel between himself and the blanket-wrapped child. The bundle shrank back away from him, so he tried to think of some other way to communicate. He rummaged around and pulled the escape kit from beneath his seat, then dug through it until he found a small, round, blue tin, labeled "RAF Special Ration Type B." *Bingo.* He shook it a few times, rattling its contents to try to get the kid's attention, then cracked the seal and worked his head and arms back underneath the silk tent.

"Sorry, these aren't great, kid, but they're the best I've got," he said. He held out one of the pale yellow barley sweets. No movement. He popped it into his own mouth, then made an exaggerated show of feigned deliciousness to try to convince the kid to try one. He held out another.

A tiny hand emerged and snatched the sweet before immediately retracting back into the blankets. A few seconds later, the same hand reemerged, palm up. Jack dropped two more of the hard candies into it and watched it disappear once again.

Satisfied that the kid must be in reasonably good shape, Jack pulled his head back from beneath the silk and gathered the fabric away from the floor below the navigator's seat. The German was barely visible down there, folded up in the semidarkness of the footwell. Jack reached down and shook him, and a low groan came back in response.

Alive.

"Hey, buddy. Hey. Can you move? You okay?"

The German was wedged awkwardly against the entrance hatch and the equipment at the bottom of the bulkhead, facing the back of the cockpit with his legs folded tight to his upper body, the boxes, briefcase, and metal toolbox Vickson had tossed into the Mosquito hidden beneath him. One eye cracked open, he reached his right hand up tentatively, and Jack grabbed him under the elbow and pulled a little. The low groans became progressively louder as the man strained to wrestle himself to a more upright position. Shaking his head from side to side, he waved Jack away and immediately stretched a hand out toward the ball of blankets in the navigator's seat.

"Das Mädchen… Uh… girl? Okay?"

"Oh, yeah, yeah. I think the kid's good." *So the kid's a girl!* "She's, uh, having a little breakfast right now. What about you? How you doing?"

Günther struggled to understand, to find the English words. "Not. Gut." His breathing was shallow, rapid.

With his left hand, Günther reached up gingerly and struggled to unzip Vickson's sheepskin jacket. Down near his right hip, his grey uniform jacket was almost black, and the fleece inside the jacket was no longer yellow-white. It was dark red. The German reached his left hand across his abdomen and cautiously pressed it to his right kidney, eliciting a pained grimace and a sharp, audible exhalation.

"I think, I...I think I am, uh, schuss," Günther groaned. "Shot."

65

It was time to move.

The first brilliant sun rays had made their appearance above the eastern horizon, and the thin film of snow that coated the cockpit canopy had begun to melt, revealing bright, clear skies.

Jack had given Günther some water and a few of the meagre rations from the Mosquito's escape kit, but the German was clearly laboring to breathe. When he'd first attempted to convince the man to let him take a look at his wound, he'd waved Jack away, but he'd finally relented and allowed Jack to try to inspect the damage. Jack was no medic, but he knew enough to understand that what he was looking at was most definitely not good. There was a jagged, deep red puncture wound near the German's right kidney area, and he'd clearly lost a lot of blood. Jack did his best to try to pack the wound with gauze, but the cramped space made access almost impossible. Finally, he stuck a syrette of morphine from the small tin in Vickson's first aid pouch into the man's thigh. There was not much else he could do.

The sugar and the activity in the steadily brightening cockpit must have made the kid a little more adventurous. She'd begun to cautiously poke her head out of her woolen cocoon from time to time in an effort to see where she was and what was going on.

"Well, kid. What do you think?" Jack asked her.

She stared back at him, silent.

He reached down and shook the German gently, spoke softly. "Hey, buddy. Hey. We need to move. We can't stay here. We'll die."

Günther opened one eye and groaned softly as he tried to speak.

"Nein. I...I cannot move. Ich denke meine Zeit ist um. My...uh, time is done." He squeezed his eyes tightly shut and gripped Jack's arm hard. "You. Promise. Dieses Mädchen...this girl. She is special. I cannot... I cannot explain."

The German was fading in and out of consciousness, but he managed to summon the energy to look Jack right in the eyes, and to communicate.

"Wir haben viel getan, sie und ich. Sie haben zweifellos meine Landsleute getötet. You have, ah, killed my...friends. I have...killed. Für was? For nothing. In einem anderen Leben, ah... In another time, we might have been...we might have...Freunde. Friends. You. Und me..." His voice trailed off, eyes closing as his head fell forward.

Jack looked over at the kid. She hunkered down in Vickson's seat, staring silently at the two men, dark eyes glistening. He had no idea if she knew what they were talking about, if she had any understanding of what was happening. *Hell, I've got no idea about any of this myself.* He put a hand on the German's right shoulder.

"Hey, hey! Tell me about the kid. Tell me why she's here."

Günther's eyes remained closed, but as he struggled to speak he slowly reached up and put his bloodstained left hand on the blanket-wrapped girl. "She is...Verantwortung, my... She has...suffered. Terribly. She is... She, ah, geändert. Special. Not like us. Promise... she, uh, werde überleben...will not...die. You...beschütze sie. Die Papiere. Papers. Why she is here. Why I am here. It is she who... wird nicht sterben. Not die. Promise..."

Günther smiled at the girl, his glistening eyes opening to lock on hers, his voice low and labored and intense as tears rolled down his cheeks. "Versprich mir. Promise. It's her...turn to live. Für alle... for all...die es nicht konnten. For all who...could not."

Confused by the German's words but wanting to ease the dying man's anguish, Jack glanced over at the girl to see her sobbing in total silence. He looked back at Günther and nodded his head. "Of course. Yes, yes. You have my word. My promise. I'll take care of her."

The German smiled weakly, looked into the girl's eyes and squeezed her arm, then he dropped his right hand from the blanket and struggled to hold it out to Jack.

"Ich kenne dich nicht, du kennst mich nicht...we, uh, we know each other, ja?"

Günther's eyelids closed as Jack took a firm grip on his hand.

"Ich bin du. Und du bist ich," he whispered hoarsely, breath shallow. "I am you...you are me."

Jack held Günther's warm, trembling hand until there was no life left in it.

66

Jack was about as ready as he was going to be.

He'd gathered as much gear as he thought he could carry—the crash axe, the flare pistol, the first aid pouch, the escape kit. From her dirty olive-green cocoon, the girl had watched him bump around in the cramped space. Jack looked over at her and smiled. "Okay kid. Whaddya say? Wanna take a walk?"

He reached up and pulled the lever to release the Mosquito's upper escape hatch, and immediately pushed the panel up and away. He'd worked up a pretty good sweat, and the rush of frigid air felt good as he pulled himself up and poked his head out of the opening.

The aircraft was resting on a gently sloping plateau of ice and snow under brilliant early morning sunshine and a crystal clear blue sky. Behind it, Jack could see various bits and pieces littered across the surface, some mostly buried but still visible under the snow, others stark against the dazzling backdrop.

The bulk of the Mosquito itself was partially covered in slowly melting snow and appeared to be substantially in one piece, although her rear fuselage was torn and shredded, its splintered vertical stabilizer and tailplane upside down in the snow some fifteen or twenty feet behind the rest of the aircraft. Jack looked down and saw bent propeller blades and a couple of unauthorized holes in the starboard engine nacelle and wing root.

Shit, that bastard did get lucky. Well so did we.

He dropped back down into the cockpit.

"Okay, sweetie. I'm going to climb out of here first and take a look around. When I get back—*if I can get back*—you're going to have to stand up right here on this seat and reach up so I can grab you and lift you out. Can you do that for me? Okay. Then we're going to walk off this little mountain and get ourselves a nice hot cup of coffee and some bacon and eggs. How does that sound?"

The girl stared at him intently but blankly. Jack knew she couldn't understand him, but he figured it wouldn't hurt to explain the plan out loud to himself, since he was basically making the whole thing up as he went along.

"Great!" He smiled, giving her a thumbs-up. "I'll be right back."

He stood and tossed the crash axe onto the plane's port wing, then hoisted himself up and out of the hatch and onto the wet surface. *Guess I'd better see what I'm dealing with. Here goes nothing.* He slid feet first off the wing's trailing edge. To his happy surprise and immense relief, he didn't disappear into six feet of powder, but instead found himself standing in reasonably firm snow that reached to just above his knees.

He scrambled back up onto the wing and lowered himself back down through the escape hatch.

The girl had moved.

She was down in the footwell, head resting on the dead German, arms wrapped around him. Her eyes were tightly shut and she made no sounds at all, but Jack could see her back heaving as the tears streamed down her face. *Oh, Jesus, kid. Who are you? What the hell have you been through?*

It was the first time Jack had seen her outside of her cocoon. She was wearing an oversize jacket over a coarse, dark woolen sweater, and black pants that were rolled up at the cuffs above her boots.

Jack smiled and held out his hands, palms up, and spoke in a soft, quiet voice. "Hey, hey. Look, I'm, uh...I'm really sorry about your friend, but we just can't stay here anymore. We've gotta get gone."

The girl stayed where she was, eyes squeezed shut. Jack had no idea what to do, so for a minute or so he simply did nothing. Just as he opened his mouth to say something, the girl suddenly pulled away from the German, opened her shining eyes wide, and worked herself to an upright kneeling position. She looked at Jack and reached out her arms to him, and Jack was startled to see what looked like dried blood on the dangling left sleeve of her jacket.

Shit! Shit, no! Is that his blood or yours? Are you hurt too?

He reached out and gently put his arms around her, lifting her onto his lap. He hadn't been around many kids, but he knew instinctively that she was terribly underweight, and even through the bulky jacket and sweater he could tell she was barely there. He couldn't believe a child could be that thin.

He suddenly thought of Marie, and of the baby they'd made together. He'd thought a lot about the kind of life he wanted their child to have. Bedtime stories and school friends and skating and sailing and family get-togethers. *Nothing like the life this kid's probably had.* The girl clung to him with a surprising strength.

"Hey. Hey. It's okay, kiddo. I've got you now. I've got you. Let's take a look at that."

He took off his glove and pointed to his own hand to show her what he wanted to see, and she slowly relaxed her grip. At the end of her left sleeve, he found two jagged holes in the darkened fabric. Carefully, he folded the blood-crusted material away from her tiny, ice cold hand. Her left pinkie finger was missing, just a partially clotted, bloody stump remained at the first knuckle. She didn't even flinch.

"Oh, Jesus, sweetie! Are you okay? You never made a sound!" He sat her back on the navigator's seat and did a quick inspection of her left side. *Maybe whatever got him, got her*, he thought. She sat passively, staring at him as silent tears continued to roll down her face. Other than her hand, he couldn't find any damage. *Goddamn. Whatever this kid's been through has made her tough as nails.*

He put both of his hands on the girl's bony shoulders and looked straight into her sad, dark eyes. "Okay, sweetie. First of all, my name's Jack." He touched his chest. "I'm Jack. Jack."

He reached out and gently wiped her wet cheeks. "Listen, I don't think you're going to be able to tell me your name, so I'm going to call you...Susie."

He'd heard the story countless times as a kid, about the time his mother, Susan, had saved her big, tough cousin. Uncle Rob said they'd been out on the pond all afternoon, him and her and Billy O'Brien and Rose Blanchette and a bunch of the other neighborhood kids, freezing their sweaty asses off but loving every second of it. It had been getting too dark to see the puck, and they were about to head back to the house when Robbie broke through. He'd almost gone under, but his stick had somehow bridged the hole and held him above the surface, from the armpits up.

They'd all been scared out of their minds—Uncle Rob said he would've shit his pants but his butthole was frozen completely shut—because they all knew from endless older sibling horror stories that the terrifyingly deep cracking-booming-ripping sound they were hearing meant that the ice might just open up and swallow them all.

Robbie had immediately started bawling at the top of his lungs, and Billy and Rose and all the other kids had stood there about as frozen as the pond, paralyzed by fear and uncertainty. It was little Susan who'd been literally as cool as ice. She'd calmly told them all to lie down, told Billy to hold her skate blades and Rose to hold his, and she'd laid all three of their sticks underneath her to distribute her weight as she belly-crawled to the edge of the hole and basically dragged Robbie the hell out of there.

When they'd finally gotten themselves to solid ground, they'd all laughed that scared shitless laugh that kids laugh when they know they just got away with something they maybe shouldn't have. All except Susan. She'd been quiet—"dead fuckin' quiet," Uncle Rob said—as they'd walked the freezing walk back toward Susan's house. Uncle Rob told Jack he'd never seen anything like what Susan did, and that it was the first time he'd ever really understood what courage was. He said that courage wasn't the lack of fear. Fuck no. Courage was the doing of something in spite of fear. Jack admired and respected and loved his mother for so many, many things, but especially for that. If his father embodied the word luck, in Jack's mind, his mother embodied that one word most. *Courage.*

The girl stared at him with confused, silent sadness, her chin trembling ever so slightly. He smiled as he did his best to wipe away her tears. "Yeah. Susie. You're Susie, okay? Susie. If we make it out of here alive, maybe one day that'll mean something to you."

It sure as hell means a lot to me.

Five minutes later, he'd sprinkled the girl's wounded hand with sulfa powder and wrapped it as best he could with what was left of the gauze, then rebundled her in her blanket and boosted her and his survival supplies out of the emergency hatch. Standing with her on the Mosquito's port wing, he surveyed their scant gear and mentally ran through his plan one last time. He knew it was rudimentary at best, but it was the only one he had.

He'd brought the plane down on a southwesterly heading, trying to get them as close to the western edge of the ice field as he thought possible. He knew there were a couple of coastal towns down below, and basically, he was planning to just walk out. *Sounds simple enough*, he thought.

"Don't go anywhere, Susie girl. I'll be right back," he said, as he clambered back up onto the cockpit canopy and dropped through the hatch. *One last look around.*

When he looked down at the dead Luftwaffe officer slumped awkwardly in the bottom of the footwell, he felt a twinge of something he couldn't quite figure—like guilt, confusion, wonder, anger, and admiration all balled up together—as he tried in vain to remember the man's name. Whoever this guy had been and whatever his motivations, Jack knew he'd probably taken some crazy risks to end up here, and the guy had protected that kid as if she were his own, though clearly she was not. He'd been absolutely adamant that the kid survive. *And I promised him she would.*

He reached inside the collar of the man's open tunic, tugged on the thin leather cord tied around his neck.

Jack had never seen a German identity tag before. It was an oval alloy disk, with identical sets of stamped numbers and letters on either side of a perforated line running horizontally across its width. He snapped off its lower half and dropped it into his jacket pocket, leaving the other half hanging from the leather.

Jack saluted the dead German. "I never knew you, buddy, but someone must have. And I don't know whatever else you might have done in your life, but it seems like maybe in this case at least, you did something really good."

As he crouched on his seat, ready to climb up and out of the upper hatch, something on the floor of the cockpit near the rudder pedals caught Jack's eye. He struggled to reach down for it. Pulling hard on the shoulder strap, he worked the dirty black leather case out from beneath the dead German. He had no idea what was in the cardboard boxes or the small metal toolbox still trapped underneath him, but they were just too much for him to even think about carrying. They were going to have to stay put. He stood up, threw the briefcase out of the escape hatch, and hauled himself up and out the cockpit.

Back out on the wing, Jack mentally ran down the instructions he'd been given, over and over, should he ever happen to find himself on the ground with an intact aircraft in enemy territory. He grabbed the flare gun and popped a cartridge into it, but he hesitated. Maybe burning the Mosquito up here wouldn't be a particularly good idea right now, given the plume of smoke it would no doubt send up. *Shit, no one even knows we're here. And we'll be long gone and this thing'll be buried under five feet of snow before anyone ever stumbles across it.*

Buried.

The word hung in Jack's mind.

There was a fallen man in that plane. An enemy pilot. But really, whose enemy? *Who the hell decides who gets to be enemies and who gets to be friends anyway?*

He removed the cartridge from the gun, shoved them both into the escape kit, and slid off the wing of EO-N for the last time.

The girl tried her best to walk, but less than fifty painfully slow steps away from the Mosquito, Jack realized that she was just too small and too weak to handle the snow, so he stopped to figure out how to carry her. And the axe. And the first aid pouch. And the escape kit. And the briefcase. Too much. He opened the first aid pouch, grabbed a couple of bandages and stuffed them into his pockets, and took the last syrette of morphine out of its small tin before tossing the empty brass container into the snow.

As he attempted to rewrap the girl, a bloodied fingertip and a jagged, razor-sharp piece of shrapnel fell, silent and unseen, from the folds of her blanket into the snow at their feet.

Without a look back, he picked the girl up and headed west.

o o o

The surface of the glacier was incredibly challenging, nothing but azure blue and blinding white for as far as he could see, and Jack was feeling it. *Can't go back. Can't stay here.* After struggling through knee-deep snow for more than two hours, he stopped to rest and check his watch. 10:56 a.m. Banff time. "Pretty much high noon here, Susie girl. Time for a little lunch." He handed her another sweet from the tin in his pocket, popped one into his own mouth, and trudged on.

An exhausting ninety minutes later, he found a wide slab of sun-warmed, dark grey rock. Jack sat the girl down carefully, dug a couple more tablets out of the ration tin, scooped some snow and wet their lips, and lay back and closed his exhausted eyes. *Just for a few minutes,* he thought.

He woke with a start.

Shit! Shit! Shit!

His watch read 2:18 p.m., and he knew that at this time of year, the Norwegian days were still pretty short. He struggled to summon the energy to get to his feet. *Two, maybe two and a half hours of daylight left. We've gotta move, but something has to stay here.* He stuffed a few things from the escape kit into the German's black case and slung the strap around his neck, then picked up the axe and the sleeping girl and trudged on.

Three hours later, the sun had dipped well below the horizon, taking whatever warmth it had provided down with it. As the western skies had turned orange-violet, a biting crispness had filled the early evening air and the surface of the snow had begun to crust over with a thin film of ice, making each step just a little more difficult. He'd seen more and more exposed rock, and Jack had sensed they'd been shedding altitude, but his strength was starting to fail. *Jesus Murphy. We've gotta be close to the edge of this stuff. Gotta be.*

The girl couldn't have weighed more than forty pounds, but Jack's arms were painfully cramped from the relentless exertion, and his legs and lungs were on fire, defying him to take one more step, then one more.

He'd noticed he'd begun to walk with his eyes closed from time to time, a dangerous sign that fatigue was taking hold of him, and he stumbled and fell more and more often. He pressed forward, but he knew his stamina was running short.

As he fought to regain his balance after another blind misstep and near fall, Jack saw something that gave him the energy boost he so desperately needed. In the deepening gloom, about four hundred yards below the ridge of snow he'd just topped, a dense black-green mass of pine trees bumped up against the dark grey and blue-white edge of the rock and ice.

When they reached the treeline almost twenty-five minutes later, he sat the shivering girl down on a bed of pine needles and wrapped her in the blanket. He knew that if he stopped moving now, he might not have the energy to get going again, so he immediately set to work. He chopped a few lush pine boughs to serve as a protective buffer to insulate them from the cold rocky ground, then gathered more and more green branches to form a lean-to over the trunk of a fallen tree. When he finally struck the first of his dozen matches, he was immensely relieved to see his tiny pyramid of pine needles and dry sticks ignite almost immediately.

Yeah! One match! My Boy Scout leader would be so goddamn proud!

He arranged a few large rocks around the fire—he knew their stored heat would help keep them warm through the long night—then flopped down beside the girl, totally exhausted.

"Well, Susie girl! Welcome to the Ritz!"

Wrapped in her blanket, nestled into a rough pine bough shelter on the side of a frozen mountain, with the arm of another complete stranger around her shoulders, the girl stared into the warmth of the flickering fire and sucked on another barley sweet. Then she did something Jack had never seen her do before, something that warmed him much more than the flames.

She looked up at him and smiled.

67

Jack didn't know who was more startled. He'd left the bundled, sleeping girl beneath their makeshift shelter and was out scouting for more dry firewood—or more accurately, at that particular moment, heeding his old man's advice and taking a piss—when he heard the rifle shot ring out. Midstream, the gun's report still echoing off the mountain, Jack jumped and immediately put his hands in the air, resulting in a minor moment of moist awkwardness as he yelled at the approaching man, whom he assumed would be a German soldier. Instead, the man—a hunter, and fortunately not a very good one—had stumbled from the trees and most apologetically introduced himself in Norwegian and halting English, as Jack had hurriedly tucked in and zipped up. His name was Moller, he said, and he lived near a small town down at the water's edge.

Less than three hours later, Jack savored his second cup of hot coffee as he tried his best to explain where he and the now-sleeping girl had come from. Mr. Moller had attempted to interpret for his wife, as Mrs. Moller had offered an almost continuous flow of questions, observations, and comments as she'd fussed over the child. She'd fed the girl, given her a hot bath and dressed her in some clean clothes, and rebandaged her wounded left hand. At one point the Mollers had politely but insistently asked Jack to explain the girl's scars, and they'd been especially curious about the cryptic alphanumeric code tattooed in dark blue on her forearm, but he'd simply had no answers.

"Look, I'm…I'm really sorry. I just have absolutely no idea where this kid came from or what she's been through. I only know someone thinks she's important enough that my partner and I were sent to Denmark to fetch her. Unfortunately, we ran into a little, ah, trouble, and we ended up here instead of home. Believe it or not"—*I can hardly believe it myself*—"there's a dead German in my busted-up plane somewhere up on the top of that mountain. That guy wanted to get her to England so badly that he died trying."

"England? Ah, England?" Mr. Moller asked. "Vil du komme til England?"

He held up a finger. "You will please…wait. Here."

o o o

They shook hands by the fire in the Mollers' tiny sitting room.

"My name is Halvorsen. My friend Emil here tells me that you would like to arrange some, ah, travel, yes?"

As the man spoke, Jack sized him up. He was tall and slender, salt-and-pepper hair. Late forties, maybe. His thin black moustache, steel-rimmed glasses, dark grey suit, and black tie gave him a decidedly businesslike air. And he spoke perfect English.

"I can make such arrangements, yes, but you cannot stay here. It's far, far too risky for these people. Do you understand?"

"Of course…yeah. What, uh…what've you got in mind?"

"In the morning you will be taken to a safe place some distance from here, away from the town. It will take some time to make the necessary contacts and arrangements for you, so you must remain out of sight until we are ready to move you. You must both wear the clothes we will provide. And most importantly, you must not speak if anyone speaks to you. Same with the child. This is imperative. Do you understand?"

Jack looked at the girl, at Halvorsen, and at the Mollers. He knew he was placing both his and the girl's lives in their hands, but something in his gut told him that was the thing to do. "Hey I've never heard the kid make a single sound, let alone speak, so yeah, I think we'll be okay there. Thank you. All of you."

68

The place had been cold, but they'd been warm.

They'd spent ten days in Halvorsen's cabin. Jack thought for sure that the girl's dark hair had started to grow out a little bit, and that she appeared to be gaining more and more strength and energy.

He'd ventured outside with her a couple of times each day, her tiny good hand squeezing his tightly as they'd explored the forest around the cabin. When a gentle rain had spattered softly through the towering pines, he'd stood and watched in silent wonder as she'd held her good hand out to catch the drops, bringing her cupped palm to her lips over and over and over. She'd been amazed at the blue skies, captivated by the aromatic layer of needles that covered the ground, and more times than Jack could count, she'd simply stood completely still, turned her face to the sky, eyes closed, and just breathed. To him, it was almost as if she'd never seen or smelled or felt any of those everyday things before, and he found himself experiencing their new surroundings with a different perspective.

On the third day, Halvorsen had arrived with a small, leather-cased box camera and had asked them to pose for a couple of snapshots in front of the cabin, to create some photographic evidence of their prior visits, he said. The girl, Jack had noticed, had seemed strangely uneasy at the sight of the camera and had almost hidden behind Jack as the shutter clicked. She'd squeezed his hand hard and unrelentingly until the photo session was over.

To help pass the evenings as they'd huddled together in front of the small fireplace, Jack had told her all about Marie. He could talk endlessly on every detail of that subject, and so he had. He'd talked about her kindness and strength and intelligence and, of course, about her elegance and beauty. He'd talked about the fact that for the first time in his life he really couldn't believe his goddamned luck. He'd talked about how many times he'd been scared of dying, of not making it back to her, but that he'd never been as scared of anything as he'd been when he'd first read the letter that told him he was going to be responsible for a new life. And he'd told the girl all about his big idea—about buying his own plane. After all, he'd said, he figured there'd be plenty of used birds for sale when the killing was all done, and he planned to make a killing instead, flying wealthy fishermen and sightseers around the Maritimes.

And he'd babbled on about his parents and his childhood, and about the dumb things he and his friends had done. Like the time he and Roddy Black had accidentally burned Roddy's old man's barn to the ground while trying to light up a couple of butts they'd pilfered. And the time that he and Walter Moser had convinced their eight-year-old selves that they could make it all the way from Lunenburg to Chester and back in Walter's uncle's dory, but how instead they'd lost an oar a couple of thousand yards out and ended up floating way past Blue Rocks for a whole lot of wet and cold hours. He wasn't sure what had been scarier: the whale that had surfaced right beside them at one point or Walter's bright red-faced but totally silent father, who'd finally, thankfully, shown up in his lobster boat to haul their near-frozen carcasses home.

Look, I've got a boatload of stories, kid, but I sure wish I knew yours.

The girl hadn't taken her eyes off him as he'd blabbered and gesticulated for hours, and still she'd said absolutely nothing. But on the sixth day, after he'd told her about getting into his first real fist fight at school because that big, dumb, freckle-faced asshole Jimmy McKay had accused him of liking Sally Hatheway—which, of course, he actually did—he'd demonstrated the arm-waving-foot-stomping-panic-dance he'd done after a swarm of bees had flown up his pant leg one summer night at his grandparents place in Mahone Bay. That one, he'd noticed with immense satisfaction, had managed to get her to crack another actual smile.

On the tenth day, they'd moved to their new home tucked behind a floor-to-ceiling wall of boxes and filing cabinets.

To say that Jack had been a little nervous casually walking into a bank in German-occupied Norway, with a briefcase in one hand and a little girl's hand in the other, would be an understatement. But they'd not been challenged.

They'd been pretty comfortable for the last three days, snugly hunkered down in their big pile of blankets and pillows and cushions during the day, and sneaking out of their padded concrete cave and up into the main part of the bank only after business hours, and only when necessity demanded it.

Jack was uneasy being cooped up down there—he sure wasn't used to that feeling—but the girl seemed almost happy. She continued to absolutely devour the steady flow of food and milk that Halvorsen brought their way, continually ran her good hand over the blankets and pillows, and constantly brought her hand-me-down clothes to her nose in order to breathe in their scent, eyes closed tight.

And she'd been completely mesmerized by the children's book Mrs. Moller had sent along. With the girl snuggled in tight against his shoulder, Jack had leafed through it by the light of the lantern. As his Norwegian was sadly lacking, he'd been forced to invent his own story—about a brave little girl who climbed to the top of a mountain in the company of a magical talking goat—to go with its whimsical watercolour illustrations. *Take a giant guess which one of us is the talking goat, kid.* She'd gazed up at him with wide eyes as he spoke softly, and she'd jumped and almost laughed out loud the very first time he'd done his impression of a startled goat.

He'd told the story for what he figured was at least the fiftieth time, and when the girl had finally been unable to keep her eyelids open, he'd dimmed the lantern, tucked the blankets snug around her, and watched her sleep. *I have no idea where you came from, or what you've been through, Susie girl. But you're with me now. You're gonna be okay.*

Over and over again, he looked at his luminescent watch dial.

And he waited.

No sleep for him tonight.

o o o

At the sound of soft footsteps above their heads, Jack checked his watch. Again. 3:14 a.m.

Go time.

His heart had begun to pound as soon as they'd emerged from the darkened bank. He'd seen the dark green Wehrmacht truck parked down the street, so he knew they had to be around somewhere, but as far as he could tell, the town seemed deserted. The four of them—Jack, the girl, Halvorsen, and a man he didn't know—quickly made their way across to the waterfront and out onto a long floating wharf.

As the man climbed down a ladder into a rowboat, Halvorsen glanced up to the black sky, then turned to Jack, his voice a whisper. "Olaf will row you out to his fishing boat, then he'll take you to a safe house on an island a few kilometres from here. After that, in about a week or so, you'll be taken by boat out to a prearranged extraction point. I…I wish you both the very best of luck." Halvorsen nodded back toward the silent stillness of the town and the Wehrmacht truck. "And hopefully this will all be over soon."

Jack shook the Norwegian's hand firmly, kept his voice low. "It won't be long now, I promise. The Jerries are done. Unfortunately a few of them are just too stupid or stubborn to realize it. But thank you. To everyone. You've all been most kind."

Halvorsen smiled and nodded, then turned back up the wharf, melting into the shadows of the darkened town as Jack helped the girl down the ladder and got her settled into Olaf's gently rocking rowboat. Olaf had hauled them, steadily, slowly and silently, about a hundred yards out into the placid blackness of the harbour when the shouting started and two shots rang out from the vicinity of the town's waterfront.

As Olaf doubled his efforts to propel them farther from the source of the noise and commotion making its way toward the end of the wharf, Jack instinctively shoved the girl away from him, down into the cold slosh in the bottom of the boat, then immediately dropped down to try to cover her. Terrified, the girl's wide open eyes stared into the almost impenetrable gloom as four more shots cracked from the shore, bullets splashing into the black water close around them. The boat suddenly rocked wildly, and Jack sensed something was wrong.

He knew something was wrong when he tried to sit up.

Shit! Must have gotten the wind knocked out of me when I hit the thwart.

Rolling away from the girl and onto his side in the cold, wet blackness, he called out to her quietly, emphatically. "Hey! Susie? Susie! You okay? Where are you?" He breathed a massive sigh of relief when he felt her moving around and her barely visible face appeared right in front of his, eyes wide with fear. He grabbed her shoulders and whispered as loud as he dared. "It's okay, Susie, it's okay. But I need you to keep your pretty little head down, okay?" He pulled her close and squeezed her tight.

It suddenly dawned on him that the sound of the oars—and the boat's momentum—had almost completely stopped. They were drifting, and Olaf was no longer in the boat. *Shit! Shit! Shit!* "Hey! Hey, buddy! Where are you?" Jack whisper-yelled, scanning the black water around them for any sign of the man. But the only sounds were the distant barking voices and the running footsteps pounding on the wharf. *Goddammit!*

Ignoring the dull throbbing in his ribs, Jack struggled to get himself into the spot where Olaf had been sitting, then quietly dipped the oars into the water and pulled steadily to get them back on what he hoped was a trajectory away from the town's waterfront. Between pulls, he could still hear the sound of boots thumping on the heavy wooden planks, and he thought he could almost make out a couple of soldiers in the darkness, no doubt desperately looking for a boat. He had absolutely no idea where he was going, he just knew that he needed to get there as quickly and as quietly as he could.

With practiced cadence, Jack pulled with everything he had, but his arms and back were aching badly and the pain in his ribcage made it harder and harder to catch his breath. He needed to take a break, just for a minute. *Back in a goddamn rowboat? Really? Pretty sure Marie likes me a lot better with wings.* He pulled the oar handles together, put his head down on his hands to rest, and journeyed back to that perfect summer day in Lunenburg harbour. Him and Will Eisnor in a yellow and green dory, sprinting like hell around a couple of buoys to try to win annual bragging rights and a few free congratulatory beers—and, of course, to try to impress the stunning girl he'd just met up on the wharf. Her scarlet sundress, wild mane of thick, dark, curly hair, jaw-dropping hazel eyes, and her incredible smile were like an irresistible magnet to him. She'd just been so goddamned beautiful that he literally couldn't take his eyes off her as he'd worked his oars like a madman to get them to the marker. And after they'd made the turn, he'd pulled harder than he ever had before, demanding that Will keep up the pace, just so he could get back to where she was standing just a few seconds sooner. He'd simply never felt anything that powerful before and, truth be told, it scared him just a little. He'd just met her, but he couldn't bear to be away from her.

Months later, when he'd finally convinced her that just maybe he was the one for her, too, he'd come to know her as strong and feisty and kind and funny and just a whole lot smarter than he was. He'd realized that more than anything else in the world he wanted to be there for her, to be the kind of man that he, for some inexplicable but undeniable reason, felt she just damn well deserved.

Just wait right there for me, okay, honey? Wait right there. I'll be back to you in a flash, Marie. I promise.

He jerked upright as he realized the girl was shaking his arm, the dull-sharp pain in his back bringing him back to cold reality.

"Sorry, Susie girl. I...I, ah, just needed to rest up for a second."

He winced as he squinted to see the dim glow on his wrist. 5:31 a.m.. He guessed they'd been in the boat for about an hour and forty minutes, and he could see the faint beginnings of daylight low in the sky. *Got to put more water between us and them.*

Forty-two exhausting minutes later, he steered them through what he thought was a narrow channel, keeping the now glowing eastern horizon to his right as he strained to stay awake and to keep the boat moving. There were no lights, no other boats, no signs of life anywhere. He hugged the shoreline to his right as the boat emerged from the mouth of the passage, then pointed them at a rocky, pebbled beach as they rounded the point.

When he felt the familiar crunch and grind of sand and rocks and pebbles under the boat, he knew he could finally rest again. He slumped forward and closed his eyes once more, totally exhausted. The pain in his side challenged each breath, each word.

"Susie? Where are you? You doing okay, girl? You okay?"

With the boat rocking and bumping from side to side, he knew she was moving toward him, but, oddly, when he opened his eyes, it was too dark to see, and it took almost his last ounce of energy just to reach out to her in the gloom. He smiled as her cold hand squeezed his, then immediately felt her trembling arms go around his neck. He sensed the fear in her warm, rapid breathing, so he spoke softly and calmly as he fought to stay awake.

"Hey, hey. You're doing great, Susie girl. You're a… You're a tough little cookie. You know that? And you're…you're gonna be okay, kiddo. I know it. You're gonna make it, Susie. You're gonna make it. You're the… You're the lucky one now."

She squeezed his neck with all of her might, and pressed her soft, wet cheek to his. And for the first time, he could have sworn he heard her say something. A tiny, soft, beautiful, pleading voice.

"Nie idź! Proszę, nie idź!"

But the bullet had gone through his lung.

And no matter how hard she wished for Jack to stay, he just couldn't.

69

He'd done as much as he could. But given the recent events at the harbourfront, the shooting and yelling and commotion he'd heard shortly after Olaf had begun to maneuver his rowboat out into the blackness, Halvorsen had no real idea of the whereabouts of either his friend or his passengers. Olaf's rowboat was nowhere to be found, his fishing boat was still moored out in the harbour, and he'd not been heard from. And the Germans had been pretty agitated for a few days, so he still hoped for the best, that they'd all somehow escaped in the smaller boat and were safely holed up somewhere.

When Halvorsen had found the airman's black leather briefcase, forgotten, despite its declared importance, in the jumble of blankets and pillows and cushions behind the boxes and cabinets in the dark of the bank basement, he'd done what he'd thought had made the most sense with its contents.

What better place to hide a folder full of papers and envelopes and notebooks than in a room full of folders filled with papers and envelopes and notebooks? He'd been sure to carefully note its location in code, figuring to lay low for a month or so before reestablishing contact and trying once again to get that part of the package to the British. But just six days later, Olaf's bloated body had surfaced.

Connections had been made.

Interrogations had been conducted.

Confessions had been extracted.

And an SS officer and four Wehrmacht soldiers had been waiting for Halvorsen when he'd left his house for work the following Monday morning.

He'd simply kissed his trembling wife and daughter as they'd huddled together and cried, and said absolutely nothing as his captors led him away through his perfectly manicured garden.

70

The girl had clung to Jack, tears silently falling until the heat of the mid-morning sun, the rocking of the rowboat, and her rising thirst and hunger had forced her to move.

Frightened and confused, but instinctively aware that she had to get herself onto land, she'd reluctantly climbed over the rowboat's gunwale and waded through the freezing cold water to the shore. Not having the faintest idea what to do next, she'd simply sat down on a sun-warmed rock and shivered and sobbed until the ebb tide had taken him away.

Hours later, exhausted and frightened but determined to keep moving, she'd managed to walk and stumble more than twenty-five kilometres along the rugged coastline. Her strength had begun to falter, and she'd fallen countless times, most recently while climbing over a rough wooden fence, a tumble that had landed her facedown in a well-trodden patch of cold, wet mud.

As she'd struggled to right herself, a fleeting moment of absolute terror had quickly given way to mild alarm and confusion, then to something much more pleasant, as a large black and white dog—its bushy tail wagging wildly—had furiously licked her dirty, tear-streaked face. When the grey-bearded old man had topped the rise to find the two of them covered in wet mud and surrounded by his confused flock of loudly bleating sheep, he'd been flabbergasted.

"Vel, hvor kom du fra?"

Despite the warm food, despite the soft bed and clean blankets, despite the woman's incomprehensible but gentle words and kind smile as she'd sat with her, the girl had sobbed uncontrollably for hours and hours, her heart and mind filled once again with the pain and confusion and desperation of loss and grief.

Early the following morning, under the attentive and concerned gazes of the farmer and his wife, she'd sat sipping hot sheep's milk and eating creamy brunost and warm lefse in their tiny kitchen.

Warmly dressed in some of the woman's clean clothes, and with a wonderful tail-wagging bundle of fur nestled at her feet, she'd only been able to think of one thing to whisper to the two new strangers who'd taken her in and shown her so much kindness.

"Mam na imię Susi."

71

Alison drove in silence, caught up in her own swirling thoughts. From time to time, she glanced over at Scott, who seemed equally lost in his own head. The early morning Norwegian landscape was breathtaking, and she let a few more perfect kilometres disappear behind them before she broke the silence.

"Oh. So, I…uh, I forgot to mention. I heard from my friend at the University of Washington. Those schematics—the hexagons and circles from the notebook pages—he agrees that they're exactly what I thought they were. Seems someone really was trying to engineer drugs around that…research. I hate to even call it that."

She knew she'd never be able to shake the horrifying images from her mind.

"And hey," Alison continued. "You never did tell me what you heard from Germany. About the ID tag. Were they able to find anything? And what about New Zealand? Anything on Robert Vickson? Or the child?"

"Right," Scott said. "I did hear something. I'm sorry. I guess I just got kind of immersed in all of the document stuff. Hold on a second and I'll dig it up." He scrolled through his phone for the emailed details. "Unfortunately there's no new information about the child's finger bone. Just speculation based on Mrs. Nygård's photo. And nothing about Vickson either. Just no indication at all what might have happened to him. It's likely he wasn't even in the plane when it went down. After all, we know that your grandfather and the German and possibly a young girl were jammed into what would have been a very tight space, so the only explanation has to be that at some point, somewhere, Vickson got out of the plane and the German and the girl got in. We may never learn what happened to your grandfather or the girl after Rosendal, and we may never know how that plane ended up where it did, but maybe having no navigator on board had something to do with it. Who knows? Anyway, I've passed everything we do know over to the Commonwealth War Graves Commission, and they're going to keep all the files open. Hopefully something will turn up there, but unfortunately this all might end up being another one of those end-of-the-war mysteries. Literally hundreds of thousands of people just vanished into that chaos. I...I wish we'd been able to do more for you, Alison. I really do."

Jesus. What kind of a shit species does these things? Kills millions of its own kind? Causes untold suffering and misery for millions of others? Sends its sons and daughters to vanish into nothingness? Alison couldn't help but feel deep sadness for the world, then and now. *Why can't we learn from our history? Why aren't we any smarter or kinder to each other now than we were then?*

"But, hey," Scott continued, "I've got some good news, too."

He clicked into a recent email from the Deutsche Dienststelle.

"Turns out the German man's name was...uh, Major Günther Joachim Graf. He was a decorated Luftwaffe fighter pilot who served with JG 54, the 'Green Hearts' they were called, first in France and then in Russia. His last known official posting was to a small town just east of Rostock, Germany, in late 1944, but his records basically disappear after that. They're going to keep looking into it for a bit, but how he ended up dead in your grandfather's plane on the top of a Norwegian mountain is maybe something we'll never figure out."

Scott paused for a second, then looked over at Alison. "But there's even more good news here. They've been able to locate a surviving relative. Major Graf's only daughter, Gisele. She'd been partially blinded as a child, in an RAF bombing raid that killed her mother—apparently sometime in 1944—and she was eventually raised by adoptive parents who immigrated to…ah, Bettendorf, Iowa, shortly after the war. She's just been notified and the appropriate arrangements are being made."

"Oh, my god!" exclaimed Alison. "My god… That's…that's just incredibly sad and wonderful at the same time. I just… I just can't imagine what she's going through right now. My god…"

The stunningly beautiful Norwegian landscape stretched out before her, completely at odds with everything she was thinking and feeling. They'd put a few more silent kilometres behind them before Scott spoke again.

"Alison, listen, there's…there's something else I think you should know. Why don't you pull over for a minute?"

Feeling an intensely unsettling twinge of anxiety at his suggestion, Alison brought the SUV to a stop on the gravel shoulder.

Scott turned to her, his voice low and soft.

"Listen, I…I really shouldn't be telling you any of this, but I know you'll never let it go any further. Your brother. James. I, ah… I did a little digging."

Alison looked into his eyes, felt her anxiety ratchet up another notch.

"James wasn't the only one killed by the IED he stepped on…" He paused for a half second. "He was just the, ah, only soldier killed."

"What? Scott, what does that mean?" Alison whispered, her voice almost unable to escape her rapidly constricting throat.

"I mean, he was carrying an injured child to a LAV when the incident occurred. The child didn't make it either."

Alison took a deep breath that caught in her chest as she swallowed hard. She felt the familiar pain rising, felt the uncontrollable tears welling up. But she felt something else too, something that she couldn't place: a complex, confusing mix of despair, hate, pride, rage, gratitude, and love.

"They were out on a long-range patrol," said Scott quietly, "and they really weren't supposed to get involved. But a school had been attacked and, well, they were trying to evacuate as many of the kids as they could. It was a setup, Alison. But they did it anyway. I…I'm sorry. I don't know what to tell you. I just know this—it wasn't for nothing."

Eyes brimming, chest tight and heaving, Alison blinked rapidly and turned her head away, squeezing her eyes shut to block out the cold, distant peaks. To block out the pain. *So much cruelty and horror in the world. So much hate.*

When she felt the warm, gentle strength of Scott's hand on hers, she opened her eyes and turned to him, smiling through her flowing tears as she squeezed back.

So much kindness.

72

Alison poured herself a second cup of coffee, opened the silver laptop on her kitchen counter, popped in her earbuds, and clicked the video conference link.

As she'd requested, her attorneys had sent copies of the translated notes and documents to Will Acton, her director of biochemistry, and Alison had asked him to tell her whatever he could.

"Hey, Will. How you doing? And what do we know?"

"Hey, good morning. And welcome back, by the way." He jumped right in. "We've done a thorough analysis of the documents and, yes, as you suspected, they appear to have their origins in something really, really awful. As you know, the Nazis used prisoners to conduct...uh, research into all sorts of things. Hypothermia, hyperthermia, extreme high and low pressure scenarios, gunshot wounds, concussion, traumatic amputation, burns, bone fractures, blood coagulants, biological weapons. Just horrible, horrible stuff.

"And these notes are obviously incomplete and nonsequential, and they appear to reference more than one type of study, so it's hard to say if we're totally sure we're interpreting and understanding all of it correctly at this point. But the bulk of the documents seem to pertain to a particular area of inquiry. As horrible as this sounds,

Alison, it actually appears that they were trying to find a way to make cancer contagious. To weaponize it."

Goosebumps stood up on Alison's arms. She hadn't given Will any hints about what Professor Lundeen had suspected might be the purpose of the procedures outlined in the documents. She breathed out hard as he continued.

"From what we can decipher, the bulk of the experiments referenced in these particular notes involved trying to cultivate tumors or haematological malignancies in very young children, through the surgical introduction of various types of cancer cells from already stricken patients into the lymphatic systems of noncancerous subjects. And it kinda looks like they were trying to develop an aerosol or liquid distribution system from extracted lymphatic fluid, bone marrow, and blood, etcetera."

Alison had always had some vague knowledge that the Nazis had done horrible things to people in the name of medical science, but that stuff had been relegated to history books. All of this, on the other hand, had become very, very real. It was right in front of her. And she was personally, intimately connected to it.

"But, Alison, there's something incredibly strange and pretty intriguing—actually pretty fucking wild, to be honest with you—in all of this. And we may be wrong on this too, okay? But…it seems that though they were unsuccessful in weaponizing the disease, they might have done exactly the opposite."

"I'm sorry, Will. What are you saying?" Alison exclaimed.

"Well, it's still way, way too early to say for sure, but I guess what we're saying is that they may have accidentally created the basis for development of a potential treatment protocol, maybe even a vaccine. It appears they may have inadvertently bioengineered natural antibodies for certain types of blood cancers in one or more of their subjects by introducing specific combinations and sequences of antigens. Of course, it's likely that any and all of the unfortunate people who might have actually developed those antibodies are long, long dead, given the amount of time that's gone by, the terrible conditions in which they were held, and the absolute brutality of the medical experiments they underwent. But there are certainly significant notes regarding, uh, certain processes and outcomes in the documents and notebooks you found."

Alison was stunned. Speechless.

She simply had too many questions to articulate even one. Mind working hard to process what she'd just heard, she stared out at the flat greyness of Elliot Bay in the distance, the foamy white wake of the Bremerton ferry barely visible.

"Alison? You still there? Did I lose you?

"Yes, yes. Sorry, Will. I can hear you."

"You know Robertson and the board will need to know all about this. They'll want all the details. They'll want to get it all into legal right away, that's for goddamn sure. And if what we think might be true is actually true, they'll want to run with it, big-time. You know that, right? Right? Alison?"

Her mind raced on, a thousand thoughts and images filling her head simultaneously.

She'd been involved in cancer research of one kind or another for almost a quarter of her life, and she'd fully committed to a specific mission when her mother had been diagnosed with a form of ovarian cancer for which, Alison knew, she personally carried the genetic markers. She felt sure that they had something, but she also fully understood the odds of that long road, and the odd mix of elation and guilt that would surely come should the drug be successful and the dreams of the money vampires were to come true.

She also knew, assuming that what Will had told her was even remotely plausible, what an incredible opportunity something like this might mean for her company and her shareholders—and, of course, for the massively lucrative business of cancer treatment.

"Yeah. Um…yeah. I hear you. Thanks, Will. Thanks," she said quietly.

"Let me sleep on this one, would you?"

73

Stomach churning as the muscles between her shoulder blades slowly knotted into a solid lump, Alison sat at the head of the walnut and stainless steel conference room table, nodding and mumbling vague good-mornings and hellos as nine board members and her executive team settled around it. Each deposited the standard meeting array— phone, notebook, laptop, and coffee cup—on the polished surface.

At 8:30 a.m. precisely, she got right to it.

"Thank you all for coming in this morning. I know this is an extraordinary meeting on very short notice.

"As some of you may already know, I was in Europe attending to a personal matter for a good part of the last month. What most of you will not know is that I was there chasing down a family ghost—my grandfather, a pilot who went missing in action somewhere over Denmark in the spring of 1945.

"Well, I—or I should say we—almost found him. In Norway. And I'm still determined to solve the mystery of his disappearance. But in the process of looking for him and his missing crewmate, we actually found something that no one could have even imagined. Something for which my grandfather and many others likely gave their lives."

She paused and clicked a button on her laptop. A series of images began to appear, one by one, on the conference room's large flatscreen TV—page after page of hand-drawn diagrams and schematics and notations.

"In my grandfather's crashed plane, buried some twenty-five feet down inside a glacier at the top of a mountain, and locked away in an old bank basement in a small Norwegian town, we discovered a set of documents that might just bring something incredibly good to the world. I believe we may have uncovered some…scientific research that may help lead to the development of certain cancer treatments, and possibly even vaccines."

The atmosphere in the room changed instantly. And completely.

Jonathon Robertson, the board Chairman, immediately amped up. "I'm sorry, what? Did you say *vaccine*? For cancer? A vaccine for cancer? Are you serious, Alison?" Before Alison could even begin to answer, he turned to Will Acton. "Have you and your team seen any of this stuff, Will? What's your assessment?"

"Yes we have," said Will. "In fact I've personally reviewed the materials that Alison's referencing. While there's obviously a lot of work to be done to prove out the hypotheses, claims, and assertions in the documents she found, my team and I believe that what she's saying may be essentially correct, pending extensive additional research, of course."

Energized, Robertson turned to his left. The company's chief legal counsel was already opening his laptop.

"Steve, you've got to get your team on this ASAP. We're going to want to move lightning fast, IP-wise. We've got to get all of the stuff Alison's talking about protected right now. And, Will, we're going to need your group to jump on this thing equally quickly. If we can prove out any of this we'll obviously have a fantastic basis for an eventual IPO. And of course, if what I'm hearing here is actually true, this could be an incredible breakthrough for all of us. An actual, honest-to-god, goddamn blockbuster!"

Alison cleared her throat. "Yes, it could be absolutely incredible, John. But that's where I have to address some…ah, personal ethical difficulty. Because the origin of these documents is too evil to even comprehend."

She clicked the button on her laptop, and a single black-and-white image of a horrendously disfigured little girl appeared on the flat screen.

"Nazi doctors and scientists committed unspeakable atrocities to learn what's documented in those papers. They tortured and experimented on and maimed and killed hundreds, maybe thousands, of innocent people, typically prisoners taken from concentration camps. In this particular case, it seems, mostly children."

Robertson tried to interject, to casually brush the horror of long-past history aside, to focus on the "opportunity at hand," but Alison completely ignored him.

"This…this research is horribly, horribly tainted. It's an absolute crime against humanity." She paused as all eyes turned to her. "I'm going to preface what I'm about to tell you next by saying that I fully understand the legal implications here, and that I'm fully aware of my fiduciary responsibility to this company and to its shareholders."

The room was totally silent as she continued.

"This information came into my possession only because my grandfather, and, it seems, many others, died trying to do the right thing in the face of so much wrong. Simply put, they risked absolutely everything to do what's right. So, in my own small way, I'm doing the same.

"In coordination with the Canadian and German governments,

and with a wonderful woman from Iowa, I've already filed for wide-ranging intellectual property protection on all methodologies, processes, and formulas contained in the found research papers. But the patent-holders will be all of humanity. All of the world's people. No single individual or company or organization or government should ever own any of this. If I could have my way, no one would ever profit from the suffering of those poor children."

Alison took a deep breath and looked at the stunned faces of the people gathered around the table. "And you should all know this: earlier this morning, I released all of the documents over the internet. I made all of it public."

74

In Seattle, the spring sun can bring a special kind of warmth. When the clouds disperse, and that fantastically brilliant glow pushes aside the seemingly incessant greyness, life can feel especially good.

Alison was in one of her favourite spots, a quiet little place in Queen Anne that, in her opinion, served exactly the kind of breakfast sandwiches and coffee that made her newly reacquired early morning workout routine worth every second.

And today, she was, in fact, feeling especially good.

The previous week's ferry trip to Victoria had been, well, a little unexpected, a little nerve-racking, and more than a little wonderful.

She'd been nervous, despite Scott's constant reassurances, but as promised, Mrs. Wilcox had been incredibly warm and welcoming. And as his mother had excitedly gushed and fussed over her mildly embarrassed but obviously loving "baby boy," her grace and elegance were absolutely undiminished—and possibly even accentuated—by the angular scar, visible beneath the short-cropped grey hair just above her left ear, where a red hot piece of mortar shrapnel had come close to ending her life almost forty-five years ago.

As Alison had stood before the carefully curated and arranged display of frames on Mrs. Wilcox's living room wall, she couldn't help but think of her own family and the incredible power of connection to the past that had somehow gotten her there, to what she was beginning to believe might actually be the start of her future.

The array of snapshots and portraits and team pictures and diplomas told a thousand stories that she yearned to know—but she especially wanted to hear the one about the tall, blue-eyed, square-jawed Canadian Forces peacekeeper and the stunningly beautiful young Namibian nurse who'd fallen so deeply in love in the middle of a violent conflict. *It's true. Becoming a combat medic really is in your DNA.*

And, of course, there were countless pictures of a gap-toothed little boy who'd grown into a gangly adolescent student and athlete, and then into a serious and committed young man who'd ultimately found his purpose in the dust and death of Kandahar—and who'd somehow, thankfully, found her.

The past few months had been incredibly strange for Alison. She'd come to realize that she'd never felt more at ease with another person than she had with Scott Wilcox, and in his own understated but to-the-point way, he'd made it clear that he felt exactly the same about her. Although they were two people who'd lived different lives in two completely different worlds, they'd discovered each other, and now they shared one. Alison was still stunned and amazed at the confluence of events that had made that possible.

She'd asked him, on that last wonderful night in Oslo, about the pattern of scars on his neck and arm and shoulder, the ones she'd been gently running her fingers over and over. He'd made light of them—*I think I must have cut myself shaving or something…* When gently pressed, he'd dismissed their presence once again by explaining that he'd been "the lucky one that day." In the warm, quiet darkness, his body had tensed and trembled a little, and Alison had kissed a tear from his cheek, and as he'd stroked her hair and pulled her closer, he'd whispered something that she'd thought about a hundred times since.

"Whenever we lose someone we love, we lose part of ourselves. But if we'd never loved at all, if we'd never cared for someone more than we cared for ourselves, never risked the pain, we never would've been whole. Does that…does that make any sense? We'd have been less than we could have been. I always want to be more."

As her own tears had mixed with his, she'd understood in that moment that she wanted to know absolutely everything about Scott Wilcox, and that she wanted him to know everything there was to know about her.

She wanted to be more.

Their time apart had been unlike anything she'd experienced. Each phone call and video chat and text message had fueled the continuous warm sensation in her stomach, her chest, her heart, her whole being. It was weirdly, heavily intense, yet tremulously, flutteringly light all at the same time. She'd eventually come to understand that the feeling was telling her that her life was no longer simply her own. The feeling was answering a question that she'd held deep inside since everyone she'd ever loved—and everyone who'd ever loved her—had left her. And it was telling her that the answer was a wonderful thing.

o o o

The package she'd received the day before yesterday had been absolutely wonderful, the elegantly handwritten letter it contained, a delight.

Dear Miss Wiley,

After you and Mr. Wilcox departed I simply couldn't sleep
for weeks. I suspected my father might have hidden more secret
treasures in this old house. And I was right!

It took quite a bit of searching and digging, but I finally
managed to find these items tucked away in a dusty old black
briefcase up in my attic. I hope they help you find the answers
you are searching for.

With my very, very, very best wishes,
Inga Nygård

Everything in that package had overwhelmed her, but it was
one particular item that had made Alison's heart pound, her throat
swell, and her tears flow. It was a sealed white business envelope,
bearing a single fountain-pen-inked word—*Marie*—and an engraved
Rosendal, Norway return address.

The heartbreaking note she found inside it—from an incredibly
brave young man reassuring the love of his life that he'd be home
to her and their soon-to-arrive baby just as quickly as he possibly
could—had completely devastated her.

Scott had held her tightly as she'd sobbed uncontrollably, and
she knew she'd never forget what he'd said to her—that he was sure
that her grandfather would be as proud of her as she was of him.

The following afternoon, she'd dropped him at Sea-Tac for his
flight to Ottawa. It had been incredibly difficult to let him go, even
though she knew he'd be back in Seattle again in just a few weeks.
She couldn't remember the last time in her adult life that she'd so
intensely and eagerly and happily looked forward to the future.

At her apartment that evening, she'd poured herself a glass of red wine and, for the first time in forever, dug into the cardboard box she kept hidden away at the back of her bedroom closet.

On her living room floor, she slowly flipped through the rigid pages of the overstuffed three-ring photo album her mom had put together for her all those years ago, lost for a while in the crackle of the thin plastic film that guarded the thousands of stories contained in its gallery of grainy drugstore snapshots, Polaroids, school portraits, and team pictures. In a cluster of loose photographs tucked into the very back of the album, she'd found it: the last picture of them all together, taken a few days before he'd shipped out.

They all looked so not like themselves. Her mom forcing a weak, tight-lipped smile, knuckles showing telltale white as she squeezed her slender hands together in front of her. Her dad so obviously proud, but clearly hiding something deep behind his unsmiling eyes. James ramrod straight in his fatigues and boots and beret, serious and intense and soldierly. And of course, eighteen-year-old Alison herself, almost expressionless, but, she remembered vividly, fighting so very, very hard to hold back her tears, unsure if she was afraid or sad or angry or all of those things, or something else entirely.

But there was no holding back her tears as she'd secured the snapshot in its new frame and carefully placed it on the bookshelf beside another recently framed photograph—the one of the handsome young man with the I-don't-give-a-shit grin.

No more questions.

I get it now.

And I forgive you.

○ ○ ○

She'd spent the last hour and a half of this wonderfully warm Thursday morning drinking coffee and combing through countless websites. The *Washington Post*, the *Wall Street Journal*, the *Times*, the *Post*, the *New York Times*, the *Globe and Mail*, the *Guardian*, CNN, CBC, BBC. It seemed there wasn't a media outlet anywhere in the world that wasn't carrying the story of the crazy American biotech CEO who'd released the potentially multibillion-dollar Nazi secret over the internet. Her phone and email had been buzzing non-stop, absolutely blowing up with countless requests for interviews and TV show appearances.

Will Acton had left her a voicemail.

Seems Robertson had been absolutely apoplectic after Alison had "dropped the fucking mic" and immediately walked out of the board meeting. He'd apparently launched into a vein-bulging tirade so intense that Will had actually been concerned the guy might pop something vital. He'd raged about his firm's massive investment in Alison's company, ranted about her dangerously irresponsible actions and how she'd betrayed the trust that he and his partners had placed in her, and finally, he'd loudly vowed to destroy her professionally and personally.

While Robertson had still been raving at the top of his lungs, Will said, absolutely everyone else in the room had simply gotten up and walked out, leaving the foaming-at-the-mouth asshole to finish his tantrum alone. She'd smiled for a long, long time at that thought, but Will's final words before he'd hung up had lingered with her.

"We've all got your back, Alison. You did good, lady. You did real good."

She knew the lawsuits would be endless.

And she felt fantastic.

○ ○ ○

Her phone buzzed again.

She smiled at the text message, characteristically to the point.

There's someone we should meet.

Then, still a little uncharacteristically, two more.

PS you rock.

Ma'am.

75

On the gloriously sunny longest day of the Norwegian year, Scott steered the SUV off the road and onto a long, curving driveway. Lost in thought, Alison couldn't take her eyes from the deep-blue ocean sparkling in the distance, or from the dark green spruce trees that lined each side of the white gravel crunching under their tires.

The young nurse at the reception desk was all smiles.

"Velkommen! I mean, ah, welcome! I mean, hello! So good of you both to come. She's just through here, in the sun room. And she's so very, very excited to meet you. Well, actually, we all are! Won't you follow me, please?"

o o o

The late afternoon sun warmed her face, the blanket was soft and comforting, and she thought nothing but good thoughts.

She thought about how incredibly fortunate she'd been to have realized that it was, in part, her own story being told on the television, on the internet, and in the newspapers.

She certainly hadn't understood all of the scientific and medical terminology—she knew almost nothing of vaccines and antibodies and lymphatic systems and the like—but the pictures and videos of the proud young boy and his dog who'd made the initial discovery on the glacier were wonderful.

The telephone call she'd received from the nice young American woman had made her feel extraordinarily special and excited, but also more than a little nervous. And the story and all of the subsequent attention and fuss it had generated had brought a lot of painful, long-suppressed memories back to the surface. But it had also rekindled some wonderful ones.

She'd smiled through her sadness as she'd thought once again of the two young men who'd been enemies by circumstance, but who'd ended up sacrificing so much for the same thing. They'd both been so kind and courageous—and done such incredibly brave and selfless things—to take her away from the terrible pain and suffering and cruelty she'd endured. To give her her life.

She'd thought of her wonderful parents, and how they'd tried so very hard, but in vain, to find her lost family so many years ago. She'd thought about how incredibly fortunate she'd been that they'd taken her into their home and into their hearts. They'd always been so loving and patient and understanding with her. And she'd never stopped thinking about her wonderful husband, Johan. She missed him more than anything, but she'd be forever grateful for the love-filled years they'd shared. Now she couldn't help but think almost constantly about the package that had arrived just days ago. From America. From Seattle. How her hands had shaken and her pounding heart had almost burst from her chest when she'd opened that small box to find something absolutely wonderful inside—an illustrated children's book about a brave little girl and her magical goat.

She'd sobbed uncontrollably as the flood of warm memories had completely engulfed her.

The contents of the crisp white envelope tucked inside that little book had taken her breath away. She'd held the small black-and-white photograph to her heart for hours and hours, been almost unable to take her tear-filled eyes off the grinning, handsome young man who stood in front of that log cabin in the woods, holding the hand of a wide-eyed, stubble-haired little girl.

And although it contained only three simple words, she supposed she must have read the handwritten note that accompanied the two pale yellow barley sweets and the half disk of grey metal alloy—stamped with its cryptic letters and numbers—more than a hundred times since she'd opened the small, blue "RAF Special Ration Type B" tin that had so carefully protected them for more than seventy years.

"You are loved."

o o o

The young nurse spoke softly as she placed a gentle hand on her shoulder. "Noen er her for å se deg, Susi."

As she opened her dark eyes and turned from the sun to face the smiling young couple walking toward her, she raised an elegant, wrinkled hand, the tip of its pinkie finger absent for so many years, and waved.

o o o

Acknowledgments

No one does anything alone.

When it comes to life in general, I'm simply indebted to too many people—my wonderful family both present and lost, my friends, my teachers and coaches, my business partners and colleagues—to list them all here.

But specific to this novel, I want to take a moment to thank a few of the people who helped bring this thing to life: Michelle Meade; Pamela Kim Lee / Multiple; Richard de Boer / The Calgary Mosquito Society; Dr. Sarah Lockyer / Directorate of History and Heritage, Department of National Defence, Government of Canada; Alistair Hodgson / De Havilland Aircraft Museum; Ryan Lee / Alberta Aviation Museum; Kimberly Hunt; Beth Atwood; and Sara Stratton.

And in particular, I want to recognize a couple of very special individuals.

To be the beneficiary of the kind of invaluable guidance and insights so generously provided by Tom Burdge, Flight Lieutenant (ret'd) RAFVR, who flew with 248 Squadron / Banff Strike Wing, and George E. Stewart DFC, Flying Officer (ret'd) RAF, who flew with 23 Squadron—two Canadians who actually piloted de Havilland Mosquitos in the dangerous skies over Europe more than seventy-five years ago—has been absolutely amazing.

I thank them for their time and attention to this project, for sharing their precious memories with me, and for the absolutely fascinating and moving and sometimes hilarious conversations, but I especially want to express my personal gratitude and admiration for their courage and commitment as shockingly young men who faced the harsh realities of aerial warfare.

EO-N is fiction.
Their incredible stories are fact.
Respect.